There Was Hate In His Eyes—
PURE HATE!

"We've got the goods on you, Flash," said Reverend Jim, "though it didn't come in just the way we expected it to come when we came here to get you."

Haddam's body had fallen into a crouch, edging away, his right hand hovering close to his gun holster.

His eyes gleamed with a terrible hatred, he curved his fingers around the butt of his gun, but Reverend Jim's lightning motion made his movement seem fatally slow in comparison. There was a glint at Reverend Jim's hip, a spiteful crash, and a piercing shriek.

His eyes ablaze, Haddam cursed and aimed his gun, wanting to kill that meddling preacher if it was the last thing he did!

"As long as there are six-guns and sunsets, *Arizona Jim* will live. More hell-bent-for-buckskin action on every page than any other Western I know."

—P. Michael Mayer

CHARLES ALDEN SELTZER

ARIZONA JIM

A KANGAROO BOOK
PUBLISHED BY POCKET BOOKS NEW YORK

POCKET BOOKS, a Simon & Schuster division of
GULF & WESTERN CORPORATION
1230 Avenue of the Americas, New York, N.Y. 10020

Published by arrangement with Aeonian Press, Inc.
Library of Congress Catalog Card Number: 74-21533

ISBN: 0-671-81953-4

First Pocket Books printing July, 1978

Trademarks registered in the United States and other countries.

Printed in the U.S.A.

ARIZONA JIM

CHAPTER I

"Smarty, Smarty, gave a party—and nobody came."

It was a tragic time for the girl, and yet the words of the childhood jingle recurred in her thoughts. She stood in the silent dining room of the big, gloomy ranch house, looking at the spotless white cover on the table, at the unused dishes, at the tempting delicacies prepared by her own hands and representing many hours of concern, anxiety and labor—all untasted, unappreciated. Her glance went from the table to the room itself, scrupulously neat and clean, just as she had left it the afternoon before, when, all her preparations completed, she had turned her attention to herself, bedecking herself in her best, spending much time in putting the finishing touches to the dress she had planned and made in anticipation of the event.

For of course it was an event. Only once in a lifetime does a girl celebrate her eighteenth birthday. It was to have been a bright spot in her life—one of the few she had known. Instead, it had been a tragedy. She had discovered that all tragedies need not result in death; that there are tragedies in disappointment, in bitter, impotent resentment. For not one of the eight persons to whom she had sent invitations had come. Worse—not by any word or sign had one of the eight indicated regret or offered excuses for nonappearance. They had simply stayed away.

The girl gulped hard as she stood looking about the room. Not until the last moment had she given up hope, for it seemed incredible that her neighbors, her former friends, could have treated her so cruelly. She had waited until ten o'clock. Then with trembling hands she had taken up the kerosene lamp that had stood in the middle of the table and with quivering lips had blown out the blaze, plunging the room into blackness that was approached in intensity only by the despair in her heart. Huddled in a corner of the porch after extinguishing the light, she had fought it out with herself—and had conquered. Now, in the daylight of the morning following, she had so far recovered from her disappointment that she was able to review the incident with calmness in which there was a tinge of bitter humor. She knew why they had not come. They were moral cowards, afraid of public opinion. She stiffened as she stood in the room, and laughed derisively—laughed to keep from crying. And once again the words of the nursery ditty sprang to her lips:

"Smarty, smarty, gave a party—and nobody came."

Her chin in the air as if in scorn of the absent eight, she went about the task of clearing the table. The dishes she placed carefully away; the tempting food she had prepared with so much care and labor she grimly threw to the pigs in the pen, lest her father, when he returned, or her brother Ben, asleep in his room upstairs, might take note of it and ask embarrassing questions. Presently all traces of the preparation for the celebration had been removed, and with flushed face and thumping heart she walked to the kitchen doorway and sat on the threshold.

She sat there long—her hair in glistening disorder, hanging over her shoulders, her hands clasped around her knees, her slippered feet hidden under the hem of her gingham wrapper, her gaze fixed upon the crenelated mountains that lifted their peaks far to the north. The misty gloom of early morning hung over the country; the ghostly solitude of space leant its mysticism to the featureless plains that stretched from the ranch house to the foothills.

It was big, this country—very big. And in the light of its inevitable contrast it made some other things seem very small. People—especially. How could anyone be mean in so vast a world—a world breathing and whispering of bigness and generosity? It was incredible, but it had happened.

Her friends! The mountains grew misty in her vision. Most of the girls she had invited she had known for years. They lived on distant ranches. Like her, they had had few advantages. What did it matter? The West had no artificial social scale with which to measure worth or character. Here values were computed by the naked rule of honesty. And she had always been honest.

But could she say that for her brother Ben? Dismay and fear crept into her, and her hands grew stiff and tense around her knees. Yet her eyes snapped with defiance. What if suspicion over Ben's friendship with the outlaw Flash Haddam *had* spread over the basin? Was that any reason why her friends should stay away from *her*, should shun her? Evidently those friends thought so, for they had done just that.

She didn't care. If they were going to punish her for Ben's sin, let them. She would not be disloyal to Ben. She didn't care for the opinions of her neighbors; still less did she regard the judgment of Red Rock, that miserable husk of squalor known as "town" which huddled its shanties on an alkali level five miles west. She cared for no one's opinion, but she must save Ben.

Concern for her brother banished for a moment thoughts of the humiliation she had undergone. There was more pity than condemnation in her heart for him. Ben's life had been narrow. He had got started wrong. He was two years older than she, and yet he had known a mother only for seven years of his life, losing her just when he needed her most. For herself—— But that made little difference. Boys needed mothering more than girls. That was a truth she had stumbled upon early, because in necessity she had taken to mothering Ben. The instinct to do so had been strong in her. But she had not been able to wield so strong an influence over him as she could have wished. For one thing, he had been too much under the domination of his father, who, since his wife's death, had been exhibiting vagaries of mind that disturbed her greatly. Ben's life so far had been confined to the limits of sleep, work and eating. It was terribly monotonous for him—worse for him than for her, because she had her books. But it was bad enough for both. And now Ben was making it almost unbearable for her.

She could see now that the disposition of her friends to avoid her had not been recently formed. Various incidents of the past rose in her recollection—incidents which should have set her to thinking. She had given them no serious thought until now. But it was very plain that all those lapses of politeness, the rebuffs, the cuts, had been deliberate and studied; that they arose from an intention on the part of her friends to ostracize her. Why didn't they try to help her save Ben, instead of deserting her in this manner? The answer to that question leaped quickly into her mind. They were afraid of Flash Haddam! The whole country was afraid of him!

She saw now why the other cattlemen of the basin allowed her father to range his cattle on the north side of the Purgatorie, reserving the territory south of it for their own herds and doing their best to keep them from mingling. They let it be known that their reason for this was the fact that Harvey Warren was "queer," or "loco," and that in a roundup he was certain to be "cranky," or "cussed mean" over a fair division of the mavericks or the unbranded calves which the roundup disclosed in his herds. But now she knew they concealed the real reason. They had made it all very comprehensible by not coming to her party.

No friends—she had no friends—she was a social outcast.

Her pride saved her from the tears that were threatening at this moment, and she laughed again as she looked around at the room. The laugh was still on her lips as she leaned against one of the doorjambs between the dining room and the kitchen, but there was a queer catch in her voice; and with ironic insistence the words of the jingle recurred in her mind: "Smarty, smarty, gave a party—and nobody came."

She could have faced them all at this instant without revealing her hurts, but she was alone now, and though she could see the sun, lifting above the rimming hills in the remote distance, the ranch house seemed infinitely somber and gloomy, as though a gleam of light could never more penetrate it. And the laugh died on her lips, giving way to sobs.

She was out on the porch an hour later, sitting very quiet in the rocking chair, her chin in her hands, her gaze upon the broad reaches of the basin, shimmering in the white, crystal light of the morning sun. There would never be any more tears over her humiliation; she had decided on that. Whatever pain she felt over her ostracism would not be for others to see.

Ben was prominently in her thoughts as she sat there. He needed advice, directing. But would he accept it from her? Had he not gone too far? How far had he gone?

She couldn't tell, of course, not having accompanied him on his trips away from the ranch house—which had been many. But long after midnight the night before, as she had been sitting at her window, not being able to sleep through speculating over the failure of her friends to come to her party, she had seen Ben ride up to the corral. And with the dismay that always afflicted her at these times she had noted that he had staggered. Flash Haddam was with him. The outlaw was steady, jocular and mildly critical. In that drawling, mocking voice that she had grown to despise, she heard him speak to Ben, as dismounting, he stood erect beside the horse he had ridden:

"Drunk again, eh? You're sure an infant when it comes to carryin' liquor."

"Ain't drunk," denied Ben, thickly. "Look here!" He tried to stand erect, but reeled to the corral fence where he laughed foolishly.

"You won't be plumb man till you can carry a jag proper," laughed Haddam.

A little later she heard Ben descending the stairs, heard him cross the kitchen, felt him standing near the doorway looking at her. He was a tall, slender youth with a shock of unruly hair and perplexed eyes that were forever squinting as though in an effort to comprehend a puzzling world. She knew he had missed a vigorous mentality through some accident of heredity, and her conviction of this increased her love and concern for him. She did not look at him until he cleared his throat, and then she turned. He was rolling a cigarette.

"Hello, Sis!" he greeted as she soberly surveyed him. "Mopin' again, eh? You've been doin' a heap of it, lately."

He had noticed that, had he? But he had not remembered her birthday. Her father had not remembered it, either. She did not feel bitter against them for it; they simply hadn't thought of it—that was all. They hadn't thought of other birthdays, either, she remembered, but she had never missed reminding them of theirs!

Ben lighted the cigarette and came out upon the porch, where he sat on the railing and nonchalantly blew the smoke upward, watching it disintegrate in the clear air.

"What's botherin' you this mornin'?" he said, after taking several puffs.

She did not answer until he had begun to wonder at her silence. Then he looked at her and was forced to meet her gaze fairly.

"You are bothering me, Ben," she said slowly and accusingly.

Guilty embarrassment reddened his face. "Me?" he responded. "Aw—don't. I ain't done nothin'."

"Don't lie, Ben. And don't pretend it's a joking matter. Do you call it nothing to associate with Flash Haddam?"

He frowned, puffed deeply at the cigarette and turned his head. He did not look up, but down—which action revealed thoughtful perturbation and guilt. "Shucks," he said stubbornly: "who says I've been associatin' with Flash Haddam?"

"I am saying it, Ben."

"Why, Sis——" He looked at her, saw knowledge in her eyes.

"Other people are saying it, too, Ben," she told him. "You *are* friendly with him."

"If you call takin' a drink with him once in a while——"

"A drink!" She knew what she was going to say would hurt him, but she felt it must be said. "Ben, I have seen you come home with Flash Haddam—have seen you stagger—have heard him making fun of you because you couldn't drink more."

"Well, what of it?" he challenged defiantly with rebellion against her assumed authority to criticize him. "I'm twenty, an' my own boss. An' if I want to take a drink with Flash Haddam, who's to stop me? It ain't no crime to take a drink, is it? Or a dozen of them, with whoever I like!"

"No harm, Ben!" she reproved. "Don't you see where the harm is? To drink—to get drunk—with a cattle thief—an outlaw? Oh, Ben!"

He shifted nervously, intolerantly. He said: "You women don't know how them things are, between men. You 'tend to your housework, Martha, an' let me alone. I know how to take care of myself."

"I wish you did know," she said.

She got up and walked over to him, putting an arm around him, but he turned his head from her and looked downward. Placing a hand on each side of his face, she gently forced him to look at her—which he did, reluctantly.

"Ben," she said, "do you know what Dal Thompson heard the other day?"

"No," he made answer, averting his gaze.

Resolutely, she went on: "He heard that people are saying it is queer that none of Father's cattle are ever stolen."

He looked at her, startled. Then rage, which she knew as guilty knowledge, paled his face. He said insincerely: "Who's sayin' that? Why, damn them, I'll——"

"S-sh!" she deprecated. "You can't stop their mouths with violence. That would make it worse. The way is for you to break with Flash Haddam, to drink no more with him—to show them by your actions that you know what is being said and that you are taking means to let them know it is a lie. If you don't do that, nothing else that you can do will convince them."

He reached up and pushed her hands away, his face alive with passion.

"I'll see them in hell first!" he declared. "Flash is a friend of mine! He's done things for me—things my own father wouldn't do!"

"Ben! Ben!" she protested.

"It's the truth!" he insisted. "Dad's a tightwad, a miser! He ain't poor, is he? Last season he marketed more than two thousand head of cattle! I figure his profit was near twenty thousand dollars! Where is it? He don't bank any of it; he don't put it into improvements; he don't spend it; he don't give any of it to us—any more than living expenses. He's got it hid somewhere. Why don't he produce some of it an' give me an' you a square deal? A man likes to have some coin to spend! He don't even pay me wages! Why don't he hire some help here, for you, so's you can go to school an' get the education you want so bad—that you ought to have? He's too damn tight, that's what!"

"Ben! Ben!" she reproved. "Hush! Do you know what you are saying? For shame! Father isn't responsible, Ben; you know he isn't." She followed him to the door, to which he had gone, putting an arm around him and holding him tightly. "Ben," she said, "it isn't any harder for you than it is for me, is it? And I am not complaining. What Father has is his own. He earned it. You haven't any right—I have no right—to dictate to him about it."

She saw a new hardness in him. He said: "Well, I ain't tryin' to dictate to him, am I? I'm simply goin' my own way an' doin' as I please. Look here, Sis," he added, his voice suddenly changing, "there ain't nothin' for you to bother your head about. I'm a man, an' I'm playing a man's game, an' if I get into trouble, I'll take my medicine like a man. Flash Haddam's a man, too. He ain't half as bad as he's painted. Anyway, I'm travelin' my own trail, an' nobody's goin' to interfere with me—not even you!''

With this word he pushed her from him and walked into the house.

He ate his breakfast in silence, and she did not again refer to the subject. After breakfast he went out, and she saw him saddling and bridling his pony at the corral gate.

''Goin' to Red Rock!'' he yelled at her as he leaped into the saddle, and with sinking heart she watched as he loped his pony down the river, presently vanishing around a bend in the trail.

An hour later, sitting in the rocking chair on the porch, deeply engrossed in a book, she heard the rapid drumming of hoofs on the trail that passed the front of the ranch house, and looking up quickly she was just in time to see a horseman appear from behind a cottonwood clump not more than a hundred yards from where she sat, and come directly toward her, his pony in the rapid chop-trot affected by the experienced plains animal.

Stirred with antagonism which was explained by the outlaw's friendship with Ben, she recognized Flash Haddam. But she professed not to see him as he rode up and brought his pony to a halt near the porch; and she did not look up until she heard his voice with the pronounced drawl that had grown so hateful in her ears, directed at her.

''Ben anywheres around?'' he asked.

She laid the book in her lap, closed it with a snap, and looked at him. He was young—twenty-eight, Ben had told her (not that she had ever asked)—tall, lithe, rugged, with a keen, hawklike face, eyes black and piercing, and a reckless, easy, self-confident bearing that reminded her of the rakish hero of an ancient romance she had once read. He did not make a bad figure, but she had always disliked him—more than ever now that she was aware of his friendship with Ben.

''Ben is gone,'' she said, reopening her book, as if to apprise him that she would say no more.

''Where?'' he asked.

''Oh,'' she said. ''You are still here. I told you Ben had gone.''

''Why, so you did! Could you tell me where he went?''

''I suppose I could. That way, I think.'' She pointed to the trail that led away from Red Rock. She lifted the book to a level with her eyes.

"How long has he been gone?" He lounged in the saddle, watching her, smiling at her, undisturbed. "I was figurin' on havin' company to town."

Color was coming back into her cheeks, sent there by the anger she felt because of his impudence in coming openly for her brother, in deliberately flaunting their friendship before her, when he must know that she was opposed to it—that any honest person must know she was opposed to it.

"Mr. Haddam," she said, trying to be calm, to speak frankly and convincingly without unduly provoking new antagonism; "I wish you would leave Ben alone, that you would quit running around with him, drinking with him, getting him drunk."

He dismounted, trailed the reins over the pony's head and stepped to the porch rail, leaning his arms upon it and looking at her with a direct, boldly admiring glance in which there was some amusement over her unmistakably hostile expression.

"You don't want him to be runnin' around with me, eh," he said. "Well, that's handin' it to me pretty straight, ain't it? You're not admirin' my company any—none at all." He laughed with low mirth, every note stabbing her. Thinly concealed in his voice was mockery which she felt was directed at her personally.

"How long has this exclusive mood been comin' on?" he added quietly.

"What do you mean?"

"Oh, nothin' special. I've been noticin' it since you throwed that party." He now grinned.

She cringed, but met his gaze. "What do you know about my party?" she said in a voice which she tried hard to keep level and casual.

"Plenty. Nobody came to it."

She shrank as though he had threatened to strike her, and sat silent, afraid to trust her voice.

"Are they saying that?" she managed to ask, finally. Oh, the injustice of it! She would have said more, but a quaver in her voice warned her.

Haddam watched her narrowly. "It hurts you, eh?" he said. "But what did you expect from the boxheads in this country?"

"They are not to blame!" she answered hotly, angered at his tone. "They are punishing me because of your friendship with

Ben. You have brought this upon me—this humiliation. If you had let Ben alone, it would never have happened."

"Maybe not. The point is—it has happened." He rested his head on his arms, looking at her sideways, insolently, speculatively. "You don't like me, even a little," he said. "Do you?"

"Of course not! Shall I tell you what I think of you?"

"It might be interestin'."

"You are contemptible!"

"Aw, don't!" he expostulated dryly. "Callin' me names, an' me a friend of your brother!"

Because she suspected that he enjoyed her rage she forced herself to calmness, though her hands were now clenched on the arms of her chair and her lips were white. The book she had been reading was lying—closed—in her lap.

He broke in on her thoughts with a smooth laugh. "You're gettin' better lookin' every day, Martha. Stirrin' you up makes you sort of sparkle."

"Keep your flattery for one who appreciates it!"

"That goes. It ain't flattery. Someday, when we're better acquainted, I'm goin' to tell you more than that." His voice was suddenly serious and she looked at him in astonishment.

Her answer was a glance of smiling scorn, which angered him.

"I don't mind tellin' you that I've been watchin' you for quite a while," he said. "For the last couple of years, anyway, since you've blossomed out. There's somethin' about you that makes me think you an' me would make a go of it."

Not answering, she opened the book again and pretended to read. She couldn't read, of course, because his words had disturbed her, filled her with an uneasy dread.

Stealing a glance at him she saw a flash of vindictive resentment light his eyes. Then they became cold and intent, as if he had been stirred by passion.

"So that's how it stands with you," he said. "Well, the Warren family ain't got no call to take on airs."

"You mean Ben, of course," she said, looking straight at him again.

"You're smart," he mocked.

Of course she understood him; she believed she had experienced a faint presentiment ever since she had discovered that Ben and he had been spending their nights together. Now she was certain. She said, in a voice that betrayed her dismay: "Do you mean that you are deliberately spoiling Ben?"

He nodded slowly, his black eyes glinting with some deep emotion. "It won't hurt you to know it. You'd tumble to it right soon, anyway. Ben wasn't hard to spoil, an' he's gone too far to back out now."

"Do you mean that he's already——" She gasped as Haddam slowly nodded an affirmative.

"Yes," he added as she sank back into her chair, her face in her hands, her chest heaving: "Ben's already run his iron on other folks' cattle. He's branded some with my sign, the Star, an' he's run the H-Bar-W, your dad's brand, on a heap more. Told your Dad he'd bought them with money he won gambling. What's more, he's been seen rustlin'. There's evidence against him—Sheriff Hawks an' someone else. He'd be a gone coon already if I wasn't his friend. There ain't no one botherin' Flash Haddam!"

"His friend!" she said bitterly.

"Well," he said, watching her with vindictive amusement, "I'm protectin' him, ain't I? I reckon you might call that bein' his friend."

"But you led him to steal!" she charged, a cold fear stifling her rage.

"Sure."

"Why?" she demanded fiercely. "Why?"

"I reckon it was because I felt lonesome. I kind of hankered for one of the Warrens to be with me on the trail I'm ridin'. I like top-notch company."

She had hoped that he had merely been trying to frighten her. Now she looked at him, a quickly growing horror in her eyes.

He answered her look. "I reckon you've got it sized up right, after all," he said. "I've been wonderin' how long it would take you." And now for the first time since he had been talking to her he had allowed her to see—at least a glimpse—the implacable malevolence of his character. His black eyes—lambent with coalescent fire—gleamed triumphantly, his voice was harsh and decisive. "You've got it figured right," he went on. "You've been too damned stuck up to suit me—you an' your dad an' Ben. I've drug you down to where I can talk to you on the level. You ain't goin' to be highfalutin with me any more. You've been too good to look at me since you got hold of them books." He stuck his chin out and glared at her over the railing. "You remember the dance at Dobble's, a year ago this fall comin'? I asked you to take a turn with me, an' you turned up your nose an' wouldn't answer me. Wouldn't notice me at all! Up to that time you'd treated me medium nice. The books was beginnin' to work, then, I reckon. Well, you'll notice me now, or I'll turn Ben over to Sheriff Hawks an' have him strung up so quick it'll make you dizzy!"

She got up after a minute, during which she did not look at Haddam, during which she fought for her composure. She succeeded in that, though it seemed that, figuratively, she was about to fall into the black pit that Haddam had dug for her. But she succeeded in laughing at him—tauntingly, and her voice was almost steady.

"I think a great deal of Ben," she said as she backed toward the open doorway. "I would do anything for him—anything except to notice you!"

She stepped over the threshold and closed the door—barred it and leaned against it for a moment as though fearful that he would attempt to follow her. She left the door presently and went to one of the windows. From behind the lace curtain she watched Haddam. He stood for a little time at the porch rail, frowning at the closed door, and then with a short laugh turned and swung into the saddle, riding toward the Red Rock trail.

CHAPTER 2

At the moment that Martha Warren, behind the curtains of the window of the ranch house, watched Flash Haddam ride down the Red Rock trail, Norman Carey, in Red Rock, was looking toward the H-Bar-W. Flash Haddam figured in Carey's thoughts, also.

Above Carey's head, affixed to the unpainted boards that formed the front of the building in the doorway of which he stood, was a weather-beaten sign which bore the legend:

THE RED ROCK ADVOCATE

The *Advocate*, one might have inferred through a casual glance at the interior of the building, noting the type cases, the press, the imposing stone, the forms, the disorder and the litter of printers' materials, was a newspaper. A newspaper, moreover, with a county-wide circulation. But one would have hesitated to conclude that the *Advocate* was Norman Carey's property. Carey did not look like a newspaperman. He wore a woolen shirt and a soft hat with a rather wide brim; his trousers legs were stuffed into his boot tops; there was a knotted scarf at his throat.

But in spite of his picturesque rigging, he owned the *Advocate*, and at this minute was wishing he didn't.

The corncob pipe in his mouth had a dolorous droop. It seemed to reflect his spirit, to lend to his attitude a suggestion of complete disgust. But the regularity with which he puffed at the pipe, sending the blue-white smoke in scurrying spirals through the doorway and out into the white, glaring sunlight of Red Rock's one street; the firm, almost derisive, set to his lips; the ironic gleam in his blue eyes—these indicated that if there was disgust in his thoughts it was tempered by other emotions.

It was a drowsy morning, and the thermometer hanging in the shade just inside the door of the *Advocate* building registered ninety-four degrees of heat. Across the street from the *Advocate* building was the Palace Hotel, its dingy front fringed with loungers draped lazily upon bench and tilted chairs. At the hitching rail that skirted the boardwalk immediately in front of the Palace were half a dozen cow ponies, fly tortured, stamping impatiently. Next to the Palace was Hitchens' Store. Bill Hitchens himself was stretched out in a chair in front of his place of business, and was drawing at a pipe which was a replica of the one in Norman Carey's mouth. A dozen or more buildings straggled down the street from Hitchens' store, and then there loomed into view the pretentious front of Dave Blanchard's Emporium—the largest and best-conducted saloon in Red Rock. Carey's side of the street was nuzzled by additional buildings not more remarkable than those on the opposite side—except Justus Castle's bank building, which was the town's only brick structure—and then, after a straggling collection of smaller buildings and dwellings, Red Rock came to an end amid a litter of old tin cans, empty bottles and other refuse.

Carey's gaze, as he stood in the doorway of the *Advocate* building, was on a picture that, a year ago, had stirred him. A year ago, arriving in Red Rock, and because it had seemed that here his ambitions might be realized, he had seen beauty in the picture. Now it was as unlovely as his thoughts. For Red Rock had disappointed Carey.

He turned away from the view and looked at the man who was lounging in a chair in front of a flat-topped desk in the *Advocate* office. The man was a personage; his manner advertised that. Here was authority—absolute, final. It stuck out all over the man, convincingly, self-consciously, ostentatiously. It was thrust upon one by the prominently displayed silver star affixed to the lapel of his vest, upon which was stamped the word *Sheriff;* it was displayed in the supercilious gleam in his eyes; it was unmistakably apparent in the thin, vain curve of his lips; in his whole attitude were the egotism and intolerance of unbridled power and despotism.

For an instant, as he looked at the man, there was a glint of disgust in Carey's eyes, but it was instantly succeeded by another gleam which was not to be analyzed by the personage. The personage grinned at Carey as the latter turned.

"An' so you tell me that the newspaper business ain't exactly jumpin' along?" he said.

Carey took the pipe from his mouth. "Are you wanting me to think that it's news to you, Hawks?" he returned, with mild derision. "I'd hate to believe that you don't know a thing the whole country knows. But if you don't know it, I don't mind telling you. The *Advocate* won't last another month unless something happens. Right now, if my mother and father hadn't been wise enough to pass over to me enough gumption to take a swipe in the pocketbook without a whimper, I'd be crying tears that would make it impossible for me to see that you are blame' glad the *Advocate* is going to the dogs."

Carey's voice was mellow and even. He used no brogue, but there was an elision here and there, a lingering accent upon some words, which revealed his ancestry.

Hawks bristled; his face reddened; his eyes drooped from the blue ones that twinkled coldly at him above a wide smile. He shuffled his feet and cleared his throat twice before he looked up again. Then he saw that Carey's eyes were on him with amused contempt, and he burst out angrily:

"Think I'm a damn fool, eh? Well, think what you like. I reckon you're done here, anyway. Any fool knows that you can't run a newspaper here if Flash Haddam don't want you to run it!"

"I've discovered that," returned Carey. "I didn't think so, at first. But I've made other discoveries along with it. I've come to the conclusion that it's harder for me to run the *Advocate* than it is for Flash Haddam to run the sheriff!"

Hawks's face darkened. The slur was direct and deliberate. Carey had said a thing that all Red Rock believed, which Hawks knew was true. Yet no man had dared hint of it in Hawks's presence until now, and he might have been goaded to violence if he had not suddenly been smitten with a doubt of the young man's earnestness. For there was a grin on Carey's face. He was leaning against one of the doorjambs, easily, his arms folded, one hand holding the bowl of his corncob pipe. In his smile were knowledge, derision, contempt, grim humor—and no fear of the personage.

"That's no secret, Hawks, though you'd like to think it is. Everybody knows it."

"You're a liar!" said Hawks. He leaned forward with provocative hostility, as if to goad Carey to some ill-considered action.

Carey had not moved. Nor had the grin left his face. He did not even change color. He deliberately pressed the tobacco into the bowl of his pipe, deftly using a forefinger. "What I said goes, Hawks," he said, meeting the latter's eyes. "The trouble is that I've no way to prove it. I'd leave it to anybody in Red Rock, if I thought anybody in town besides myself had nerve enough to tell the truth. Put your gun away; I'm not afraid of it. In fact, if you'd use it, I'd be getting just what I ought to get for being fool enough to come to Red Rock in the first place. Put it away," he said jeeringly as Hawks hesitated and blinked at him uncertainly. "I don't like to be called a liar, of course, but I'll admit your provocation was great, and I'll excuse you."

Hawks sheathed the weapon with a jerk. "You're a fourflusher!" he snarled.

"Thanks," said Carey. "Anyway, we understand each other now. In tomorrow's issue of the *Advocate* I'm going to print what has been said here. Along with it I am going to charge that you are not doing your duty in letting Flash Haddam run at large. I've played a losing game here long enough. I'm going to stir things up. I've sunk my money in this newspaper, and if I can't get it out I'll get its equivalent in excitement."

Hawks got up and walked to where Carey stood at the door. Carey did not move. Hawks leered at him. "You print a word of what's been said here, an' I'll herd ride you, sure as the devil!"

"It's as good as printed, Hawks," said Carey. "Go as far as you like."

He stepped aside and watched Hawks walk down the street. Then, still in the doorway, he took in Red Rock's ugly dimensions. He had made a mistake in coming to Red Rock.

Justus Castle was to blame, of course, for it had been at Castle's solicitation that he had come to the town, and it had been through Castle's advice that he had bought the *Advocate*. He had sunk his last dollar in the paper, only to find that he had made a bad investment. Red Rock had failed to fulfill Castle's enthusiastic forecast of a prosperous future; it had not met his own rather doubtful expectations. Yet the town was well located for progress. It was in the heart of a good grass country; the railroad had built a spur and corrals with which to facilitate the shipping of cattle; there was no other town within a hundred miles in any direction—except Twin Adobe, a mere water-tank station some thirty miles east—and ranchers throughout the country were glad to come to Red Rock for supplies. It seemed inevitable that Red Rock would one day become an important town.

These advantages had all been pointed out to Carey by Justus Castle, when the latter had induced him to buy the *Advocate*. Carey had realized them himself. But Flash Haddam's malign influence had retarded the town's growth. His reputation had gone abroad. The exchanges that came to Carey's desk spoke slightingly of Red Rock's inability to cope with the outlaw. Prospective residents and merchants looked elsewhere for locations; some solid citizens had quietly packed their belongings and decamped. Others were contemplating the same step.

Red Rock, Carey decided, needed law and a church. Or, what was more to the point, it needed a courageous representative of the law and a religious instructor who could not be bullied or bluffed—as Red Rock had bluffed the mild-mannered little man who had formerly attempted to elevate it. The meetinghouse caught Carey's gaze as he stood in the doorway, and it seemed a thing distinct and apart from the town. Carey smiled as he looked at it. His sympathies had been with the reverend gentleman who had once reigned there, but still the incident of his abrupt leave-taking had not been without its humorous side. He grinned at one of the loungers on the other side of the street, who had waved a hand to him, then turned and entered the *Advocate* office.

Carey went to his desk and tried to write, but it was no use. A queer impatience possessed him; a strange elation was upon him, reddening his cheeks, brightening his eyes. Concentration was out of the question while he was in that mood; and at the end of an hour he had not written a line, so he stood up, puzzled, and not a little disgusted with himself. It was ridiculous, preposterous, this premonition. He wondered if his defiance of Hawks had not brought it upon him, for there was something to be said about a positive decision bolstering a man's spirits.

"Holy smoke!" he said. "If I yield to such thoughts they'll

soon be comparing me to old Harvey Warren! I'll go down and talk with Castle."

He found Castle stretched out in a chair beside an open window of his banking room, smoking a pipe. Castle waved to him, blandly.

"Come in!" he invited. "The distinguished editor, owner and general manager of the *Advocate* seems a trifle worried this morning," he remarked after Carey had dropped into a chair, in a position from which he could see Red Rock as far down as Blanchard's Emporium.

"Wrong," denied Carey. "The aforementioned distinguished gentleman has passed that stage. He has reached the point where he is beginning to have dreams and visions and—well, the main thing is that I've been bothered all morning with a hunch that something is going to happen."

"Umph!" said Castle. "Fishing for an invitation for a drink. Well, I'll buy."

"I live near the Emporium, and my credit is still good," said Carey.

"What is it, then?"

"I don't know, myself. It's just a hunch with no especial foundation."

Castle blew a ring of smoke upward, at the same time glancing covertly at his friend's face.

"Humph!" he said. "No foundation for it, eh? Usually, hunches are not worth the thought we give them—if any. But it happens there is something in yours." He got up and went to his desk, returning with a paper which he tossed into Carey's lap.

"Read that," he directed. "It's a letter from Cunningham, the Sante Fe resident buyer for the Chicago Livestock Company, which I represent here."

Carey ran through it rapidly. Mainly it was devoted to matters of a personal nature, and these Carey tried not to grasp. But presently he came upon a paragraph that gripped his interest. It read:

I have some good news for you: The governor has at last yielded to our entreaties and is going to remove Sheriff Hawks from office. I don't know when this is going to happen, for the governor would tell me no more. Your last letter to me did the work; the governor said he had no idea that conditions over

*there are so bad. I need not impress upon you the imperative
necessity for secrecy.*

Carey passed the letter back to Castle. "That's the best news I
have heard in a long time!" he fervently declared. "And, by
George! it does vindicate my hunch! The only bad feature of the
news is that I can't print it. But I can weather that disappointment
in view of the fact that the wabbly spined Hawks is to be kicked
out. Lord, what a fourflusher that man is!"

"Uh-huh," agreed Castle. "We jibe on that statement. This
letter was written a week ago, in spite of the fact that I got it only
yesterday. Evidently the governor is not going to blunder in this
game, for I note that Hawks is on the job this morning, as usual. I
don't pretend to anticipate the governor's actions, but it seems
reasonable to suppose that if he fires Hawks he will have to
appoint someone to his place."

"Inevitably," drawled Carey; "I never heard of a political
job that went begging."

"Naturally, since the governor is disposed to observe secrecy
in the matter," pursued Castle, "he wouldn't notify Hawks of
his dismissal until he is ready to name his successor. And it is
also reasonable to suppose—also keeping in mind the secrecy
surrounding the matter—that the new appointee will not be
announced with a blare of trumpets. Indeed, it is highly probable
that he will arrive in Red Rock incognito, or otherwise uniden-
tified, in order to sort of size up things and get a line on the
character of the people."

"Clever," mocked Carey, drawling.

For a moment Castle smoked his pipe in silence, watching
Carey refill and light his own. Then he smiled.

"You newspapermen profess to be observant, don't you?"

"Meaning what?"

"Meaning that in my opinion the new sheriff is already in Red
Rock—has, in fact, been here since yesterday."

Carey sat erect. "Good lord!" he gasped weakly. "How do
you know?"

"Evidence," grinned Castle. "I was doing some work at my
desk yesterday when a strange horseman rode up, tied his nag to
the hitching rail and came in. He wanted to know if Justus Castle
was anywhere around. I told him I was the person he wanted and
he sized me up right carefully. Then he asked me if I knew W. G.

Cunningham, of Santa Fe. Upon being assured that I knew the gentleman, he asked me if I had received a letter from Cunningham recently. The man didn't seem to be trifling, and so I told him I had got a letter from Cunningham. He then pulled a letter out of a pocket, compared the handwriting with Cunningham's letter, and handed over both letters. The second letter was short and sweet. It read:

DEAR JUSTUS: *This will introduce you to Dave Lawler.*
                                                    CUNNINGHAM

"Then the man drew a photograph from a pocket and tossed it over to me. The photograph was a dead ringer for him. On the margin was written: 'To Justus Castle: You can identify Dave Lawler from this photograph.' This was signed by the governor and bore his official seal.

" 'Right?' said Lawler, grinning at me.

"I told him it was 'right' and he gave me a letter of credit from the Territorial Treasurer, signed by the treasurer and the governor, which makes Lawler due to pull up to ten thousand dollars out of this bank whenever he wants it.

" 'Right?' he says again. 'Quite right,' I had to tell him. 'Want it now?' I asked. 'Nothin' doin',' he returned. 'Just want to know it's here for me. You're not a gassin' man,' he said as he went out. 'Cunningham says you ain't.' ''

"Then he didn't say he is the new sheriff," said Carey, disappointedly. "He may be only a special man sent here to investigate."

"Whatever he is," said Castle, "he's evidence that something is coming off."

"And whatever that something is, I suppose we should be duly thankful," added Carey. "Where did this man put up?"

"At the Palace."

"If it isn't asking too much, would you mind letting me have a look at the photograph?"

Castle passed it over and Carey stared long at it. The face was typical of the country—lean, strong, rugged, with steady, serene eyes. A distinguishing feature was the extra-high cheekbones, over which the skin was tightly drawn, giving the upper portion of the face a bold, intent expression.

"Striking mug, that," commented Carey as he returned the

photograph. "Its owner isn't telling everything he knows; you may depend upon that."

"That's how he impressed me. Anyway, it's none of our business what he's here for. Only—I'm hoping he *is* the man the governor has made sheriff; he looks to be a match for Haddam, Hawks or any of them."

Carey turned to the window. He did not sit in the chair, however; elation and anticipation would not permit him to be quiet at this minute.

Castle continued to talk, his conversation hinging upon trivialities. But presently he stopped when he discovered that the distinguished editor of the *Advocate* was returning monosyllabic replies to questions which required extensive answers, and that he was staring with intense interest at something in the street.

"What on earth has got into you?" demanded Castle as he leaped toward the window.

"Holy Moses!" exclaimed Carey in an awed voice. "Look! Right out in front here! Am I seeing things, or is that a parson?" He grabbed Castle and pointed toward the street.

Castle took one quick glance, and gave a yelp of delight. "By George!" he said, "it's a parson as sure as you're a foot high!"

A sigh of relief escaped Carey. "Lord, Castle!" he grinned, his blue eyes alight with joy, "the *Advocate* is going to live. Something is coming off, for sure! A sheriff and a parson! My hunch was a double-barreled one!"

CHAPTER 3

A buckboard, old and dust covered, to which were hitched two horses that drooped as if they had been driven a long distance, had come to a halt in front of the bank building. A man and a woman sat in the low seat of the vehicle. Another horse, saddled and bridled, trailed the buckboard, secured to the endgate by a strap.

The woman, Castle and Carey instantly noted, was young and good looking. There was no mistaking the parson. The soft, black Stetson and the somber black coat suggested the clergyman quite as clearly and definitely as did the white collar that adorned his throat, in its turn adorned by a flowing black tie. As he descended from the buckboard and walked forward to hitch the horses to the rail, the two watchers saw that he was tall, slender, vigorous looking. Yes, he was a clergyman—and also something more than a clergyman, for a certain bulge in his coat at the hip suggested that he was carrying a good-sized gun in a holster.

While the "sky pilot" hitched the horses, the young woman turned and saw Castle and Carey watching her. Both flushed at the straight, inquiring look she gave them—whereat her eyes kindled a little with some emotion and she looked away.

Red Rock was interested—as interested as Carey and Castle. From where Carey stood he could see groups of men watching the newcomers from doorways. Heads were stuck out of windows; necks were craned; it seemed that instantly there was a suspension of all activity. Red Rock—for the moment—was dumb with astonishment, for if the clergyman intended to grace the town permanently he had sent no advance notices.

After their discovery that the young woman was aware of their presence at the window, Carey and Castle politely backed away from it. Castle went to his desk and pretended to be busy with some papers, and Carey suddenly discovered that a last year's calendar on the wall near the window was intensely interesting.

Embarrassment sat heavily upon each as they heard the clergyman's voice from the doorway. There was a note of quiet amusement in it, which led them to believe that he had not been unaware of their glances from the window.

"Good morning, gentlemen!" he said cheerily. "I wonder if I could have a bit of your time?"

"All you like," said Castle.

"We work in spasms," added Carey. He had turned from the calendar and had stolen a swift glance at the young woman, who had entered with the clergyman. Castle rose from his desk and went to the counter. Was Carey mistaken, or was there mirth in the slightly twitching corners of the young lady's mouth? At any rate she was pleasing to look at, and Carey, knowing that he was supposed, in this situation, to pretend polite disinterest, found it difficult to turn his head and gaze out of the window.

She wore dusty garments, it was true, and yet her wearing apparel was not of the slightest interest to Carey, except that he had got a general impression that the things she wore fitted her with entrancing grace. Her hair, arranged in tightly caught curls and waves, had a film of dust upon it, yet it glistened through as if the dust were a gray veil. It softened the brown, glistening sheen of it into gloriously rich tones. Perhaps the dust veil accentuated the clear whiteness of her skin, but Carey could not have told, because, at a stroke, he was in the grip of a yearning ecstasy which made his judgment unreliable.

The clergyman resembled the young woman. He had her eyes—which were so serene and steady that they created a queer but definitely calm atmosphere around their owners—calmness which Carey instantly translated into confidence. Yes, the clergyman and the young woman had qualities of character which could be seen and felt at a glance—they could not be frightened or intimidated. Red Rock would not drive this man out of town, exulted Carey.

Evidently the clergyman had observed the interest of Red Rock's citizens, for he nodded in the general direction of the street.

"Do you think they're wanting religion?" he said.

Carey looked quickly at him—caught a subtle glow in his eyes. Carey's first impression of him was strengthened. Here was no pretense, but natural depth. Carey's respect for him increased.

"They want religion as much as they want law and order, Reverend," he answered.

"Then I expect I won't be popular."

"Were you expecting to be?" asked Carey.

"I was hoping to be." He turned and looked at the young woman, who was accepting a chair that Castle had offered her. "Tired?" he asked, with tender solicitation. "Well," at her nod, "we've been traveling mighty lively since daylight. If these men have no objections you might stay here and do a little resting while I hunt up the chairman of the trustees." He turned again to Carey. "You know him, I expect?"

Carey told him that the important office was held by Dave Blanchard, the proprietor of the Emporium Saloon, and the clergyman did not exhibit horror. Far from it. Carey saw the corners of his mouth dimple; saw his eyes twinkle.

"It's paradoxical, rather," said Carey. "I presume you will not find another such case in the country. At least I have never heard of one. But Red Rock calls Blanchard 'square,' and that's a tribute in these parts."

"A man's business need not keep him from knowing there is a God," said the clergyman.

"Dave's a straight-from-the-shoulder believer," grinned Carey.

The clergyman's eyes narrowed and gleamed with amusement. "I expect Dave and me will get along," he said. "But I'll have to see him before going any further. My sister," he added, indicating the young woman, who smiled and caused Carey's pulses to leap unaccountably, "Ellen Mc Donald. You gentlemen can supply her with your names; and I think we may as well get acquainted. My name is James Mc Donald—'Jim' for short."

"Reverend Jim," smiled his sister. "It's a combination of theological dignity and human humbleness that particularly fits him, as you shall see when you get to know him better.

" 'Jim' is a handle I've been used to since I was born," said the reverend gentleman, unsmilingly. He smiled at his sister. "I'm going down to see the chairman of the trustees. I expect it won't take long. Then we'll go right down to the parsonage." He looked at Castle and Carey—longest at Carey, his eyes twinkling again. "No objections to entertaining Ellen?" he asked. "Thank you," he added at Castle's and Carey's fervent "Certainly not!"

With a nod and a smile he stepped out of the doorway. Carey and Castle turned to the sister. Both spoke at the same instant, and both would have said the same thing, had not Carey, with the first word forming on his lips, had a sardonic divination that Castle had anticipated him. Indeed, as the verb trembled on Carey's tongue, Castle uttered it.

"Are," he said, and then scowled with one side of his face at his friend, "you intending to stay in Red Rock, Miss Mc Donald?"

"That is my present intention," answered the young woman. "That is, of course, if Jim finds Red Rock in a receptive mood. I shall not desert him, whatever happens."

"To be sure you won't," said Carey.

"I think Red Rock will receive your brother," confidently announced Castle, thinking of the suspicious bulge at Reverend Jim's hip.

She rewarded both with a smile—the same smile. "I hope so. I believe I shall like Red Rock, in spite of its bad reputation. So much depends upon the sort of support Jim receives from the best citizens. I am sure that you and Mr——" She hesitated, looking from one to the other.

"This is Justus Castle," cut in Carey, indicating his friend with a triumphant half-grin. "He is the owner of this bank, the Red Rock representative of the Chicago Livestock Company and my friend. My name is Norman Carey, and my presence in Red Rock may be accounted for by the fact that at my friend's solicitation I bought the Red Rock *Advocate*—which, in broad, general terms, may be described as a newspaper—which has been a losing investment. I may add that my friend has never indicated that he has repented his action."

Castle flushed, and Ellen Mc Donald laughed.

"Let us hope you may ultimately realize on your investment," she comforted.

"Carey has the impatience of the very young," came back Castle, and Carey felt Ellen's appraising glance without looking at her.

She saved him from any possibility of embarrassment by changing the subject. "As I was about to say," she resumed, "I am sure both you gentlemen will support my brother."

"Certainly!" they answered in unison.

"Red Rock needs reforming," instantly added Castle.

"A spiritual uplift," supplemented Carey.

"Yes," said Miss Ellen; "though the work will be difficult. I happen to know that my brother has no illusions in the matter, however.

"Indeed, this will be his first charge, his first call. I feel a little doubtful of him—that is—of his ability to distinguish between the spiritual and the material in his attitude toward the people of Red Rock. For he is likely to be less a minister of the Gospel and more the man, if he is imposed upon. Before he began attending the theological university he was a cowboy in Arizona, and he makes no secret of the fact that he was what you men call a 'hard case.' "

"Ah!" said Carey. "I perceive that Red Rock is due for a surprise."

"The bishop has evidently not forgotten the experience of your brother's predecessor," grinned Castle.

"The bishop," added Carey, "knows something besides prayer is necessary to the saving of Red Rock."

CHAPTER 4

The coming of Reverend Jim to Red Rock was an event rich in potentiality. Red Rock did not want to be "saved"—would not be saved—defied anyone to save it. And so Red Rock's interest in Reverend Jim was merely the interest of a great, sullen beast in the approach of a pest for which it has an innate fear slightly tinged with contempt. Its interest, a trifle abated by Reverend Jim's disappearance into the Castle bank building, was revived by his reappearance, and as he strode down the street toward the Emporium, Red Rock regarded him, appraised him and expressed its various opinions. There were smiles, laughs, sneers covert and open, good-natured jibes, and some curses.

There were many men in front of the Emporium, because they had gravitated there to discuss him and to speculate upon the probable purpose of his visit. Most of them hoped it would be a *visit*, only. But now, watching his approach, they divined his errand, for they knew that Dave Blanchard was the chairman of the trustees of the church and that if the reverend gentleman was seeking a charge in Red Rock he must first see Blanchard. And seeing Blanchard meant that he would have to enter the saloon, for Blanchard, having observed the approach of Reverend Jim, had withdrawn from the crowd and was now inside, having

33

divined Reverend Jim's errand and leaving word that he could be found behind the bar.

Blanchard's action had been deliberate and ironic. A former clergyman had incurred Blanchard's displeasure by inveighing against his business, insisting that as a trustee of the church he should set the citizens of the town a good example by closing his place. As it had been due entirely to Blanchard's efforts and money that Red Rock had a church at all, it might have been expected that the clergyman would have avoided friction with Blanchard. But the former clergyman had been uncompromising, and the result had been that when the hostile element had rose against him Blanchard had not interposed to save him.

Presently, now, Blanchard heard a quiet voice inquiring for him, and he was conscious of the distinct jeer in the voice of the man who answered, saying:

"Blanchard's in his rum joint."

There was a moment of silence and then Reverend Jim was inside the Emporium, standing just inside the doorway, peering about him. The subdued light within made objects a little dim after the white glare outside, and for an instant Reverend Jim stood uncertain.

And then came a voice from outside—the voice which had spoken to Reverend Jim.

"Hell!" it said. "He can't be a heap parson, runnin' into the devil's place that deliberate."

Blanchard waited. He saw the reverend gentleman smile with humor that seemed almost feline. And instantly, before the sound of the man's voice had died away, Reverend Jim replied.

"My friend," he said, turning to the man, whom Blanchard could not see, "are you the devil's defender?"

There was a roar of laughter; it rose above the growls of the discomfited owner of the voice.

Reverend Jim walked over to the bar and leaned an elbow upon it easily and carelessly. He looked straight at Blanchard and there was no diffidence in his manner.

"I am looking for Dave Blanchard," he said.

Blanchard cleared his throat. The former clergyman had not had this man's confidence of bearing, certainly not his assurance. "I'm Blanchard!" he returned gruffly.

Reverend Jim's right hand went across the bar. Blanchard reluctantly took it and his own was quickly in a grip that was manly and warm.

"I have come to talk with you about the church," said Reverend Jim. "I am Jim Mc Donald. The bishop sent me in reply to some correspondence you had with him. Where shall we talk?"

Blanchard's gaze was defiant. "Ashamed to do your talkin' here?" he said.

"No," answered Reverend Jim quickly, "this suits me."

Blanchard's smile contained approval. "Then we'll go into the back room," he suggested. "There's too many guys here to butt in."

Blanchard was bulky and tall, and he moved slowly from behind the bar and walked to a door that led to a rear room. Reverend Jim followed him. Gambling tables stood about; chairs were scattered around in disorder; wooden boxes partly filled with sawdust and reeking with tobacco juice were prominent; the air was foul with stale smoke and fumes from the liquors dispensed from the bar. Once in the rear room Blanchard looked intently at Reverend Jim—not without a certain vindictive amusement on his florid face.

"Not exactly a fit place to talk church in," he suggested experimentally.

"It won't hurt the church to be talked about in here," smiled Reverend Jim.

"How about yourself? You got your esthetics adjusted to the smell of tobacco and stale booze?"

Reverend Jim met his eye with a level gaze. "I punched cows around Tombstone for ten years," he said.

"Then you're set for what you see here," said Blanchard, giving Reverend Jim a glance that was very near approval. "Most parsons is a little finicky about such things." And now, as he motioned his visitor to a chair, he for the first time saw the butt of a six-shooter peeping from beneath the black coat. His eyes dilated.

"Lordy!" he ejaculated. "Did you come here to save souls or to disconnect them from bodies?"

"To save them, I hope," said Reverend Jim slowly. His smile was subtle and gentle. "I carry this," he said, "partly from force of habit and partly because I haven't got godlike enough to let anyone herd ride me without protesting."

"Then you ain't preachin' the gospel of 'turn the other cheek?' "

"I may reach that point—give me time." His eyes met Blanchard's—and Blanchard's gleamed with newborn astonishment and respect. "I expect I sure would make a stubborn Jesus," he added.

"Well, now!" said Blanchard. "Well, now!" His eyes glowed with some deep emotion as he regarded Reverend Jim. "I reckon I've been travelin' the wrong trail. I've been thinkin' that parsons was pretty much all alike, but I'm beginning to see there's some difference in them, same as there's difference in ordinary folks. Red Rock ain't never been shocked by no parson, but I reckon she's about due." But now a glint of doubt flashed in his eyes. "I reckon you don't work that gun any too clever," he said.

Reverend Jim had not yet taken the chair offered by his host. As the latter asked the question, Reverend Jim's right hand moved with a gliding, downward motion. There was a gleam of dull metal, a crashing roar, and a whisky bottle that stood on the sill of one of the rear windows was shattered to atoms. It was rapid, accurate work.

Blanchard grinned his admiration. "Plumb slick shootin'," he complimented. "An'," he added, "you draw like an old-timer. I reckon that even Flash Haddam ain't got nothin'——"

The door leading to the saloon was flung open; a dozen heads were stuck into the opening; a bartender in a white apron looked in with popeyed surprise.

"What in——" he began.

"Shut the door!" growled Blanchard. "The new parson has just took his first shot at the demon rum!"

The door was closed and Blanchard drew a chair to a table and motioned Reverend Jim into another. "I reckon you're some man, along with your religion. We'll have that talk."

An hour later Reverend Jim and Blanchard emerged from the rear room. Blanchard was smiling. The crowd which had been about the door of the Emporium when Reverend Jim had entered was now inside, and there was a hum of voices which abruptly ceased.

Blanchard halted midway of the length of the bar-room and faced the crowd, his right hand resting upon Reverend Jim's shoulder.

"Gents," he said in the quick silence, "this here's your new parson. He's come to open up the meetin'house, to glorify God an' herd ride sin. He's got his papers all regular an' O.K. from the bishop. He's a simon-pure parson, an' he's man's size. He ain't allowin' that he's goin' to preach the eternal damnation of booze, because he says he's fit booze, an' if any man can't quit guzzlin' it of his own accord he wouldn't have sense enough to heed any gospel in that line. But he's allowin' you all has got plenty more sins which is a heap worse than drinkin'. An' he's goin' to yawp some to you about them, soon's we can get the meetin'house hoed out an' set to order. I reckon we——"

There was a stir in the crowd surrounding Blanchard, and Flash Haddam stepped into view. He had only just entered, but had heard Blanchard's words, introducing Reverend Jim.

He brushed his way through the crowd and strode in front of Reverend Jim. He was cool, insolent, contemptuous. He spoke to Blanchard, ignoring Reverend Jim.

"Did I understand you to say there was a parson comin' to Red Rock—to stay?" he said.

"I reckon you heard me gassin' some to that effect," returned Blanchard, his ruddy face paling a little. "Also, you butted in before I was done talkin'. I was about to hook onto that statement that I'm backin' the parson in this here little deal."

Haddam laughed, still ignoring Reverend Jim, who stood there quietly, knowing that all the men in the crowd were critically watching him and enjoying the prospect of Haddam's violence. In seeming playfulness, though there was a dawning, wild intolerance in his eyes, he placed an open hand against Blanchard's chest and shoved him backward. The gesture was an expression of disdain for Blanchard's championship of Reverend Jim. Blanchard, enraged, endured the laughter of the crowd, which was obviously in sympathy with Haddam's provocative words about Reverend Jim. They remembered Reverend Jim's predecessor, who, one day during the later hours of his stay in Red Rock, had endured passively the disgraceful ordeal of having his nose tweaked by the outlaw.

Haddam, now speaking to Blanchard, said: "Every man plays his own hand in this country. You ain't slippin' no one any cards from your bootleg, Blanchard. You ain't in this—understand?"

He turned to Reverend Jim, his slow, insolent gaze traveling from head to heels. What he saw seemed to amuse him.

"A parson, eh? Well, Red Rock ain't allowin' it needs any damn parson to shoot off his gab. Red Rock has got along medium without any sky pilot blazin' the way to heaven for it. Parson's is mostly wind an' four-flushin', accordin' to Red

Rock's experience.'' He took a step closer. ''I'm givin' you the
first warnin' that we don't want you in Red Rock, stranger,'' he
added. ''If it's disregarded, we'll come stronger the next time.''
He reached up slowly, very slowly, a twisting, disparaging smile
on his lips, and seized Reverend Jim's nose between a thumb and
forefinger, holding it very, very gently, so that everyone in the
crowd might see what he intended to do.

Men other than Reverend Jim's predecessor had suffered this
indignity at Haddam's hands, and the crowd voiced some gig-
gles in anticipation of the clergyman's humiliation. But it was
evident that one day, in perpetrating the indignity, Haddam had
met with resistance or violence, for now, with the motion of his
hand toward the victim's nose, he dropped the other hand to his
gun holster in readiness for expected counter hostility. A savage
twist with the thumb and forefinger, and Reverend Jim would be
standing before the crowd, full of physical pain and mental
humiliation.

But Flash did not twist Reverend Jim's nose. At the instant his
fingers touched the butt of his gun he felt the muzzle of Reverend
Jim's six-shooter making a deep dent in his stomach, and he
heard Reverend Jim's voice, low, cold, intense:

''One twist and I'll blow you apart!''

There was a gasp of astonishment from the crowd, a grin of
savage delight from Blanchard. Awed, the crowd was silent,
filled with wonder over Reverend Jim's temerity and his uncan-
ny rapidity in drawing his weapon. Followed an instant's gaping
speculation as to how Haddam would meet this challenge. And
then the crowd relaxed from the unusual tension, for it saw the
color slowly recede from the outlaw's face—watched the contempt on his lips turn to a shallow, abashed grin of surrender. For
an instant he hesitated, and then his hand dropped from Reverend Jim's nose, while his gun hand moved carefully away from
the holster at his hip.

''I reckon I've got into the wrong pew, Parson,'' he said.
''But,'' he added, stepping back; ''you'll be holdin' meetin'
again, an' I'll sure be on hand.''

Reverend Jim smiled faintly, his six-shooter still in hand.
''Meeting is still going on, Haddam,'' he said gently. He looked
at the heavy Colt in his hand.

''Tweakin' parsons' noses ain't goin' to be so popular,
hereafter,'' said a voice from the crowd.

Frowning, his eyes blazing, Haddam faced toward a point from which the voice had seemed to come.

"This parson is man's size," he said, his voice hoarse with passion. "I'm wantin' the man who's feelin' so damn funny over this nose-pullin' deal to step up an' see if he's got nerve enough to pull it off on Flash Haddam!"

There was no answer. The men around Haddam stepped back. There was a tense silence. Haddam broke it with a low laugh.

"Nobody's allowin' he wants any of that game, eh? Then I reckon you all won't be jumpin' onto the parson, an' he'll be saved for me. I'm runnin' in with him again. He sure ain't no greenhorn." He laughed mockingly, bowed with extravagant politeness to Reverend Jim, and strode out of the front door, his spurs jingling in the silence.

CHAPTER 5

Reverend Jim's clash with Flash Haddam merely served to intensify Red Rock's interest in him. The clash, however, had wrought a difference in the quality of that interest. Red Rock had been prepared to receive Reverend Jim with skepticism and ridicule, but after the meeting with Haddam it thought of him with feelings akin to respect.

During the week that followed his appearance at the Castle bank building, however, Red Rock saw little of him. The clergyman had taken his sister to the parsonage. Carey had ridden down there once and had brought back word that Reverend Jim and his sister were busy getting their house in order and that, until they got settled, there would be no service at the meetinghouse.

Meantime Blanchard, as chairman of the trustees, had been busy turning his promise to "hoe out the meetinghouse" into reality. Blanchard's remark, delivered a few days following Reverend Jim's clash with Haddam: "The parson's got a way about him that's mighty convincin'," seemed complete and comprehensive, and reflected opinion in Red Rock, if the interest which attended the work at the meetinghouse was to be accepted as an indication. To Carey and Castle, Blanchard's remarks was a vindication of Miss Mc Donald's illuminating description of her brother's character.

Carey's reception at the parsonage had been as cordial as he could have wished, and in addition to the word concerning the Reverend's intentions with regard to the date of the first meeting, Carey brought back a vivid picture of Miss Mc Donald in a house dress, standing at the door waving a farewell to him.

The parsonage was not a large building. Formerly it had been a ranch house, abandoned by its owner for reasons which had been too slight for Red Rock to remember. But when the former parson had come Blanchard had had the house prepared for him, had furnished it and made it habitable. Reverend Jim and his sister found it to be not unattractive.

It was built of logs, hewn smooth inside, with plastered interstices. A big porch, more picturesque and substantial than symmetrical, stretched across its front. There were six rooms, all on the ground floor; four bedrooms, a kitchen and a large sitting room.

Behind the ranch house was a stable, a small affair of the lean-to type, with a larger stable near a distant corral, and a few outbuildings in a fair state of repair. Close to the corral was the river, which wound its way in serpentine fashion through the basin.

North of the river, opposite the parsonage, the basin extended only a few miles. It widened farther down, toward the H-Bar-W ranch, and then it merged into some barren foothills behind which were somber mountain peaks. But, standing on the edge of a butte that fringed the river back of the parsonage, Miss Mc Donald could see the beauty of the mountains despite their somberness, and gazing across the river at a point where it doubled sharply, she could see a ranch house and outbuildings which Carey, on the occasion of his first visit to the parsonage, had told her was the property of Harvey Warren—the H-Bar-W.

Carey frequently called at the parsonage, but Ellen had not been permitted to monopolize all his time. From the editor of the *Advocate* Reverend Jim had learned much about the inhabitants of the vast section of country in his charge. Of these, Harvey Warren, Ben and Martha had been most seriously discussed, and Reverend Jim's eyes had glowed with interest during Carey's recital of their misfortunes.

At dusk on a day two weeks following their arrival at the

parsonage, Reverend Jim and Ellen were sitting on the front porch. Ellen was sewing, and Reverend Jim was stretched out comfortably in a rocking chair, his feet on the railing, a pipe in his mouth.

"Like it here?" he asked presently, breaking a long silence.

"Very much. Do you?"

"Better every day."

Ellen stopped sewing and folded her hands in her lap.

"You'll be careful of that man Haddam?" she said, solicitously.

"Oh, Haddam." Reverend Jim's face grew grave and his lips straightened. But when Ellen caught his eyes they flashed with a fire that she knew well. "I think Flash has more respect for clergymen than he had," he said.

"Yes," she answered. "Norman Carey told me your conduct that day had shocked Red Rock more than anything else had ever shocked it."

Reverend Jim smiled. "Norman Carey's plumb man."

He smoked in silence for five minutes, during which time he alternately watched the night shadows steal over the basin and stole glances at Ellen. Finally the pipe spluttered in depletion and he knocked the ashes out of the bowl and put the pipe into a pocket. Then he got up and walked to where Ellen sat, standing beside her and laying a hand affectionately upon her head. "Looks like we've got a big job in front of us, Sis. A clergyman, or law and order, is about as welcome in this country as a rattler in a prairie-dog town."

"You'll win," she said, looking up at him with a confident smile.

He patted her shoulder and stooping quickly, kissed her forehead.

"I'll go and look after the horses," he said. Instantly he turned swiftly, catching a sharp, strange sound, and saw, not more than fifty or sixty feet away, a man on a horse, watching him and grinning widely and derisively. The horseman had apparently ridden around a bit of concealing timber, and must have been watching for some time, for his pony was browsing the tips of some long grass, the reins hanging loosely over his head.

The rider was Ben Warren. He had left Flash Haddam only a half-hour before; he was intoxicated, and obeying a maudlin impulse of curiosity, had ridden some distance out of his way to catch a glimpse of Reverend Jim. He had seen Reverend Jim's exhibition of affection, had noted Reverend Jim's discovery of his presence, and his derisive grin indicated that he had formed an uncomplimentary and suspicious conclusion regarding Reverend Jim's action in kissing his sister.

Reverend Jim took a step toward him, smiling cordially. He had been anxious to meet as many of his parishioners as possible. "Hello, my friend," he said. "Get off your horse and visit!"

Ben laughed loudly. "His sister!" he derided, addressing no one in particular. "An' mushin' over her! Hell! Somebody else's sister, I reckon!" He jerked the pony's head erect, jammed the spurs into its flanks and raced recklessly away from the ranch house, his mocking laugh floating back to Reverend Jim and Ellen on the porch, reddening the girl's face and bringing a pallor to Reverend Jim's.

CHAPTER 6

Nothing had occurred to break the monotony which had surrounded the H-Bar-W ranch house since the departure of Martha's father, more than two weeks ago. No roaming cowboy, no chance traveler, no neighbor, had passed the ranch to speak a word to the girl. Her isolation had been nearly complete. Her father had set no definite date for his return, and when he rode in early one morning with Dal Thompson, the foreman, he stayed only a few minutes—long enough to eat the breakfast Martha hurriedly prepared for him, and to refashion some branding irons needed by the men of the outfit. Then he rode away, saying that he would return about the third day. But before he left, Martha beguiled him from the house, away from Dal Thompson. She halted near the corral gates and faced him.

Warren was grizzled and tanned; his beard was rough and bristly from the rigors of a half century of life in the open. His eyes were bright and lacked the serenity of expression common to men of his calling who have communed with vast solitudes and great stretches of vacant world. The brightness of his eyes told of his mental affliction—told that the silence of solitude had pressed in upon him. His expression sometimes had that vacuous immobility indicative of a dull, puzzled brain with its resulting slowness of perception. He looked at Martha with a grin.

"You look a lot like your mother—like she looked when we got married, Martha. Brown hair, brown eyes, fair skin, roses in your cheeks. She had them—lord! She had them!" He peered hard at her. "You've got a different disposition, though; you're one of them kind that stand up for their rights. But your mother—it's kind of lonesome without her."

She placed an arm affectionately around his waist. "Daddy," she said, "I have been lonesome, too. Why not sell the H-Bar-W and go away—to some place where things would be a little livelier? We have been here a long time, you know."

His face hardened as he stared at her in astonishment. "Shucks!" he said. "You're talkin' foolish. I've been in these parts too long to go gallivantin' around now—lookin' for somethin' I mebbe couldn't find. You've talked about that more'n once, lately. But it ain't goin' to do any good. I'm stayin' here. Why, girl," he added, his eyes gleaming with the unnatural brightness that she dreaded to see, "what would your mother say if I was to pull my freight an' leave her here alone? Why, she's here, Martha! I see her nights! Some folks say it ain't possible, but folks ain't as wise as they think they are when they say Harvey Warren's wife has left him!" He laughed lowly and weirdly, and Martha turned away from him with white face and trembling lips. Half an hour later when he left with Dal Thompson, she stood in a doorway, watching dejectedly.

She had no word to say to Ben about her conversation with Flash Haddam. To have done so would probably have precipitated a clash between Ben and the outlaw. She knew Ben's temper, and she knew of Haddam's deadly rapidity with a weapon—knew also, since her last conversation with him, the wantonness of his character. She must keep her knowledge to herself, even though she was convinced that silence would ultimately result in Ben's ruin. In fact, it seemed inevitable that Ben was already lost, for this very morning, despite her reproofs over his condition the night before, she had caught him laughing into his plate at the breakfast table. He had been at home only once during the past two weeks.

A quick pang shot through her. That he could laugh after her protests showed he had no sense of responsibility, no conception of his danger. And yet, so deep was her affection for him, she could not help smiling in sympathy with him.

"Shucks!" he said aloud, after a period of silent laughter. "I reckon Flash must have been some took back!"

"What is it, Ben?"

He grinned broadly at her. "I forgot you ain't heard. There's a new parson at Red Rock—at the parsonage. Calls himself Reverend Jim, they say. Jim Mc Donald. Come here two weeks ago—him an' his sister. He says it's his sister," he added laughing harshly, "though there's some of the boys have got their doubts."

"Ben!"

"How's a man to tell? Anyways, I'll say this: I run into them last night when I was comin' home, an' I seen him an' her mushin' on the porch. An' I reckon there ain't no *man* mushin' none over his sister. It ain't natural."

"Not for some men. Some men seem to care very little for their sisters." Her voice was regretful, wistful.

He bristled. "I reckon I care as much for mine as the next man, but I ain't gettin' sapheaded about it!"

"I wouldn't think any less of you if you did make more of a show of your affection, Ben. If I am not mistaken someone has said that no real man is ashamed of his demonstrations of love to his own people."

He reddened. "You got that way from readin' some of your mushin' books. I say a man can like people without showin' it—to his sister, especially. A man that mushes over his sister ain't a heap man. Anyway's that ain't what I'm tickled over. The new parson ain't all parson—like that other critter which spread his smooth palaver all over Red Rock. This guy's got nerve. Brought Flash Haddam up with a short turn the first crack out of the box!"

Martha gave an exclamation of vindictive satisfaction.

"Fact," said Ben. "Flash allowed he was goin' to twist the parson's nose; an' the parson, not feelin' in the humor that particular time, bent his gun on Flash an' made him crawfish. It sure must have been amusin'!"

"It is time somebody did something to Flash," she said. "But did Reverend Jim know what he was doing, making an enemy of Flash?"

"He wasn't sayin'. But accordin' to what I hear, the parson ain't no greenhorn when it comes to handlin' a gun."

"But Flash is sure to do some mean thing in return."

"I reckon so. But from all the specifications noticed by them which was so fortunate as to witness the deal, it ain't goin' to be no picnic for Flash. The parson's been a cowboy around Tombstone; he totes a gun, an' Dave Blanchard says he's a wizard at gettin' it into workin' position. I don't reckon that Flash will try to run in no cold lead proposition on him. It's goin' to be a different game than that!"

"How different?"

"I don't know. But Flash is pretty slick himself."

Following this conversation, Ben saddled his pony and rode away without telling her where he was going.

She found it lonesome again, after his departure, and for an hour after washing the dishes and "straightening" up, she sat at the table, her elbows on its top, her chin in her cupped hands, gazing out of the window at the cheerful, peaceful world. It called to her in tones insistent and irresistible, speaking of its wide spaces, its beauty, its silence, its amazing variety. And presently she got up, put on her riding garments, caught up Ginger, her favorite pony, threw a saddle on him and rode down the river trail.

The Reverend Jim's eyes twinkled, as sitting on his pony at the edge of the parsonage porch, he looked at his sister.

"I'm thinking of riding up the river to the H-Bar-W to have a talk with the Warrens," he told her.

"Well, if you are thinking about it, you'll go," she said. "And it's about time. You haven't called upon them yet. So get along."

"If Carey happens to drop in here, peddling his *Advocates*—those that are now a week late—you might tell him that I'm going to preach at the meetinghouse Sunday at ten A.M. sharp."

"I don't think he will come today."

"How long has it been since he was here?"

"Five days."

He looked at her with narrowed eyes as he said: "I suppose you've been counting them."

"You are hopeless, Jim," she said, reddening.

"He that hath eyes——" began Reverend Jim.

"Shall not see things that are forbidden him," she interrupted.

"How could he help it," he grinned, "if he looked at all. And so you are admitting——"

"I am not admitting anything. Won't you ever outgrow your

habit of poking fun at people?'' She shook a threatening finger at him. ''One of these days, when you meet a woman who makes an impression on you, I'll pay you for your teasing with interest.''

''You'll never be getting even then. I'm too bashful to do any courting. The woman would have to do it, with me doing the retiring and dodging.''

''The woman always does it, I think. But she permits the man to think he is taking the initiative.''

''So that's it, eh? Interesting and informative. Well, we learn, it seems. So that's how it's done. You want a man, but you don't let him know you want him. And you lead him along until he falls head over heels in love with you, and——''

''Hush! Every woman knows that.''

''I expect I've been foolish.''

''Why?''

''For forgetting that you're having some experience in that line with——''

''Go along to the Warrens!'' she told him, blushing. And she stood on the porch, smiling at him as he rode down toward the river. He waved a hand to her as he entered some timber.

Reverend Jim went on his way, smiling to himself. Ellen's susceptibility had afforded him many moments of pleasure. And he liked Norman Carey. But presently, as he rode, his face grew grave, for his thoughts went to the Warrens and to a word that Norman Carey had spoken concerning them. It had been about Ben Warren, chiefly, and Carey told Reverend Jim that he would not have mentioned Ben if he had not been convinced that Reverend Jim might be able to lighten Martha's burden of care.

Many smiles wreathed Reverend Jim's face as he reflected upon his talk, a few minutes before, with Ellen. He was riding a dim trail that led through some timber skirting a grassy promontory overlooking the river, and he had just laughed audibly over Ellen's confusion over his skillful reference to her attitude toward Norman Carey, when he became aware of a pony on the trail in front of him. It was a little beside the trail and was unconcernedly browsing the river grass.

It was piebald, with a dark yellow predominating. The reins were trailed over its head, indicating that it was abroad with its owner's consent, and after a short nicker of interest, which

Reverend Jim's pony returned, the animal resumed its uncon-
cerned browsing.

Reverend Jim spent a moment in silent contemplation of the
strange pony and then swung himself crosswise in the saddle to
await the appearance of its owner. The presence of a pony alone
on the trail was not an occurrence to be passed by lightly, since it
might mean that the rider had met with an accident. At all events,
etiquette would compel the investigation of such an incident. He
intended to wait.

Meanwhile he inspected the landscape in the vicinity for signs
of the rider. There were none. But when, after a time, Reverend
Jim returned to the promontory, he straightened in the saddle.
For at the base of a cottonwood tree, seated on the grass close to
the edge of the promontory, was a young woman.

She was resting. Her hat was off, her hair was in a tangle of
disorder, with some stray wisps hanging down over her temples.
Her cheeks were red, and though her hands were folded in her
lap in a manner indicating lassitude—or possibly mere unconcern or indifference to Reverend Jim's presence—he could see
from the brightness of her eyes that she was speculating about
him.

But Reverend Jim was also speculating about her—and striving mightily to conceal the amazement and admiration that, as a
clergyman, he should not permit to find expression on his face.
He thought he did rather well, though to accomplish it he was
forced to feign surprise. But though his chest was swelling with
the most ecstatic thrill he had ever known, he managed to be
natural. He rode his pony close to the edge of the promontory,
passing within a few feet of the young woman, hoping by this
subterfuge to be able to steal a glance at her without her seeing it.
But when, after a long look into the valley below, he turned his
head, the young woman was looking straight at him, still
speculatively, but with the vestige of an enigmatic smile—
which, Reverend Jim thought, made her more beautiful than
ever.

Her gaze was direct, challenging, and he knew she was
expecting him to speak, to explain why he had invaded her
privacy, but having finally met a girl who had set him to tingling
with admiration, he had no intention of permitting the meeting to
become a prosaic contact between a parishioner and a clergyman, merely. Yet, fearful of frightening her by being too abrupt,

and perhaps too formal—to make her self-conscious and spoil her natural charm—he proceeded obliquely.

"Well, ma'am," he said, bowing to her, but making no move to dismount, "if I was a horse thief, now, I would have thought I'd have had a chance to run off with your pony. You see, I didn't know you were sitting there, watching me."

"How do you know I have been watching you?" she asked, her chin lifting a little—a slightly hostile gesture.

He divined her mood, and smiled with satisfaction. She was just as he hoped she would be—as he felt she must be after his first look at her—entirely capable, and sturdily independent.

"Why, I don't exactly know," he said, as if reviewing the scene. "Why, of course," he added, as she watched him curiously. "It must have been that way. You were looking at me when I first looked at you, and so you must have been looking first."

She did not reply. Reverend Jim was beginning to think that this exchange of words would be a brief one, and not wishing to make the mistake of annoying her, he had tightened the reins to urge his pony on, when she spoke again:

"I suppose you are the new minister?" Her voice was less hostile. She had noted his preparatory movement and it had convinced her that he had no intention of forcing himself upon her.

Reverend Jim gravely considered her. Of course she must have known him for a minister at first glance. So that she, too, was pretending a little.

"Why, you've guessed it!" he said. "Right away—almost. I'm the new minister. And I'm on my way to make my first visit to the nearest family in my flock—which happens to be the Warrens."

"I am Martha Warren," she informed him. And now, for the first time, he saw her lashes droop a little as she gazed downward. She was thinking of her brother, of course. Enduring the humiliation of his departure from honesty. "There is no one home at the H-Bar-W," she added.

Reverend Jim had suspected her identity, but did not intend to tell her so. He grinned, pushed his hat back from his forehead and scratched his head doubtfully. It was purposeful exaggeration of mental confusion, and Martha smiled wisely.

"I expect I'm a boxhead for not tumbling to it sooner. Why, it's right plain that you're Martha Warren. You're right near the

H-Bar-W; you're the only girl living there, and there is no other ranch close around. Sometimes I come pretty close to not thinking at all.''

''I'm sure you are more of a thinker than you pretend to be,'' said Martha. There were two emotions struggling within her—skepticism and amusement. Amusement predominated. For the minister was strikingly good looking, his dignity was vulnerable with humaneness; ministerial dourness was absent in his glances at her. She was strangely glad he was not different.

''Oh, don't!'' he said in a tone of gentle remonstrance. ''You don't mean to accuse me of knowing who you were all the time?''

''Yes,'' she said, positively. ''You overdid it, I think. You are not a hypocrite—though you came dangerously close to acting like one.''

''There's one thing I couldn't be hypocritical about, no matter how I tried,'' he said. ''It's that you are a mighty observing girl. I'm glad you are; and I'm glad to know you. Now, if you'd shake hands with me, I'd feel that we are beginning to become acquainted.''

''Of course,'' she said. She got up, brushing her skirt with feminine daintiness, and tucking in the stray wisps of hair at her neck and temples with the deftness that always arouses man's admiration. By the time Reverend Jim had dismounted she was ready to greet him. And Reverend Jim shook her hand warmly and sincerely, though her grasp, he noted with delight, was as friendly as his own; and her smile, though shy, contained consciousness of his admiration.

Reverend Jim's aim was achieved, though she had seen through his ruse. It had not been the stiff and formal meeting of preacher and prospective church member, as it might have been; he had made it what he had wanted to make it—an encounter between a man and a woman.

Gentle respect mingled with Reverend Jim's admiration as he watched her. The greeting over, they stood as they were, each tingling from the encounter, both stirred to thoughts that were new to them, both aware of the romance of their meeting. She had folded her hands at her waist, but was standing straight, her gaze direct, but somewhat abashed, smiling at him.

''I expect I did come pretty close to playing the hypocrite,'' he said. ''I'm planning to be careful, after this.''

''I don't know whether to believe you or not,'' she declared, seeing a gleam in his eyes which gave the lie to his promise of future reformation.

"Why, you'll certainly believe a parson!" he said, astonishment, which was not all pretense, in his voice.

"Why should I?" she laughed. "A preacher is merely a man, isn't he? Because he professes to believe the word he teaches and wears a black coat is no indication that he is not as human as other persons. It has always seemed to me that the quality of a person's manhood is more important than the depth of his belief in what he preaches."

"There's a heap of truth in that statement," he returned, soberly. "You've been looking the truth straight in the face. A man's got to be right with himself before he can be right with God. That applies to preachers as well as to other men. But if a man is right with himself and with God, that needn't keep him from funning a little when he feels like it. A man don't have to go around with a long face to be a Christian."

"Of course when you played the hypocrite a few minutes ago you were only joking. I knew it—somehow."

"That's a bull's-eye," he told her. "I don't aim to be stuck-up with the members of my new flock, to keep on doing things in the same old way. You see, I couldn't be dignified if I tried. I've had no practice yet—this being my first charge."

She had no reply to make to this, and for a moment silence came between them. Finally he said: "You in a hurry to get home?"

"No indeed. I've been lonesome all day."

"Then we'll rest here for a while and do some talking," he said. "That is, if you're not afraid that I'll go on acting the hypocrite."

As she arranged her skirts and sank to the grass she for the first time noted the breadth of his shoulders, his lithe, well-knit figure, and she remembered Ben's words: "The parson's been a cowboy around Tombstone." She could not help thinking that as a cowboy he must have been more in his element than as a minister.

He stretched himself out on the grass near her, resting on one elbow, facing her.

"I suppose you know the country around here pretty well?" he said.

"Very well. I have lived here all my life."

"It's a pretty good country. Plenty of grass, water—plenty of room. A person can move around and not feel crowded. You like it?''

"Yes. But it seems rather lonesome lately. Sometimes I feel as though I would like to get away from it.'' Her voice was a little wistful.

He smiled knowingly. "It's a heap natural for folks to feel that way. Talk to a man in a place like this, and he'll tell you he'd like to go some place where he could touch elbows with somebody once in a while. Listen to a man from town, and you'll find he is yearning to get out where he can stretch himself and look at the sky and breathe the air without anybody being around to interfere. It's not exactly crowded around here, but there's plenty of folks to touch elbows with—if a man wants to. It depends. There's people who are lonesome in a crowd.''

She was silent; her face lost a little of its color and there was the ghost of a bitter smile on her lips. The "crowd,'' as he had termed it, was responsible for her lonesomeness.

"The 'crowd' is injust, or one could not feel that way,'' she said.

He eyed her sharply, and thought instantly of his conversation with Norman Carey, concerning her brother. Carey had told him that suspicion of Ben Warren's intimacy with Flash Haddam was quite general, though no man had dared to publicly voice it. But her words and manner seemed to indicate that in some way the people in the vicinity had contrived to show her they were aware of her brother's delinquency.

"Why,'' he said, "you're too young to be a pessimist—to have the idea that there is no good in the world—either among people or things. And so it must be that someone has treated you mean recently. People are like that, sometimes, when they don't understand. Of course there are others who act mean, not intending to.''

"Of course it is your business to think kindly of people,'' she said smiling mirthlessly. "That's why you are ready with an excuse. But the people I charge with being unjust understand fully, and have made their intentions very plain. There is no excuse for them.''

"Well, now, that's too bad,'' he said quietly, detecting the emotion in her voice. "They sure must have treated you mean to make you feel that way about them. Usually, though, there's two sides to a story or a question. But I'm not qualified to judge because I have heard nothing of either side.''

He did not state a literal truth here, for he *had* heard something of one side of the question, but he felt that his departure from the exact truth was justifiable. He had professed ignorance merely for the purpose of leading her into a confidence, for in that manner he would be very likely to learn more of the truth about Ben than he would otherwise hear.

She did not tell him that she was yearning to make a confidant of him, yet that had been one reason why she had ridden down the river this morning toward the parsonage. She *must* have a confidant, must have someone whom she could trust, to whom she could communicate the doubts and fears that had beset her. She felt now, looking at Reverend Jim, and noting his serious manner, that she might confide in him without fear.

She spoke simply, "They say my brother is a cattle thief!" She looked straight at him, though her cheeks were crimson, and her next words came quickly and jerkily: "That is why people around here have been so mean to me. I suppose you think they have that right," she went on when he did not answer, and watched her with expressionless face. The color slowly receded from her cheeks, and her lips stiffened.

"Have they?" she insisted.

"You can't be held responsible for your brother's sins—if he has sinned," he said slowly. "Nobody's got any excuse to treat you mean on that account. But *some* people will do it. Have you talked to Ben about it? Did he tell you that he had been stealing cattle?"

"Flash Haddam told me," she said.

Some expression came into his face now—and his lips straightened. He sat erect, the ease gone from his attitude. "Haddam told you?" he repeated after her. "Haddam told you that Ben has been running his iron on other men's cattle?"

Carey had told him that her brother was suspected of being a friend of Haddam, and now Martha was telling him that Haddam had told her of Ben's crime. It was not a friendly action. He was puzzled until a new flood of color flooded her face, and she answered.

"Yes," she said, "Flash Haddam told me. He is at the bottom of it all. He spoiled Ben—got him to drinking—spoiled him purposely. He told me he did it because he felt the Warrens considered themselves better than he; that he wanted to drag us down—me, especially—to where he could meet me on terms of equality. He wants me to marry him!"

"Ah!" said Reverend Jim.

He sat for a moment, digesting this news, while Martha, embarrassed and uncomfortable, looked downward at some bunch grass at her feet. She had not failed to hear a note of cold astonishment in Reverend Jim's voice. It told her that he was not pleased with the news. But when she presently looked up she saw a faint smile on his lips.

"I expect no one could blame Haddam for *wanting* to marry you," he said.

"I am not looking for flattery," she said coldly.

"Flattery?" he returned, his smile becoming sober. "Oh no. I'm not the kind of man to deal from the bottom of the deck to a woman. I'm just telling you what I think. No one could blame Haddam for wanting to marry you. Even an outlaw can know a good woman when he sees one. But it takes two to make a bargain. Of course you told him his ideas were running a little wild?"

There was scorn in her eyes.

"Well, then," he said slowly, with satisfaction in his voice, "I expect there is nothing to worry about—except Ben," he added. "Flash has showed his hand; he has spoiled Ben—so you say—thinking that you will marry him to save Ben. I expect you are not afraid of Haddam on your own account. It's Ben who is worrying you. I expect, too, that the reason you've been telling me this is because you want me to help you keep Ben out of trouble. Well," he went on, with what she thought was a mysterious smile, "maybe I *can* help Ben. I expect it can't be so bad, after all. Mostly our troubles don't stand up and look us in the face when we go after them right hard. I expect yours looked big enough to you, though, having to rassle them alone. Has your father any influence over Ben?"

He saw her lips quiver, and he frowned as he suddenly remembered a word that Carey had uttered in reference to her father.

"Well, it's right bad when a father has no influence over a son or a daughter, as sometimes happens. A boy or girl will get to imitating other people. And so there has been no one you could talk to about Ben?" His lips grew tight; his eyes narrowed. "That crowd we've been talking about—that I was gassing about so fluently a minute ago—not using my brain any—ain't allowing that it's any friend of yours?" He caught her negative shake of the head and went on, disgust in his voice. "Folks are like sheep—sometimes; they play 'follow the leader.' They've been letting you alone a heap since they found out about Ben, eh?'' His voice was gentle with sympathy. ''I expect they've been crowding it onto you pretty hard, to get you to feeling like you do toward them. When trouble comes to a man he'll make a heap of fuss about it and try to rope and hog-tie it, pronto, so's to have it over with. But a woman is different. She'll put in a heap of her time keeping quiet, brooding and thinking and waiting for something to come and help her out. She wants sympathy. Wasn't there any woman——''

Reverend Jim hesitated, for he saw the girl gulp hard; saw tears well up into her eyes, her lips tighten near where her teeth were pressing them in a vain endeavor to keep them steady. She had not meant to speak to him about her ostracism—to go into detail about it; but neither had she expected his sympathy to be so sincere, so deep—had not expected it would affect her as it did. Suddenly her feelings overwhelmed her; the tensed lips opened, and the accumulated disappointment and bitterness of days of lonesomeness and brooding burst forth in one sentence:

''They wouldn't even come to my party!''

She leaned forward and buried her face in her hands, yielding to sobs that shook her violently.

Reverend Jim got up quickly and stood, looking down at her. His face was white, his chin thrust forward, his teeth clenched.

''Your party?'' he said with a tense coldness that made her lift her tear-stained eyes to his in surprise. ''Do you mean that you gave a party and that nobody came to it?''

She got to her feet before replying, wiping her eyes, smiling shamefacedly at him.

''Oh, I didn't mean to let anybody know that it hurt me,'' she said, ''and here I am, crying like a baby. I—I stood it as long as I could—without crying, I mean, though there were times when I came pretty near it. It wasn't anything—that is, I shouldn't have expected anybody to come. I don't think I should have cried about it, anyway, if it hadn't been that I kept thinking of that nursery thing—'Smarty, smarty, gave a party—and nobody came.'

''You see, I hadn't been a 'smarty.' If I had been——''

Reverend Jim interrupted her with a very unparsonly remark:

''The damned cowards!'' he said.

At her quick start of astonishment, he grinned coldly.

''That goes!'' he said. ''I wouldn't give a snap of my fingers

for a God that wouldn't damn such a lot of weak-kneed critters!
Wouldn't come to your party? Shucks!'' He suddenly laughed.
''Why, I'm letting my feelings get the best of me right immoder-
ate. But I ain't been used to seeing a woman cry like that, and I
expect——'' He hesitated again and went close to her, looking
at her with a critical but impersonal interest. ''You ain't had such
a big drove of birthdays, either, have you?''

''That was my eighteenth.'' She was smiling, now, and met
his gaze steadily, though she was frankly embarrassed.

His hand came out and was placed on her shoulder, where it
rested lightly.

''Shucks,'' he said; and again: ''Shucks! And they left you to
celebrate it alone! Afraid they'd get their characters soiled,
coming near you, because your brother don't happen to be
walking in the straight-and-narrow path! If I was the Lord I'd
give some people souls that they could take off and wash, and
then put back on again, like an apron or a shirt. They wouldn't be
so scared of risking them, then.''

''Well,'' she said, ''I didn't blame them—very much. You
see, in this country, a cattle thief——''

''You're plumb grit, not to blame them,'' he interrupted,
patting her shoulder, ''and I expect it's just foolishness to get
worked up about it. I'm going to try and help you. No more
crying, though,'' he grinned. ''No more moping around and
brooding about all the mean things that folks think and say.
Why, if a man was to sit around and think of all the mean things
that people say about him, he'd feel so sour that he'd think he
was swimming in a jug of vinegar. You're eighteen! When you
get as old as me you'll know better!''

His reference to his age brought her to the sudden realization
that she felt less a child in his presence now than when she had
needed sympathy. And with her clearer vision came the knowledge that he was a man and she a woman. She blushed and
looked at his hand as it rested on her shoulder, at which he
withdrew the hand and smiled a grave, pleased smile.

''You looked so much like a kid, crying that way,'' he said,
apologizing.

Again there was no guile in his look, and she met it frankly.
But her burden had been lifted, and between them she placed the
bar of demure reserve abetted by the wisdom of eighteen.

''You are not so *very* old yourself, are you?'' she said.

If she had expected to embarass him, she failed. He grinned

broadly, and she was forced to smile with him. "In years I ain't a heap older—being twenty-five last month. But in experience my age is a different thing. Sometimes, looking back on what I've gone through, I get to thinking I'm Methuselah." He looked at his watch. "I've got to be getting on," he said, stepping toward his pony. "I'm figuring on getting over to Dobble's and back before dark. How far would you say it is to Dobble's?"

"Fifteen miles," she told him.

"Well," he said, bowing to her, "I'll be getting along, then. I'm right pleased to have met you. If you ain't got a heap to do now, and it won't inconvenience you any, you might ride over to see my sister. She's allowing it'll be a little lonesome for her while I'm gone. Though I expect," he added, thinking of Ellen's confusion over his references to Norman Carey, "that there's times when she's glad, too."

"I shall ride over right away!" she promised, pleased to take advantage of this opportunity for companionship with one of her sex.

He smiled with pleasure. "You'll like Ellen," he told her. "I expect *she* won't be afraid of spoiling her soul."

He got on his pony, not offering to help her to mount hers, remembering the swift shyness that had overtaken her a few minutes before. He did not want to embarrass her. But his help was not needed; she was on her pony almost as soon as he was on his, and as they faced each other for a moment, each ready to depart, a silence fell between them. Their ponies were nuzzling each other with inquisitive muzzles, while hardly a bridle's length of space yawned between their riders. The delay to start was mutual.

Martha nervously smoothed her pony's mane, Reverend Jim watching her with a grave smile.

"I hope you'll like my sister," he said, presently. It was not the clergyman talking to a child now; it was a man talking to a woman. And it was no child who looked up at him.

"Oh," she said, gathering the reins more firmly into her hands: "I know I shall like your sister!"

And then her pony lunged forward in answer to the quick lash of the quirt, and it seemed he *must* know that she had meant the words, not for his sister, but for him!

Reverend Jim did not know, but he speculated much over her words as he turned in the saddle and watched her pony going down the river trail. His thoughts lingered on the girl as he rode his own pony into the wild country toward the Dobble ranch, and humorously he considered an impulse to ride after her. "You've talked like a fool to Ellen," he told himself, "because she likes Norman Carey. I wasn't thinking that what has happened to her would happen to me. Gentlemen, hush! Don't tell me what you'll do when the right girl comes along!"

Never had a woman impressed him as Martha impressed him. He had told Ellen the truth when he had told her that he had never loved any woman. And though Martha had stirred him deeply, he was not certain how. And what was he to think of her attitude toward him? He had lingered, delaying the leavetaking, but had she not lingered, also? Her blushes, too, were infallible signs, but he could not so easily surrender to vanity, and he told himself that her blushes had been due to gratitude over his offer of help for her brother. He was wondering if it had not been his self-consciousness and regret over her calling him a hypocrite that had been responsible for the blushes, when he looked up to see a horseman on the trail in front of him and not more than a dozen feet distant.

The horseman was Flash Haddam. He was sitting erect in the saddle, a six-shooter in hand, its muzzle menacing Reverend Jim, and on his face was dark hatred.

Reverend Jim brought his pony to a halt and sat motionless, steadily looking at Haddam. In this situation custom commanded that he also raise his hands in token of submission to the will of the rider who had "got the drop" on him, but he disregarded the custom, did not even think of it in his curiosity regarding Haddam's intentions—which seemed plain enough, after all. He watched Haddam, his hands resting on the pommel of the saddle, more astonished than fearful, disgusted to find that he had been dreaming instead of watching the trail.

"Hello, Haddam," he said. "So you've got your gun bent on me? I expect, if I hadn't been dreaming——"

"You've been palaverin' plenty," interrupted Flash. He was shaking with repressed fury; his voice was hoarse, almost a whisper, and his eyes were burning with a fire that needed only the slightest hostile movement on Reverend Jim's part to make it wanton.

Reverend Jim felt the danger, but by no sign did he indicate it. True, his lashes flickered once, but the eyes they veiled were steady, clear and unafraid. He did not look at Haddam's gun, but he referred to it.

"Well," he said coldly, "I expect you're doing the driving. Are you figuring to use that gun, or are you considering that I let you down easy in Blanchard's Emporium?"

A mighty mental struggle seemed to be going on in Haddam. His narrowed eyes bored into Reverend Jim's, and Reverend Jim looked back at him, curiously, unwaveringly, his hands still resting on the pommel of his saddle. Haddam, evidently, was looking for something in Reverend Jim's eyes—something that he could not find. For presently the malignance of his gaze began to fade, and a glint of doubt, in which there might have been a little respect, mingled with it. Slowly the intense emotion he had exhibited was subdued. His lips ceased to quiver and grew to straight, hard lines; his free hand unclenched, and the paleness of reluctant composure came into his face. He leaned forward and spoke, his chin thrusting, his lips writhing.

"You can go on livin', I reckon. But damn you, if you had showed yellow, I'd have salivated you!" He stared hard, obviously still uncertain. "Any man that can look at death that way ain't goin' to try to make a monkey out of a woman!"

"Thanks," said Reverend Jim dryly. "I'm passing you a compliment that's just as good. Any man who can use his brain like you used it in deciding not to shoot, ain't exactly a common critter." He smiled slightly. "And so it was my morals that was bothering you?" He watched Haddam jam his gun back into its holster. His interest in the operation was almost casual. And when Haddam looked up Reverend Jim's gaze shifted to his eyes.

A change had come over Haddam. All that sinister deadliness of attitude which had been so evident before, had vanished with magic quickness, as though it had been a cloak which he could put on and take off at will; and when he holstered his gun he became the reckless, easy, self-confident figure that had leaned over the porch railing talking to Martha Warren—the figure that Red Rock and the basin knew.

"Don't go to complimentin' my brain box none," he said. "You'd have cashed in by this time, if——" He broke off and laughed heartily, seemingly without visible cause. Evidently a thought in which Reverend Jim was concerned had brought him pleasure. He hesitated in his laugh long enough to remark, as he looked at Reverend Jim: "I reckon that'll be pilin' it onto you some, even if you have taken a shine to her!'' Then he continued his laugh.

"If you're propounding a riddle——"

"A riddle!" said Haddam. "Why, I reckon a riddle would be easy alongside of what I'm thinkin' about you!"

"Be careful you don't go loco, wrestling with heavy problems," warned Reverend Jim.

Flash guffawed. "No," he said, as if estimating Reverend Jim's probable attractions, "I reckon you ain't no lady-killer. Swappin' palaver for more than an hour with a good-lookin' girl, an' didn't get no further than puttin' a hand on her shoulder!"

Reverend Jim wheeled his pony so that his right side was toward Haddam. It was a position which would facilitate the drawing of the heavy Colt in the holster at his right hip and which would give him a decided advantage, should Haddam meditate accepting the challenge. And Haddam did not attempt to wheel his horse, being aware that such a movement would be interpreted as an acceptance. And now, both men knowing what impended, the outlaw listened to Reverend Jim's voice, which was low and earnest, and cold with sinister determination.

"I expect you were watching us. There wasn't a thought in my mind like you are thinking. But I'm getting that thought out of your head, forever. Be mighty careful what you say when you talk, for you won't get a chance to reconsider. Listen, Haddam. Martha Warren's a good girl. Don't you think so?"

Haddam sneered experimentally. He was measuring the distance between them, their positions, considering the possibilities. And now, meeting Reverend Jim's eyes, his own were hooded with guarded humor, derisive and malicious.

"Martha Warren's a good girl?" repeated Reverend Jim. He was watching Haddam closely, trying to solve the enigma of his expression.

"Why, I reckon she must be—if you say so," laughed Haddam.

"We'll call that sufficient," said Reverend Jim. "Though I don't like that grin on your mug. You're thinking thoughts that you ain't got nerve enough to express right now. Well, maybe you'll express them later. Right now, if you've got any more riddles that you think need expounding, we'll get them cleared up. If you ain't, and it's understood that there will be no more hinting about Martha Warren, I'll be hitting the trail over to Dobble's, and you can mosey along to where you're going."

He had told Haddam that he was going on his way to the Dobbles', but he made no move, sitting motionless in the saddle, watching the outlaw, still puzzled by something which was guarded by the latter's lowered eyelids, narrowed so that they squinted.

"Get goin', then!" said Haddam.

Reverend Jim smiled. "You're traveling first, Haddam," he said. "What you've got in your eyes might be a bullet for me when my back is turned."

The outlaw laughed and spurred his pony past Reverend Jim's. Turning in the saddle when several feet distant, he looked back, still laughing.

"Plug you in the back!" he said. "Not a chance, parson! I'm savin' you—savin' you for the big day!"

Reverend Jim rode on, toward the Dobbles'. Haddam had given him something to think about—a riddle to solve. The mystery of his words and of something guarded and derisive in his manner.

CHAPTER 7

So great was Red Rock's interest in Reverend Jim that the publication, in the *Advocate*, of Carey's bold defiance of Sheriff Hawks, failed entirely to create the sensation Carey had expected it to create. There was some talk about the article, to be sure, but it was secondary to the chief subject—the proposed uplift by Reverend Jim. Any new readers gained by the *Advocate* was because the people of the section were interested in Reverend Jim's activities—which were recounted at some length in the newspaper. Carey still hoped that excitement would emanate from—something. Hawks had not carried out his threat to "herd ride" him; Carey had met him several times, but the sheriff had merely scowled at him. Dave Lawler, so far as Carey and Castle could see, had done nothing. Lawler spent his days idling in the saloons, though several times Carey had seen him returning from trips into the basin. What significance these trips had, no one knew, for Lawler took counsel with no one. But toward the second week following Lawler's appearance, a rumor reached Carey's ears to the effect that Lawler intended to take up—or buy—some land in the basin, and go to raising cattle.

This news brought a grin to Castle's face. He spoke of the matter to Carey.

"That solves a mystery which has been puzzling me since Lawler came," he said, "why the governor should place ten thousand dollars to Lawler's credit. It's plain, now, though, that the money is to be used to finance Lawler's entrance into the cattle-raising game. I don't see, though, how anything is to be gained through a move like that. If I was the governor I'd depose Hawks first, and then go after Flash and his gang through the sheriff's office."

"You'd be like a half-baked lawyer without any clients," grinned Carey. "You'd be playing a waiting game. Maybe you'd get evidence, and maybe you wouldn't. There isn't a cattleman in the basin who would appear against Haddam. It looks to me as though Lawler is going about it the right way. Nobody knows he is the sheriff—we're only guessing and are obligated to secrecy—and if he starts a ranch of his own, and Flash's gang rustles any of his stock, he's got them dead to rights. I'd call Lawler's idea a clever one."

But the rumor of Lawler's proposed enterprise had not detracted from Red Rock's interest in the new clergyman. Carey had brought word that Reverend Jim was to hold his first meeting at ten o'clock Sunday morning, and on the Saturday preceding the day set, the meetinghouse was ready.

At nine o'clock Sunday morning the town was agog with speculation. Lookouts were stationed in front of the saloons to watch the trail leading to the parsonage. Wagers that Reverend Jim would not appear at all were made. But at nine-thirty a lookout reported dust on the trail to the parsonage, and there was a general exodus from the saloons. A man leveled a pair of field glasses toward the dust, and then with a chirp of delight announced that in the dust was a buckboard, and that in the vehicle were a man and a woman.

"His sister!" many voices declared.

Blanchard, alone, met Reverend Jim and Ellen as they descended from the buckboard at the door of the meetinghouse. He grinned as Reverend Jim looked in the door, noted the yawning emptiness of the place and turned an inquiring eye upon him.

"The boys are taking advantage of the last chance," he said.

Reverend Jim ushered Ellen inside. As she vanished, he spoke to Blanchard, quietly.

"I expected the other trustees to be on hand."

"They ain't allowin' they're goin' to let religion interfere with their poker game," said Blanchard. "An' I reckon we'll have to fight sin without them.'' He looked narrowly at Reverend Jim. ''There'll be a crowd on hand,'' he added. ''I've counted fifty men, an' there'll be some women. I expect, this bein' your first meetin' here—or anywhere—you're some flustered, ain't you? A little redeye, now——'' he invited.

Reverend Jim smiled a refusal. And Blanchard placed an encouraging hand on his shoulder.

''It's likely the boys will be a little loud, religion not bein' doled out to them regular. But I'm puttin' you wise a few. Give it to them straight from the shoulder. If Red Rock ever gets religion it'll have to be shot into it, I reckon. I expect you ain't got any too much coin—parsons is never long on it, I've heard; an' so you'll have to play your cards close to your belly for a little while. Red Rock's got plenty of money for booze, but mighty little for parsons, an' you'll find the contribution box as empty as an orphan's stockings on Christmas mornin'. But I'm figgerin' to pass the contribution box, an' any son of a gun that don't come across is goin' to be bawled out right in meetin'. I figger that I can make some concessions to religion, an' them yaps can follow suit.''

Reverend Jim's glance at him was subtle. His voice was low and full of concern.

''I'm glad to see that I can depend upon you, and that you are going to set the boys a good example. But how are you going to do it? Are you going to close your saloon on Sundays?''

Blanchard grinned widely, wisely, for he had not failed to note that Reverend Jim's concern was spurious.

''I reckon I ain't goin' to be *that* religious,'' he said. ''But I'm goin' to hire an extra bartender for Sundays an' stay out of the saloon myself.''

''That's right,'' laughed Reverend Jim. ''A trustee ought to make some sacrifices.''

Blanchard grinned at him in open admiration. ''I reckon you're a knowin' cuss!'' he said. ''You savvy that Red Rock can't be reformed in a day—that whatever is done must be done gradual and sympathetic. If you're ready, I'll shoo the boys in.''

Reverend Jim watched him as he crossed the street, the alkali dust, kicked up by his boots, swirling around him. And then, his face suddenly serious, Reverend Jim entered the building.

He went to the improvised pulpit—a crude one which Blanchard had covered with black cloth—and laid on it a small Bible. In one of the front seats sat his sister, watching him closely.

When he laid the Bible down and turned to her, she smiled at him.

"You are not a bit nervous in your new role," she said.

"Not any nervous, but feeling a little strange, maybe. I expect it will wear off."

He sat down in a chair behind the pulpit. From where he sat he could look down the entire length of Red Rock's deserted street. The white sunlight of the morning beat fiercely down upon the dust-covered roofs of the buildings. There was peace in Red Rock's desolation. One could not ignore the solemn beauty of the distant mountains, could not fail to feel the lure of the mystery that sat on their silent peaks. The broad sweep of plain and valley that stretched to infinite distances made an impression that inspired awe. Over it all was the brilliant sunlight; and coming through the windows of the meetinghouse was the clear, pungent aroma of the sage.

Reverend Jim turned, after a little, and looked at his sister.

"Did you invite Martha Warren to the service this morning?" he asked.

He had not spoken of the girl since the morning he had met her on the river trail.

"Of course—but she declined to come."

"Did she tell you about how everybody declined to come to her party?"

"She told me everything. I am sorry for her."

"Like her?"

"I like her very much. She is a good and sensible girl."

Reverend Jim's eyelashes flickered. "I suspected that. Flash Haddam vouched for it. Discerning man, Flash is." He was silent for a moment, and then he spoke, meditatively. "It must be disheartening to give a party on your eighteenth birthday, to invite people and have nobody come. Sort of a tragedy for the one who gives the party, I expect. Do you think it has made Martha bitter?"

"No. She is too sensible for that. The poor thing! She cried when she was telling me about it."

Reverend Jim said, earnestly: "I would like you to be friendly to her, Ellen. She'll need a friend she can depend upon before this thing is over, if I'm not missing my reckoning. Flash Haddam has something up his sleeve in connection with her. Did she tell you about Flash wanting to marry her?"

Ellen nodded.

"Well," continued Reverend Jim, "he does not admire her because of her character; I guessed that much from the talk I had with him. She's made an impression on him in another way—her looks, I expect. She's a right pretty girl."

"Oh, so you've noticed that," said Ellen. "I thought you told me that girls had never interested you?"

"She's just a kid, Ellen."

"You didn't think that of me a year ago—when I was eighteen." She smiled. "Do you remember the day you told me I was 'grown up'?"

"You always seemed older than your age, Ellen," he told her gently. "And smarter."

"Smart enough to know what's going on," she smiled. "Smart enough to see what is happening between you and——"

"Don't, Ellen."

"Of course not, Jim. Not even if you say things about"—she glanced quickly about her, and then added—"Norman."

"So it's gone *that* far," he laughed.

Carey was the first of the congregation to arrive. He quietly, but immediately, took a seat beside Ellen. And Reverend Jim, taking up his Bible, pretended to read, but found time and opportunity to steal glances at Ellen and Carey—who were so absorbed in each other that they were not aware of his interest in them.

Castle sauntered in after a while, greeted them all, and secured possession of a chair on the other side of Ellen, to the somewhat obvious annoyance of the editor, but to Reverend Jim's secret enjoyment. Then came Blanchard, and following him, straggling by twos and threes, came the "cohorts of sin," with faces embarrassed and expectant.

Blanchard took a position at the door, greeting each arrival with exaggerated politeness and in a tense whisper which seemed startlingly resonant in the silence of the room. As each man entered he was gently but firmly requested by Blanchard to pass over his weapons.

"Guns an' religion ain't got nothin' in common," he told those who would have entered without submitting to his disarmament command. "The only shootin' that will be done here will be done by the parson shootin' off his gab. An' I reckon that will be plenty."

The six-shooters were deposited in a corner. The number

grew in volume and variety as Red Rock's population continued to shuffle in, red of face, self-conscious, awkward, but undoubtedly interested. Seats were taken gravely, quietly. This was because there were women present in the congregation.

"Not one in ten of these men will be influenced by any word your brother may say to them," whispered Carey to Miss Ellen at a propitious moment, "but you will note that they are observing the solemnity of the occasion with impeccable decorum."

Buckboards began to arrive at the door. They came from distant parts of the basin; several of their occupants having driven forty or fifty miles.

"There are the Dobbles," Carey said as a red-whiskered man descended from his seat in a buckboard and assisted a florid, wide-girthed woman to alight. "He's been saying something about his *Advocates*, undelivered."

"Why haven't you delivered them?" asked Ellen innocently—though she remembered Reverend Jim's insinuation of the editor's dilatoriness.

"I'm beginning to discover that I need a distributor," lied Carey brazenly, wondering if she had noticed the bulky appearance of his saddlebags during his visits to the parsonage.

"I really believe you do need a distributor," she said, looking at him with demure eyes. "Both times you visited the parsonage you seemed to be terribly overworked."

"Oh, Lord!" groaned Castle in a hoarse whisper. "Overworked!" He laughed sardonically at Carey's furious blush.

The situation was saved for Carey by the arrival of another buckboard, and he seized the opportunity to elucidate the identity of its occupants.

"That's Hexter, of the Diamond Dot," he whispered to Ellen: "and his wife and daughter. They've got a son, too—Henry. They live thirty-five miles down the Purgatory—nicknamed Picketwire."

The meetinghouse was full. Reverend Jim got to his feet and looked at his watch. It was ten o'clock. Red Rock's population was well represented, even to the trustees, who had interrupted their poker game through recklessly anticipating the services to be more interesting. The congregation now settled into their chairs expectantly.

Reverend Jim's opening prayer was short, simple and pithy, and when it was finished he opened the Bible and announced his text. It was: "I am with you always."

He preached for an hour—slowly, forcibly, convincingly.
The congregation gave him its undivided attention. During the
first few minutes Ellen watched him anxiously, but when she
saw that he was perfectly self-possessed, exhibiting no evidence
of self-consciousness or of nervousness, the anxious expression
left her face. As he proceeded a smile began to steal around her
mouth. Once, when he paused to take a sip of water, Carey
whispered into Ellen's ear, admiration in his voice:

"He's the most effective kind of preacher, for he makes you
forget he is a preacher—makes you think he is merely a big
brother, pointing out your faults and the remedy. He's going to
be mighty helpful to those who need help. And," he added as an
afterthought, "there's nobody here—except his sister—who
doesn't need help."

"Wait," she said, smiling wisely, "he may say something
about flattery."

Reverend Jim kept to the text he had selected, telling them of
the omnipresence of God and of their inability to escape His all-
seeing eye. He told them that here, even here, in a country as
desolate as this, the eye of the Creator was upon them, noting
their shortcomings and their sins, and that His hand was ready
and willing to help them. Only toward the end did he refer to
himself.

"I am not here," he said, "to attempt to force you to accept
the word of God. That is a matter which you must consider for
yourselves. But you can't sneak away from God. He's got you
hog-tied and branded, so that He knows every one of you—and
whether by your deeds you belong to Him or the devil. There are
some men in this basin who are running their irons on cattle that
belong to other people; and there are other men who are helping
them by not having the courage to tell the representatives of the
law about it. For a while all these folks may escape the law, but
one day the law will catch up with them and then there will be a
day of reckoning and punishment. The rules of decency and fair
dealing apply to our material, as well as to our spiritual lives.
You can't cheat God or man and get away with it forever.
Remember that when Flash Haddam and his gang of outlaws ask
you to help them break the law.

"You can't see how God has got you hog-tied. But I expect
none of you has ever laid on your back out on the range and
looked up at the stars, without doing a heap of thinking—serious
thinking. You've thought about the bigness of the world, and

wondered about the size and shape and the looks of the Boss who's running it all, and who makes you and your own little piece of it look so insignificant that you feel kind of cheap. And when you were looking and thinking of these things, you didn't forget to think of what sins you'd done, and what a lot of them you wouldn't have done if you had it to do over again. You felt kind of small-like, and sorry—like you'd feel if someone who'd always treated you square had trusted you with something and you had double-crossed him. Well, that's where God has you hog-tied and branded—in your conscience. Your conscience is the machinery inside of you which makes you wish you hadn't done things; it's the rope that keeps you from running maverick and making a total fool of yourself. I'm not asking any of you boys to chuck away all holds and try to grow angels' wings in a night—some of you couldn't grow pinfeathers in a hundred years. It's asking too much. You grew into sin gradual, and I expect you'll have to pull out gradual, or not at all. But if any of you do want to pull out, you can call on me to help. That's what I'm here for. And that goes for any man who is sorry he's in cahoots with Flash Haddam!''

He began to pronounce the benediction. As he reached its close and raised his head, a woman who had been seated in the rear of the room arose and came slowly and hesitantly toward him. The eyes of the congregation followed her as she made her way up an aisle near the wall, and Reverend Jim, an encouraging smile on his face, stood waiting.

The girl—she could not have been more than twenty—was pale; her lips were pressed tightly together; and as she came forward, she looked at none of those who were watching her. Not until she stood in front of him below the pulpit, did Reverend Jim note that her eyes were moist with tears and that her lips were quivering. She was pretty, but it was evident that dissipation was responsible for her fading color, the hardening lips. She was slight and delicate of figure, and Reverend Jim, who had sensed the situation at a glance, looked down at her and spoke softly:

"Do you want to speak to me, miss?"

"Yes."

"Here?"

"Yes. There's no secret about it. Everybody knows me. I have been living at the Bulldog,'' she said falteringly. "I have sinned. I want to get away from that life. I want you to help me.''

"Of course we'll help you. It's the surest thing you know!''

He was down at her side in an instant, with an arm over her shoulder, patting her head. He led her directly to Ellen who tried to rise. But the girl, after one searching look at Ellen's face, dropped on her knees in front of her and buried her face in Ellen's lap, sobbing.

Reverend Jim looked straight into the faces of the people of the congregation. The people were restless and their voices were buzzing. Reverend Jim raised his hands for silence.

"The congregation will please pass out," he said.

Blanchard disturbed the deep solemnity of the moment. His voice rose above the sudden shuffling of feet that had set in a tide toward the door. He stood, blocking egress, a militant look in his eyes; and the congregation paused.

"I reckon the parson's forgot somethin'," he said. "I'm swingin' the cashbox in this here deal, an' you wild an' woolly speciments which has got an earful of religious palaver has got to cough up plenty. Any son of a gun which thinks he ain't got his money's worth can talk serious to me outside!"

Thus reminded that there was a material price to pay, even though they might deny the good of the spiritual lesson that had been taught to them, Red Rock's citizens responded handsomely. Not all of the men left immediately. Many stayed outside to discuss Reverend Jim's sermon and to speculate upon the concluding incident. Lize Ebbets was going to reform! The Bulldog would be minus one of its most attractive characters. Reverend Jim had struck a heavy blow at vice right at the start. What would be the attitude of Wes' Vickers, the proprietor of the Bulldog? Would he agitate humiliation for Reverend Jim? Would he attempt reprisal? There were doubts. And Reverend Jim's attack upon Flash Haddam in open meeting? What would be the result of that? And his appeal to those who were secretly working with Haddam—those who were afraid of him? At least Reverend Jim was not afraid, for the story of his clash with the outlaw was still a vivid remembrance.

The Dobbles, the Hexters and those others who had come from a distance got into their vehicles and set out for their homes. Ellen and Lize Ebbets were still in the front seats near the pulpit. Lize was still sobbing, softly now, and Ellen was trying to comfort her. Reverend Jim had stood watching them for a few minutes until Ellen motioned to him and whispered a low word into his ear; then he had gone to the rear, where Dave Blanchard waited.

Blanchard took Reverend Jim's hand. "I reckon that might be called dealin' sin a knockout blow right at the start," he said. And now he narrowed his eyes at Reverend Jim. "But it's one thing to take a girl away from that life, an' another thing to keep her away. If she stays in Red Rock she'll be back in the Bulldog in a week. What are you going to do with her?"

Reverend Jim looked him straight in the eyes. "She's going to the parsonage, to be a companion to my sister."

Some emotion moved Blanchard; his eyes gleamed. "I understand," he said, watching Reverend Jim's face intently, "that church folks don't consider it just the right thing to associate with such people. There's folks that listened to your talk today who will turn their noses up at you when they find out you've took her in."

"Do you think that will make any difference to me?" said Reverend Jim, his lips tightening.

Blanchard squeezed his hand hard. "By Jupiter," he said, "I don't believe it will!"

CHAPTER 8

Flash Haddam and Ben Warren had ridden to Haddam's ranch on the Saturday preceding the delivery of Reverend Jim's first sermon.

On a level in the basin, near the bases of those hills on the southern edge of the great rim, was an adobe ranch house surrounded by other buildings of like construction. Buildings and level were known to the cattlemen of the basin as the Star Ranch. No trails led to the Star, and Haddam's range was shunned by cattlemen as though it were a plague district. Smuggled on the level, concealed by slopes and draws and hills from any rider who might follow the regular trails, the Star's isolation was complete.

The sandy level surrounding the ranch was not vast. It merged into the hills on the south; grass slopes to the north and west descended to it; the Purgatory doubled sharply to the east and flowed broadly between two flat banks of dense timber, beyond which opened a grass range that stretched its green level many miles. It was a fertile country upon which other cattlemen looked enviously, when they were so bold as to look at all—an ideal location for the prosecution of Haddam's unlawful enterprises.

Flash had been apprised of Reverend Jim's intention to preach in Red Rock on Sunday, but his interest had been negative. He had spent Friday night carousing with Ben Warren and several other friends in Red Rock's saloons, and early on Saturday he and Ben had ridden to the Star. At about the time Reverend Jim was beginning his sermon, Ben and Flash were sitting in the shade of the eaves of the Star ranch house. They were smoking as they talked, and occasionally Haddam's gaze sought the green sweep of level stretching beyond the river.

He turned suddenly and caught Ben looking at him. A twisting grin wreathed one corner of his mouth.

"Got the makin's?"

Ben slid tobacco pouch and papers along the bench on which they were sitting. He watched Flash roll a cigarette, caught the pouch and papers that were tossed in his direction and began to manufacture a cigarette himself. When he had completed it he saw Flash scowling into the southern distance.

"Snedden was due yesterday," he said.

Ben stopped smoking, the cigarette drooping from his lips, which had become loose from surprise.

"Snedden!" he said. "Snedden coming here? Why, Snedden is Dobble's foreman!"

"H'm, so he is," snapped Flash, as if moved with sudden passion. "But he's comin' here; he was due yesterday, to bring back the coin from that last haul of yearlin's. Took them to Laskar's, across the line from San Pablo, as per regular. Been gone four days—him an' six of the boys. Somethin's wrong."

Ben sat rigid and silent for a moment, astonishment over the revelation of Snedden's relations with Haddam shocking him to speechlessness. He knew that a number of cowboys employed by various ranchmen in the basin were associated with Haddam—were members of his gang—for one after another, as his intimacy with Haddam had grown, their identity had been revealed to him. But Snedden! Snedden had been above reproach; his reputation in the basin was spotless; he was Dobble's most trusted employee! A flush grew slowly over Ben's face. His vanity was pleased. This signal confidence indicated that Haddam's trust in him was great. He laughed as though his astonishment had been merely fleeting, and was apprehensive when he thought Haddam might think his surprise boyish.

"Maybe Laskar didn't come across immediate," he suggested.

"Oh, I reckon he did. It's more likely that Snedden is four-flushin' in San Pablo. Gamblin' an' drinkin'."

He puffed slowly at his cigarette, the scowl deepening, his lips jerking, curving.

"Snedden's gettin' too swell headed lately," he said, after a silence. "He's due for a tumble." He relapsed into silence again, and sat smoking steadily. Presently the cigarette was consumed. He motioned, and again Ben passed over the tobacco and papers. When the cigarette was made and lighted, Flash spoke again without looking at Ben. Decision was in his voice.

"Snedden is quittin'!"

Ben looked quickly at him. The cold gleam in the outlaw's eyes made a chill run over him.

"I've been groomin' you to take his place," said Haddam. His teeth flashed into a grin of feline amusement as he looked at Ben, noting the latter's quick start and the instant pallor that came into his face.

"Some shocked, eh?" he said, laughing. "Well, you couldn't have expected it, that's a fact. But it's straight goods. We're friends, ain't we? Well, then"—at Ben's nod—"I reckon that settles it. From now on you take Snedden's place."

"Snedden goin' to drop out?"

Flash looked quickly at him. "I reckon he'll drop out," he said, smiling oddly. "Some of the boys has been complainin' about Snedden. He's been playin' hawg. Twice, now, he's had ideas different from mine, an' has aired them to the boys—not so's I could hear him, you understand. But it's got to me in one way or another. He's got to his limit."

Once more Ben was silent. His thoughts were not of Snedden at this moment, but of himself. Gradually he had yielded to Haddam's influence, but not until this minute did he realize how far he had yielded, how entirely he had linked his fortunes to Haddam's. He had not intended to effect a permanent coalition with the outlaw, and he was not gratified over Haddam's offer—his plan. He felt at this minute very little desire to become a leader in Haddam's gang. There had been, to be sure, a certain lure in the knowledge that he was breaking laws; there had been a tinge of reckless enjoyment in the work of "running his iron" on cattle not belonging to him, in robbing banks in distant cities. It had all provided him with that romance which his life, until he had taken up with Haddam, had lacked. He had been satisfied until now; but he did not want to go any farther.

"I reckon I'll drop out. I ain't takin' Snedden's place," he suddenly blurted.

To Ben's surprise, Haddam seemed unmoved by his refusal. He did not look at Ben.

"I reckon you won't drop out," he said. "You're talkin' like a kid now. Cold feet, eh?"

"Call it what you like. I've gone far enough, Flash."

"Too far, you mean, I reckon." Flash turned and looked at him. "Too far, Ben," he mocked. "It's easy enough to get into this game, but it's no cinch gettin' out of it. You recollect the night we snaked twenty calves from Billings? Well, Hawks wasn't far away then; he saw you cuttin' them out—was right close when you hobbled a cow an' drove her calf off."

"But Hawks is with us," said Ben.

"Sure—he's with us. But he'll be against anyone who figgers on pullin' away."

"You mean——"

"I reckon you're on. If you're with us, all well an' good; Hawks is your friend. But if you drop out, Hawks might take it into his head to make an example of you. The folks in the basin has been cryin' for an example to be made of someone."

"So that's it," said Ben, dismayed over the realization of his danger. "You got me into this deliberate, knowin'——"

"Easy, Ben," warned Haddam. "I reckon you're beginnin' to find out what it's all about. But there ain't no sense of gettin' reckless. You're in, an' you ain't gettin' out. You ain't runnin' no risk. Half the cowhands in the basin are your friends, Ben," he continued, silkily. "You don't reckon I'd have got you into this if I thought you was runnin' any risk?" His voice took on a note of disappointment and regret. "Shucks," he said, "I'm beginnin' to believe I was mistaken in you. I hear your dad ain't treatin' you right—lettin' you work your head off an' not payin' you for it, an' I try to put you in the way of makin' some easy money. I'm even figgerin' on promotin' you, so's you'll come in for a bigger divvy, an' you set down hard on the proposition. Call that repayin' my friendship?"

Ben was silent, reviewing each act that had led him to his present serious predicament. He saw how logical it all appeared from Haddam's standpoint, how illogical and puerile it seemed from his own. He had been entirely to blame, for Flash could not have led him had he not permitted himself to be led. Still, one loophole remained through which he might wriggle out.

"I'd keep my mouth shut about what I know," he said.

"It don't go, Ben. If you ain't with us, you're against us, an' you'll take the consequences accordingly. I'd be sorry, but there's the other boys of the outfit to be thought of, an' they'd take matters right out of my hand. Shucks," he added, "ain't I treated you white? Don't have me tellin' the boys I misjudged you! Be a man, Ben. Don't have me makin' excuses."

Ben's lips stiffened and then curved into a mirthless smile as he reflected upon the unenviable position he would occupy should he refuse Haddam's offer. In the eyes of his present companions he would lack manliness. Respectable people would be suspicious of him—would never trust him. Yes, he had gone too far to ever return.

"I reckon I'm a man," he said.

Haddam laughed. "I didn't doubt it at all," he declared. "I knowed you'd stick, soon as I could make it plain to you that you ought to." He paused and then went on: "Them six boys that was with Snedden was to break an' scatter back to their outfits as soon as they drove that bunch over to Laskar's. I got word in Red Rock yesterday that the boys was all back. Snedden's laggin' behind as usual. He's done it more than once, lately. It's the last time. The boys are comin' here tonight, an' we'll settle with Snedden. Your dad ain't brightenin' up none, lately," he went on, abruptly changing the subject. "Seems to me that he's gettin' worse. Too bad! Makin' coin, too, ain't he? Wasn't you tellin' me that he shipped two thousand odd head last year? An' he ain't handed you nothin'! I reckon he must have a pile in Castle's bank."

"He ain't got a cent in Castle's bank," denied Ben in a voice that was now nearly normal.

"In Las Vegas, then? Or Raton? Or somewhere's else?"

"He don't believe in banks, far as I can find out."

"What's he done with the coin he's made, then?"

"Ask me somethin' easy."

"Shucks! Got it hid out somewheres, I reckon," said Haddam. "That's one of the first signs that a man is gettin' queer—when he won't trust his coin to banks, preferrin' to hide it out where he can get a look at it once in a while. I reckon if you could find out where he's hidin' it, you'd just naturally make him wish he *had* trusted it to a bank, eh?"

Ben scowled. "I ain't thinkin' as much of myself as I thought awhile ago; but I ain't figgerin' to be dog enough to lift no coin belongin' to my dad.''

Haddam's lips curved with amused contempt, but a hand hid the expression from Ben. ''Of course you wouldn't,'' he said. ''No man would. But there ain't no law against funnin' about a thing.'' He now looked at Ben speculatively. How much did the boy know of his intentions concerning Martha? Had she told him anything?

''Does Martha know you've took up with me?'' he asked.

''She was tellin' me the whole basin knows it.''

''What else is she sayin' about it?''

''She's against it. But I'm runnin' my own trail.''

''Why, sure. Women is just natural butters in. She wasn't confidin' anything else to you?''

''No. Martha ain't much on gassin'—to nobody.''

Haddam smiled. He had not cared whether Martha had told Ben of their conversation, but it pleased him to discover that apparently she had not taken Ben into her confidence.

''No,'' he said. ''Martha's a wise girl.'' He turned again to look into the southern distance. Almost instantly he sat erect and leaned forward.

''I reckon that's Snedden comin' now,'' he said.

Just topping a rise was a rider. He was too far away for the two men to be certain of his identity, and they watched him in silence while his pony shortened the distance, and when he reached a point a few hundred feet from the opposite side of the river, Haddam said shortly:

''It's Snedden.''

A change had come over Haddam. He had been talkative, smooth, suave, while discussing Martha. His manner now was that of cold, prepared alertness. His eyes were narrowed; there was a saturnine smile on his face as he watched the rider splash his pony through the water of the ford, mount the slight slope on the near side and come toward them.

Ben had seen Snedden many times. He was a young man, not over thirty-five, good looking, dark, reckless eyed, self-confident. Long before he drew his pony to a halt he had scrutinized Ben intently, and the expression in his eyes as he rode to within ten feet of him and sat looking at him showed that he had recognized him and was surprised at his presence at the Star. But he grinned cordially, swinging a leg over the pommel of his saddle.

"Howdy," he said. "I seen you two from out there a piece an' thought mebbe you'd like a little company."

Evidently this was said to mislead Ben. But Haddam spoke, a grin on his lips.

"Ben's with us. Talk straight."

Snedden climbed down, trailed the reins over the pony's head and stepped forward. "I wasn't sure," he said, halting in front of Ben. "But I'm right glad——"

"I'm waitin' for your report," interrupted Haddam. He looked straight at Snedden, his face expressionless except for a very little downward twist at the corners of his mouth. His eyes were squinting with a light that might have meant cold humor or derision.

His manner did not appear to affect Snedden, for he laughed lightly.

"I'm reportin', then," he said. "Laskar——"

"You got the coin with you?" interrupted Haddam.

"Sure. In my saddlebags. Laskar——"

"How much?" interrupted Haddam once more—gruffly.

"Two thousand, three hundred," said Snedden. "Laskar wasn't allowin'——"

"To hell with Laskar!" sneered Haddam. "You ought to have three thousand. The boys——"

"Who's makin' this report?" said Snedden coldly. "You send a man to do a thing, ask him for a report on it, an' before he can make a report you go to interruptin' him. Do I make the report, or are you shootin' off your gab?" He was on edge with passion. It was plain that between him and Haddam there was a clash of wills and little respect. "I'm tellin' you about Laskar," went on Snedden wrathfully. "He's sourin' on the game. Says folks in his neighborhood are talkin'. Stood pat at twenty— wouldn't go a cent higher. Even then he wouldn't come across immediately, as per usual. Kept me in San Pablo a day an' a night, waitin' for him to make up his mind. That's why I'm late. I'd have been here yesterday, accordin' to——"

"You're a liar, Snedden," said Haddam softly.

Snedden's muscles jerked. Astonishment, passion, sudden realization of Haddam's intentions seemed to fill his eyes as for an instant he stared and stiffened. For now Haddam was on his feet. His heavy Colt was out; his face was flaming with poisonous hate and rage. This wild and ruthless side of him was what had made him the legendary figure he had become—a figure from which men of ordinary valor shrank, and which the law had not been able to subdue.

For an instant Snedden was motionless. If he had anticipated this moment he was not prepared for it, and his face whitened to an almost grayish pallor. Then with desperate swiftness his right hand dropped to the stock of his six-shooter. The weapon flashed out, came almost to a poise.

But Snedden had no chance. Haddam meant that he should have no chance, and Snedden's gun was still rising when Haddam's six-shooter roared thunderously. Snedden staggered; the pistol dropped from his hand; the arm fell limply, paralyzed by the bullet that had gone into his shoulder. Snedden reached with his left hand for the weapon on the ground, doubtless thinking Haddam had failed to hit a vital spot through excitement. But there was no excitement in Haddam's manner. He laughed as Snedden lunged for the fallen gun, and sneered, his lips writhing in mockery. Then, pitilessly, as Snedden grasped the pistol, he fired again. Snedden jerked, shuddered; his knees doubled under him, and he sank slowly, clutching with his uninjured hand at his chest. For an instant he rested on his knees, his head sagging forward, swaying oddly back and forth; and then as Ben shouted hoarsely in protest, Haddam fired again. Without uttering a sound Snedden pitched forward, face down in the sand, his legs slowly stiffening.

Ben had sagged back against the wall of the house, his face pale, his soul sickened by the sheer brutality of the crime. It was not the first killing he had seen, but this murder appalled him. No such sensations afflicted Haddam. He stepped close to Snedden, looking down at him coldly, critically, appraisingly—and then at Ben with a stiff grin.

"Didn't I tell you he was quittin'?" he said.

Ben was silent again. He felt that if he attempted to speak his voice would fail him. He got up and walked around a corner of the house, to get away from the Thing that lay stretched in the sand, and to try to regain his composure. He returned after a little, yielding to a morbid curiosity, and saw that Haddam had dragged the body to the edge of some brush fringing the river. At the instant Ben observed him, he was searching the saddlebags on Snedden's pony. Haddam did not see him, and, obeying a sudden, wild impulse, Ben dodged around the corner of the house again, ran to the corral, threw saddle and bridle on his pony, leaped into the saddle with the animal running, and raced up a long slope away from the scene.

And now panic seized him—a wild disorder of fear, horror and remorse. He rode many miles while in that mood. He did not know in what direction; he took no heed of the breakneck speed at which his pony was traveling, until, long after leaving the Star, he began to regain control of himself and saw that the animal's flanks, neck and muzzle were in a foaming lather. He brought the pony to a halt and sat, loose lipped and shaking, looking about him. When he saw some buildings near him, he started and sat erect, for in his blind panic he had ridden to Dobble's ranch—the Arrow. He wheeled his pony and raced back—toward the Star. And as he now rode he grew more calm, for a realization of his own grave danger was slowly lessening his horror for what he had seen.

But he did not immediately return to the Star. It was dusk when he rode back and turned his pony into the corral, but during the time he had been away he had hardened himself, had steeled himself against his pity for Snedden, against the impulses in him which had fought in protest against his continued intimacy with Haddam. He had chosen his life and would follow it; he was irrevocably committed to crime. And perhaps he knew that if he failed Haddam he would meet Snedden's fate. When he went around a corner of the house and saw Haddam sitting on the bench, several of his men lounging near him, he was almost calm again, and managed to smile at Haddam.

Haddam grinned cynically at him.

"Just ridin'?" he said.

"Just ridin'," returned Ben. "An' thinkin'."

"Don't crowd your brain any," advised Haddam, with an intent, searching look. "I've just been tellin' the boys about Snedden—how he tried to ring in a cold-lead proposition in on me, an' how I had to perforate him. Who would you say was to blame?"

"Snedden," lied Ben. Dusk hid his flaming cheeks.

CHAPTER 9

It was Norman Carey who, a week later, brought to the parsonage the news of the killing of Snedden. There were no details. It was rumored, merely, that a clash had occurred between Snedden and Haddam, and that Snedden had been fatally slow in drawing his weapon after having unwisely provoked Haddam to anger. Sheriff Hawks had ridden over to the Star, and the report of his inquest was that Haddam had acted in self-defense. Therefore, unmolested by the law, Haddam rode abroad as usual. By the unknowing in Red Rock, Snedden's name was mentioned with respect and reverence, and he was considered a martyr to honesty.

To Reverend Jim, however', there came a moment of illumination. Dobble was responsible for it. Dobble had been much impressed by Reverend Jim's first sermon, and when on a day following that upon which the news of Snedden's death leaked out, Reverend Jim rode over to the Arrow, he received a warm and sincere welcome. It was not until he was ready to go that Snedden's name was mentioned. And then Dobble drew Reverend Jim confidentially aside.

"You're a minister," said Dobble, "an' I reckon you won't abuse no confidence. I've had my doubts about Snedden. I've

seen him talkin' confidential to Flash Haddam. More than once
he's been gone days at a time. I've noticed that it's usually been
when there'd be some stock missin'—not from the Arrow alone.
I missed a bunch of calves about two weeks ago. Usually, I'd
leave lookin' for them to Snedden. Maybe I'd send the straw
boss out to tell Snedden about it. This time I went out to hunt the
outfit myself. Snedden was gone. The boys said he'd swung
around the range, lookin' for calves. Rats! No bunch of calves
can get away from under an outfit's nose without the outfit
knowin' something about it. There was a bunch of cows hobbled, and some of them had their hoofs burned. Snedden was
gone five days. Then a man I know right well told me he'd seen
Snedden hitting the booze over in San Pablo with a tinhorn
rustler named Laskar. Then comes the news that Snedden has
cashed in, monkeyin' with Flash Haddam. Mighty suspicious
actions, I call them. What was he doin' at the Star?''

"Do you suspect any of the other men?''

"I didn't, until Snedden was killed. But there's some of them
that are not ridin' a straight trail. That's certain.''

"If you'll mention their names to me—the ones you suspect—I'll take note of them, and someday I'll have a talk with
them, not letting on I know they are crooked.''

Dobble's laugh had almost a sneer in it. But his face had
instantly sobered. ''That ain't such a bad idea after all,'' he said.
"There ain't any way of gettin' the law to doin' business, an'
maybe the next best thing would be to try an' argue them into
givin' a fellow a square deal. Anyway, here's their names.'' He
mentioned several, and Reverend Jim rode on his way toward
the parsonage, his face genially wrinkled.

He came upon Lize Ebbets when he dismounted at the corral
gate. It was two hours after noon, and both Reverend Jim and his
pony had partaken of food at Dobble's; so when Lize, who had
been standing at the corral fence watching him, asked him if he
was not hungry, he told her that he had already ''grubbed.'' He
saw Carey on the front porch with Ellen. They were absorbed.

"Not a bit lonesome here for Ellen, after all,'' he said. He
pulled saddle and bridle from the pony and hung them from the
corral bars. ''Lonesome for you?'' he asked Lize.

It was the first time since Lize's coming to the parsonage that
he had even hinted of the change that had come to her. There was
something in Lize's gaze that made Reverend Jim look at her

again, quickly. Something smoldering there, deep, guarded, but vital with significance.

"Lonesome for me?" she said. "Oh no. It's like being in heaven."

A strange softness in her voice made his senses record something unpleasant, discordant, but he laughed playfully, fearing she might notice. "The next thing we know, you'll be calling Ellen and me angels."

"You are angels to me," she said quietly.

"That's laying it on pretty thick, don't you think?" he expostulated. "I wouldn't want to think I was getting *that* good. Why, I'd go to getting swelled up and folks would think I was loco! I don't think anyone ought to think of himself as an angel because he's done his duty to a fellow human. Let's forget it and be just folks who are glad to be around one another."

"I'm glad to be here," she said, adding softly: "With you."

"And Ellen," he said, with a dawning realization of a belief that Lize's thoughts were not trending toward angels, but toward men.

"Yes—Ellen—of course," she amended hesitantly.

He nodded, smiled at her with concealed skepticism and sympathy, knowing how hard it was for her to break away from her old associations, and from the many temptations that would enticingly lure her.

"Wes' Vickers watches me," she said. "I want him to let me alone, but he won't. I wasn't going to tell you, because I didn't want to bother you. But Wes' Vickers was here yesterday, and threatened that if I didn't go back to the Bulldog he would stir up trouble for you."

Reverend Jim's lips straightened.

"What did you tell Vickers?"

"I'm afraid it wouldn't sound just right for me to repeat it," she said.

"Strong language has got a place," he declared. "*That* was a place. Trouble is a heap better than sin, Lize. If it comes to a question of sinning or of bringing trouble on anyone, bring the trouble mighty quick."

"But I haven't any right to bring trouble upon you," she protested, moving closer to him.

"Look here, Eliza Ebbets," he said gruffly, though there was gentleness concealed somewhere in his voice, visibly accentuated by a sympathetic glow in his eyes. "Who's the loser in this deal—you or Wes' Vickers?"

"Vickers, I suppose."

"Well, then, if there's any bawling to be done, you let Vickers do it. Also, if Vickers is hunting trouble let him hunt it. You forget it, and run along and tell Carey and Ellen that I'm here, so's they won't be embarrassed by me coming upon them suddenly."

He started to walk toward the stable; then, when he observed that Eliza had not moved but was standing with drooping head, looking at him, plainly filled with indecision, he halted, turned and came back.

"There's something you're wanting to say, I expect," he said.

She looked down at the space between them, nervously clasping and unclasping her hands. "Yes," she said. "It's about Ben Warren."

"What about Ben?"

She did not look up. "Hasn't Ellen told you?" she said. "I—I wasn't all to blame—for the life I led in Red Rock. Ben——"

"Ellen told me," he interrupted. "But I'd guessed it. Usually a man's to blame. Usually, too, it's the man who keeps the woman in the pit he's dug for her. Much depends upon the woman, though. She's got to decide one way or the other. Does she want to live right? Or does she——"

She looked at him with level, steady gaze. "I don't want to see Ben again," she said. "I'm through with that—all of it."

"That's right," he returned earnestly. "That's the only way. But I wasn't going to interfere. I want to see you fight it out with yourself. You make your own position stronger by doing your own thinking and deciding. Maybe I could give you advice, but you'd get nowhere if you don't want to."

"Will you keep him from coming here?"

"You're trying to side-step now. If I'd tell Ben to stay away he'd think I was butting in. There's times when a man can't interfere. If Ben comes he'll have to see you. Then, if you tell him you don't want him and he comes again, I expect it would be my duty to keep him away."

Her face suddenly lost its color; she looked up, her eyes alight with fear. "I'm afraid of him," she said, shuddering. "He said he'd kill me if ever——"

"We won't take any chances, then," said Reverend Jim. "I'll see him if he comes. Maybe that's the best way, anyway." He walked to the stable, and she watched him, longingly, until he vanished inside.

That evening Reverend Jim sat smoking on his porch, and meditating over the three-cornered problem presented by Martha, Ben Warren and Lize Ebbets. It was not an easy problem, and in an hour he had made no progress toward a solution. So at length he got up, knocked the ashes from the pipe and stepped down from the porch, walking toward the timber grove to the west of the ranch house, on the Red Rock trail.

As he walked, his face lighted, his eyes gleamed and he smiled.

"Why, it's all plain enough," he said aloud. "It's simple as rolling off a log." He halted at the edge of a clump of oak brush and yielded to the humor that moved him. "I've been sort of reluctant to see Ben, but I expect if he'd come now——"

He stopped short and wheeled swiftly, for he heard a sound behind him, the sharp crack of a breaking twig. Standing in the brush, one hand holding the branches apart, the other clutching the stock of a heavy Colt, his face pale and his lips writhing with hate, his eyes blazing, was the young man whom Reverend Jim had seen on the pony the night he had caressed Ellen on the porch—the rider who had hurled the taunt at him: "Hell! Somebody else's sister, I reckon!"

Reverend Jim stood looking at the young man. He instantly divined the truth—that the young man was Ben Warren. He knew, too, that if Ben's intentions had been murderous he would have used his weapon before now. Yet there was no doubt that murderous passion blazed in his eyes.

"Talkin' to yourself about me, was you, you bleatin' sky pilot?" said Ben. "You was sayin' what you'd do if I was to come right now! Well, I'm here! I've been watchin' you! I saw you clamp your dirty paws on Lize Ebbets' shoulders while you spread on the palaver. You're slick, ain't you? But there's them that's slicker!"

"I expect you don't mean to compliment me any," said Reverend Jim dryly. He had been startled by Ben's sudden appearance; but he was now quietly watchful and cold and alert. Yet he was more occupied with a study of Ben's face than concerned over his threatening attitude and words. The boy looked little like Martha. There was a faint resemblance around the eyes—though Ben's were squinted with a perplexed expression—for they were brown, like his sister's. But the features were unlike hers; the calm poise was absent; the challenging honesty was not there. Reverend Jim felt that the young man must resemble his father, for he noted instantly a certain vacuity of expression which fitted Red Rock's description of the elder Warren.

"Not complimenting me any," he repeated, his inspection complete. "Not by talking that way, or by pulling your gun on me. I'd been hoping you would happen along. There's something I want to talk to you about."

"Four-flush!" sneered Ben. "You're talkin' for time!"

The passion in Ben's voice had changed its tone, revealing indecision. Reverend Jim laughed and said: "Were you going to shoot me for sure? In that case, I'll certainly talk for time." He saw doubt in Ben's eyes, and he was certain the young man had not come seeking him with murder in his heart, but with curiosity tortured with jealousy that rose out of injured vanity. "No, I expect I'm not any scared that you'll do any shooting. Grown-up men don't let a gun off at a man until they know what it's all about. And you don't know. That's what you came here for, I expect—to find out?"

"I'm findin' out, too." The fire was going from Ben's eyes. He now stared at Reverend Jim in sneering appraisement. The weapon in his hand wavered uncertainly.

"You'll find out sure—give you time," said Reverend Jim. "But I'm not a pleasant talker with a gun gaping down my throat that way. I keep thinking about it. So if you'll just put it where it won't go off—accidental—and spoil our talk, I'll be doing some explaining to you. Does that meet your present ideas?"

Ben sheathed the gun, a little shamefacedly, for there had been quiet sarcasm in Reverend Jim's voice. "Talk!" he said. "An' do it fast!"

"That's better," said Reverend Jim. A change had come into his voice. It was still quiet, still controlled, but in it now was a note of cold earnestness. His eyes were narrowed and watchful, his lips straight and hard. "Things are even with us now," he added, "and we'll talk—talk straight. There's *two* things I've been wanting to talk to you about. The first is for what you yelled at me the night you saw me showing affection for my sister. There'll be no talk about the second thing until the first is settled. It's going to be settled right now. After we get done here I'm going to tell my sister that you have explained what you said about her and me that night. What's it going to be?''

In Reverend Jim's eyes there was something that made Ben gasp with a realization that he had done the minister an injustice. Ben was not afraid of Reverend Jim; he was merely confounded by the knowledge that he had done a mean and miserable thing in hurling the insult at him. Also, he was able to detect the implacable determination in Reverend Jim's eyes. A sense of justice compelled him to acknowledge his fault.

''I reckon you can tell her I was talking through my hat,'' he said.

''I wasn't expecting anything less from Martha Warren's brother,'' smiled Reverend Jim.

Ben flushed. ''What you knowin' about Martha?'' he asked belligerently.

''That she's too good a girl to have a sneak and a coward for a brother,'' returned Reverend Jim.

The red in Ben's face deepened. He shot a swift look from his perplexed eyes at Reverend Jim, for the latter had laid subtle emphasis on his words. But he saw nothing but kindliness in the gaze that met his.

''We've come to the second thing now,'' said Reverend Jim. ''It's known that you like Lize Ebbets. But the question is: How much do you like her?''

''Plenty. But I ain't allowin' that it's any of your business!''

''Plenty, eh?'' said Reverend Jim gravely, taking no note of the sneer in Ben's voice. ''Well, that's pretty indefinite, for all it sounds as if it might cover the case. There's too much delicacy and not enough straight talk and looking the facts in the face in a thing like this. Lize wants to be straight; she told me she didn't want to see you again, because it was you who started her to going wrong. You like her plenty, you say. But do you like her enough to bust up your relations with Flash Haddam?''

Ben started; the color left his face; he crouched.

''Easy, there!'' warned Reverend Jim, his voice sharp and chill. ''We'll do that talking, and there won't be any gunplay, either. You'll play it straight across with me, using your brain instead of your gun. There's no secret about your associations with Haddam; everyone in the basin knows about them; your sister has been bearing the brunt of it—they've been sneering and turning up their noses at her because she's been taking your side. And you've been going on, letting Haddam make a monkey of you, and helping the folks in the basin to pile it onto your sister. I'm offering you a chance to get straight. If you want Lize—want her honest, like she wants to be—you've got to ride a straight trail yourself. This reformation business can't be a one-sided affair.''

"Lize tell you that?'' asked Ben. He was breathing fast; his eyes were now glowing with impotent rage and hatred.

"Lize told me she didn't want to see you again,'' said Reverend Jim. ''I'm talking reform to you on my own responsibility. I reckon she'll change her mind if you come to her honest.''

"Honest!'' fumed Ben. His composure had gone; his hands were clenched—his lips were quivering as they had quivered when Reverend Jim had caught his first sight of him. Reason had departed from his eyes, and they blazed with an intolerant light; he had again dropped into a crouch, and profanity gushed from him.

"You're a damned liar!'' he screamed. ''Honest! She honest, an' you mushin' with her, your hands on her shoulders! Honest! Why, you soft-soapin' fool! You sneakin' pulpit pounder! You come here—a stranger—an' try to interfere between a man an' his woman! You try to run things! Why, you—you—I'll——''

Whatever other words Ben would have added were stifled in a gasp of astonishment as Reverend Jim suddenly lunged forward. Ben grasped at his gun, but at the instant his fingers gripped the stock, Reverend Jim tilted full against him and his hand was seized in a grip that almost crushed his fingers. The hand was wrenched from the stock of the weapon, the arm was bent backward. He struck at Reverend Jim with the other hand, curses writhing through his lips. But the blow was blocked, the arm caught, and like the other, it was pinned to his back, above the hip. Ben ceased cursing and fought silently, furiously, to escape. His efforts were unavailing, for Reverend Jim's strength was prodigious. His arms crushed Ben's arms into his sides so that they cracked with the strain; and he was suddenly lifted, twisted, turned—and fell backward into the long bunch grass at the side of the trail, Reverend Jim on top of him.

Ben struck with an agonized grunt of pain, and lay breathless, glaring impotently up at his conqueror. Reverend Jim was breathing fast from the exertion, but he did not seem to be angry, and Ben lay still and watched him, amazed and incredulous.

"Now,'' said Reverend Jim, ''you won't be kicking up your heels while I'm talking to you.''

Ben loosed a torrent of invectives, of vivid, picturesque but unavailing profanity. He tried again to free his arms, but they were forced away from his sides and extended to their full length straight out from the shoulders, and were pinned down into the grass by Reverend Jim's weight. The grip on his wrists was like iron. Ben could move his head and his feet. His body, like his arms, was in durance, for Reverend Jim was sitting on his stomach.

"Let me up!" screamed Ben, adding a string of oaths.

"You'll get up when you can talk sense and act like a man—not a minute before," said Reverend Jim. "I'm not going to beat you up, like I ought to," he went on, his face close to Ben's, "because you're Martha's brother, and she's got enough to bear without having you come home to her looking like you'd been through a stampede. But I'm going to tell you a few things, which, if you've got the manhood of a prairie dog, will make you wake up and realize that there's other folks in the world besides you, and that they have feelings which have got to be considered.

"You get that nonsense about me cottoning up to Lize Ebbets out of your mind right now—if you've got any mind. And get this in place of it: What I said to you about you not having anything to do with Lize until you ride a straight trail is gospel facts. If I ketch you trespassing around here I'll bust you up proper. But if you're playing square I'll qualify as matchmaker, and think I've done a good job. You get that, you suffering shorthorn? I'm wanting Lize Ebbets as much as I'm wanting a short poker and a front seat in Satan's inferno, stoking Number One furnace. Can I be more convincing to you? What have you got to say? Quit turning your head that way and look at a man, can't you? That's better"—as Ben looked up at him in scowling reluctance. "You come straight, now, and tell me if you think I'm a man who would try to steal another man's woman from him?"

Ben grunted a negative reluctantly, and Reverend Jim continued:

"That's settled, then, and don't need referring to again. But there are other things which have got to be rubbed into you. You know you've got a bang-up, dyed-in-the-wool, yard-wide sister? You know she's been eating her heart out, worrying about you? You know that she's carrying the weight of all your blame foolishness? I met her on the river trail the other day, and she told me a few things. Folks in the basin won't look at her; they've cut her off their visiting list. You know she had a birthday not long ago—her eighteenth? No, you didn't know that; it had slipped you, hadn't it, because you've had your brain box so full of yourself that you couldn't think of anybody else. You didn't get her a present—not any present—on a day that means more to a girl than a thousand of your birthdays could mean to you. Do you know that she gave a party on that day, inviting all her friends and neighbors, and that not a blamed one of them came to her party? Of course she didn't tell you, you pinheaded idiot. How could she have the heart to mention it to a brother who forgot her himself, who was the cause of none of her friends coming to her party!

"What's Flash Haddam done for you? Drug you down to where you're like him—a cheap, ranting, roaring tinhorn, no-good, cowardly, sneaking thief! What do you and Flash Haddam know? Enough to gamble and drink and steal. That's all. I'm giving it to you straight, and it's not a sermon, either. It's the plain truth as decent men see it!" He paused, and then went on, more quietly, this time persuasively: "I'm asking you, for Martha's sake, to bust up with Haddam. I'll help you if you'll say the word. What do you say?"

Ben rolled his head from side to side. He was awed by Reverend Jim's strength, subdued by the truth of his words.

"Let me up," he said.

"Why sure," agreed Reverend Jim, "if you're over it." He got up and watched Ben clamber to his feet, and then stood looking at him as the youth stared downward, red of face and embarrassed. All of Ben's bluster was now gone, and Reverend Jim saw him in a new light—saw him as Martha saw him always, a big boy aping his elders, assuming a bravado which was as ridiculous as it was artificial, a boy who needed guidance rather than condemnation. Obeying a sudden impulse, Reverend Jim stepped forward, as he had done with Lize, placed his hands upon Ben's shoulders and forced the youth to face him. Ben looked up quickly with a glance of mingled shame and hostility, but instantly dropped his eyes and stood with his shoulders sagging.

"Buck up, Ben," said Reverend Jim in a low voice. "I expect you are not entirely responsible, boy; you just got the wrong start. You straighten up, and show them! It's not so big a disgrace to go wrong when you haven't had a right view of things. It's the ones that keep on doing wrong after they've discovered what is right who are deserving of all the devil can hand them. The people who are making it hard for your sister have never been tempted, and maybe they've never experienced what you have experienced with your father. And maybe there's never been a Flash Haddam around to attract them with his cheap, show-off life, which, after all, has a certain romance in it for people who don't know that only straight people get any real kick out of life.

"Maybe the people who wouldn't come to your sister's party have never been able to look things straight in the face, and maybe they'll be patting themselves on the back and telling themselves how good they've been. But I expect they're not fooling anybody but themselves. You jump on your pony and go right back to Martha. Tell her you've tumbled to your faults and that from now on you're going to be different. I'll bet she'll be so tickled about it that she'll forget all about ever having had a birthday. It'll be a new birthday for both of you. It'll be like being born again. You go on, now, and tell her."

"I dassen't," said Ben huskily. "I'm in too deep. Flash——"

"Why, I reckon we're holdin' revival meetin' right out here in the brush, ain't we?" came a voice from a thicket near by, and Flash Haddam stepped into view. He was smiling crookedly; his manner was that of cold confidence and ease, and his black eyes were gleaming with amused interest. They fell on Ben, who paled and shrank from the significance of their gaze. From Ben he looked at Reverend Jim with cold, enigmatic mirth, suppressed and sinister. Reverend Jim faced him. He was not able to conceal the contempt he felt of the man. Haddam's presence could probably be accounted for by the fact that Reverend Jim and Ben had created quite a disturbance in attempting to settle their differences, and that Flash, having ridden up unnoticed, had recognized them, had concealed himself and his pony in the thick brush at the side of the trail, to reveal himself when he thought the time propitious.

"Well, it's a meeting, Haddam," answered Reverend Jim.

"An' you're tryin' to reform Ben," laughed Haddam. "Aw, don't! Why, Ben wouldn't reform any more than he'd stick his head into a rope necktie that Sheriff Hawks would be tickled to make for him!" He looked at Ben, and again the boy shrank from the cold significance of his expression.

But Reverend Jim noticed that Ben was laboring under some

deep emotion. His face had gone dead white; he licked his dry lips with his tongue. It was evident to Reverend Jim that he was fighting a mighty battle with himself, and that it was to be won or lost within an instant.

The outlaw observed the signs, too, and drew himself slowly erect as he watched, the sneer on his lips growing cold and set. His eyes, though, were filled with astonishment; it was evident that he understood the emotions that were battling in the boy's mind as well as Reverend Jim knew of them; and with as much interest, though with less anxiety than Reverend Jim, he was awaiting the result.

It came quickly. Ben's lips stopped quivering; his voice came sharply, the words rushing out as if he feared he would reconsider before they were uttered:

"Ben Warren is goin' to reform right now!" he said. "Damn you, Flash Haddam, you got me into this! I'm gettin' myself out! I'm through—understand—through! Through, I tell you! I didn't know it then, but I got enough of you and your crowd the day you murdered——"

"Look out, Haddam!"

It was Reverend Jim's voice. He had crouched, his right hand poised, the fingers spread, tense, curved, above the butt of his pistol. For at Ben's last word Haddam's hand had moved with a gliding downward motion. Reverend Jim's warning had stopped the hand at his gun holster.

Haddam heeded the warning though he snarled at Reverend Jim, and Reverend Jim watched him narrowly as Ben finished his interrupted speech, his voice high pitched and shaking:

"The day you murdered Snedden! You shot him down in cold blood—didn't give him a chance—shot him like you'd shoot a dog! I'm through with you, I tell you! An' you can do what you damn please!" He turned and walked past Reverend Jim, ignoring Haddam.

"I'm thanking you," he said as he passed Reverend Jim, meeting his eyes. "I'm goin' back to the H-Bar-W, to tell Martha. I'm goin' to make it up to her."

Haddam and Reverend Jim did not change their positions until Ben had vanished around a bend in the trail, going, no doubt, to the place where he had left his pony. When he could be seen no more, Reverend Jim and Haddam looked at each other.

"It was a meeting, all right, Haddam. One convert is hitting the straight trail!"

Haddam looked toward the spot at which Ben had disappeared, as if meditating riding after him, then again at Reverend Jim, steadily, as if indecision and frustration were slowly yielding to feline humor, to a thought of future discomfiture for his enemy. "A meddlin' parson, eh?" he said. "I reckon someday we'll have it out, Reverend. But not right now. I'm savin' you."

He laughed at the puzzled expression of Reverend Jim's face, then turned and walked rapidly away. He had given no warning of his presence until Ben had been about to pronounce Snedden's name; and he was equally mysterious in the words he had uttered as he took his departure. Reverend Jim watched the Red Rock trail for a long time, but Haddam did not appear on it. But a little later, from the porch of the parsonage, he saw Haddam riding along a ridge on the river trail. He was headed away from the H-Bar-W, and Reverend Jim smiled his satisfaction—a smile which was somewhat strained with mystification over the outlaw's concluding words: "I'm savin' you."

CHAPTER 10

Norman Carey's corncob pipe was drawing beautifully, and he sat at his desk in the *Advocate* office, blowing clouds of blue-white smoke ceilingward and writing despite Justus Castle's frequent interruptions. Castle was straddling a chair directly in front of the door, and had been told by the editor that he was preventing what little breeze there was from entering. But Castle had not moved. "Huh!" he said, "the hotter you are, the better stuff you'll turn out. Maybe it'll get so hot after a while that you'll write a sizzler at Hawks and he'll walk in here and send you to join the angels, and then I'll have a chance to talk to Ellen Mc Donald once in a while."

"I'll blue pencil a paragraph right now," said Carey. "It was a corker—about Hawks. I'm glad you warned me." He grinned and kept on writing.

Castle was in a garrulous mood. Any hope that he might have had of getting into the good graces of Ellen Mc Donald had vanished long ago. He had not failed to observe certain unmistakable signs which told him of the young lady's preference for the editor. He was more disappointed than resentful, but he got a certain satisfaction from coming down to the *Advocate* office after closing his bank, to harass his friend.

"I believe you could write if the building were being torn down over your head," he remarked.

"Sure." The pencil moved steadily.

"How's the circulation?"

"Increasing."

"Humph. Miss Mc Donald and Reverend Jim on your circulation list?"

"Uh-huh!"

"Dave Lawler a subscriber too?"

"Yep."

Castle looked across the street, where, in front of the Palace, a number of cowboys and others were congregated. In the crowd were three men that Castle had never seen until two or three days before. They had come into town quietly. Apparently they were strangers to the country and to one another, for as he watched them now, Castle noted that they took no part in the talk and laughter that was carried on by the other men, and that they seemed to hold no communication between themselves. One of these men sat, his chair tilted at an acute angle against the pine-board front of the Palace, his broad-brimmed hat pulled well down over his eyes, as he smoked a cigarette while listening to the other men. His profile was slightly toward Castle, and Castle could see that he was a lean-faced fellow with fiery red hair. Another of the strangers was sitting on the edge of the hotel porch floor, leaning languidly against one of the slender columns, apparently deep in meditation. Like the first man, he was tall and slender. Castle could see his face clearly; he also was listening. Plainly, what he heard was of little interest to him, for the droop of his lips told of ennui. The third man was small, and a ferocious mustache distinguished him. He was sitting straddle in a chair on the boardwalk in front of the hotel, near the hitching rail, and he got up at the moment Castle looked at him. Castle grinned; the third man's legs were grotesquely bowed. He was small, but not of a retiring disposition, for his yawn, as he stretched himself, his arms above his head, could be heard distinctly by Castle. And the words that followed the yawn drew the attention of the other men to him.

"Lordy!" he said. "This town's smaller than a sheep camp!"

Castle squinted his eyes at the man with a new interest.

"What's he?" he said to no one in particular.

"What's who?" inquired Carey.

"A locoed stranger testifying to the utter degradation of our beautiful city."

"He's a liar!" declared Carey. "Civic pride will rise in its outraged might to smite so bold and reckless a defamer." He got up and stood beside Castle. "Which one are you referring to?"

"The guy with the bulging accent at the knees of his pants legs," indicated Castle. "He's just compared Red Rock to a sheep camp."

"Cowboys out of a job, those three," said Carey. "They've been here a couple of days—hanging around the saloons. Blanchard's got them spotted. Hard cases, he says they are. 'Notice their cayuses,' he said to me yesterday. 'I can always tell—ornery looking, leathery pintos. Cow saddles weigh almost a ton.' Exaggeration, of course; that Blanchard's way of saying they weigh more than an ordinary saddle. Grass ropes, oxbow stirrups—general don't-give-a-damn atmosphere around them."

"Out of a job, eh?" said Castle. "Well, if I was hiring men, I'd pass up those fellows. They look straight enough, but there's something about them that gives me the creeps. The little man puzzles me most. Reckless-looking devil, isn't he? I wouldn't want to hire any of them."

"You haven't given them the best recommendation in the world," returned Carey. "But it strikes me that if I owned a cattle ranch in this part of the country right now, and was in need of men, I'd grab those fellows quick. Too bad Dave Lawler doesn't know they are here; I don't think he'd hesitate to hire them."

Castle looked quickly at Carey. "Do you mean that Lawler has his eyes on a location?"

"Dave has committed himself more deeply than that. I meant to tell you when you came in, but you talked so fast that I couldn't get a chance to spring it. Prepare yourself for a shock. I haven't the least idea who began the negotiations, and I can't even guess how they are going to get along—to agree, I mean. But Dave Lawler has gone to live with Reverend Jim and Ellen——"

"Oh," said Castle. "Ellen."

"Ellen," repeated Carey, defiantly grinning. "Dave Lawler has gone to live at the parsonage, using the place as his headquarters."

Castle looked blankly at the editor. Carey was in earnest and went on:

"At first glance such an arrangement seems ridiculous. It struck me that way when I heard of it. But when you remember that Reverend Jim has been a cowboy, and therefore knows the game—very likely likes it—it doesn't appear so ridiculous, after all."

"But it takes money to go into a thing like that," protested Castle. "And Reverend Jim doesn't seem to be overburdened with it. I wonder what arrangement they made? Do you think——"

Carey smiled dryly, a certain subtle reserve in his manner. "You might satisfy your curiosity by asking Lawler about it," he interrupted. "Here he is, now."

Lawler was loping his pony down the street as Castle turned. Lawler was heading toward the *Advocate* office, but when he saw the crowd in front of the Palace, he urged his pony toward it, dismounted and hitched the animal to the rail.

The crowd had become animated; men were laughing and talking loudly; there were some jeers and some curses—all good natured. The little man's words, comparing Red Rock to a sheep camp, evidently had not provoked the storm of indignation and resentment that Castle and Carey expected. But the movement, the voices, indicated the imminence of unusual action, and there was an atmosphere of repressed excitement which penetrated across the street and affected Carey. He grinned at Castle.

"There's too little happening in this town to miss anything that's liable to happen," he said. "And if I'm not mistaken there'll be doings over there. Work's over for the day," he declared. "I'm hanging out across the street for the rest of the afternoon."

Castle followed him across the street. There were perhaps a score of men in the crowd, mostly cowboys in town for a holiday, and they were congregated around the little man, being evidently inclined to treat his vigorous statements with levity. Lawler did not mix with them, but leaned against the front of the building, his face expressionless as he watched and listened.

"This town," the little man was saying in a loud voice as Carey and Castle reached the Palace porch, "don't grade up, nohow. She's dead slow an' yearnin' for the mourners. No excitement—nary a chirp which could be diagnosed as indicatin' trouble. No nothin'—not even no job!"

"I reckon you used up all the work where you was—you're such a hell warmer for it," said a voice.

"Boss wore himself to a frazzle, lookin' for jobs for me, tryin' to keep me busy. I done took pity on him an' blowed before he'd leave a widow who'd be accusin' me of killin' him," retorted the little man. "No jobs around here, I reckon. I'm thinkin' of hittin' the breeze out."

"You got any qualifications besides your gab?"

This was Lawler. He still stood beside the building, and there was an ironic smile on his face as he spoke.

"For," he went on as the crowd turned to look at him, "you've got to measure up to man's size to hold a job in these parts."

"Disparagin' my height an' my legs," said the little man, sneering at Lawler, his chin outthrust, his eyes belligerent.

"Disparagin' your gab, as I told you," returned Lawler, unruffled. "You got anything else on tap? Ropin', shootin' an' such?"

"I'm a heap accommodatin'," said the little man, coldly, as he crouched, his fingers curved and tensed, clawlike, above his gun holster.

Lawler's smile was unperturbed. "I've seen men who was quick on the draw that couldn't plug the front of the Palace at ten feet," he said. "I'm wantin' men. But I wouldn't have no man around me which couldn't score a bull's-eye from any angle I give him. Also, he's got to be some slick at ropin'. You wantin' a job bad enough to make good on them specifications? I'm payin' forty-five a month to that kind of a man."

The little man looked at him intently.

"Why," he said, "I reckon you're talkin' business. I'm yearnin' to hear them shootin' specifications. If I make good on them mebbe you'll take my word about the ropin'."

"That goes," agreed Lawler. He pointed to a post at the extreme end of the hitching rail. It was considerably beyond the building and in front of a wide-open space which the proprietor of the Palace used as a place in which to store miscellaneous articles—crates, empty barrels and boxes and a litter of refuse and litter from the kitchen. "See that post?" Lawler added. "We're takin' a whisky glass, of which the Palace boss has just got in a new consignment, an' we're settin' her on the top of that post. You hop on your cayuse at the other end of town an' come down here, your cayuse runnin' his level best, an' if you bust the glass in three tries you're on the way to qualifyin' for that job, pronto.''

The little man grinned widely. ''Oh, say, give me a man-size trick!'' he said. ''Make it shootin' the buttons off your coat, or somethin'!''

''Salivate the whisky glass,'' declined Lawler as the crowd laughed. ''You'll earn Reverend Jim's thanks for takin' a shot at the demon rum, an' I won't have to requisition the mourners.''

The little man turned and walked around the side of the building toward the stable in which he had left his pony. The crowd watched him as he walked away, his bowed legs accentuating the bagged condition of his trouser legs. Another man dived into the Palace and emerged with a whisky glass, which he placed daintily upon the post indicated by Lawler. The crowd waited, impatient for the little man's appearance, some of them wagering upon the outcome of the feat.

Carey had been greatly interested. He had watched the little man narrowly during his talk with Lawler, and had detected a certain insincerity in his face and in his voice. This had been his conviction, at any rate, but he was sure no other person had noticed it, for every man's face was alight with anticipation or doubt—even Castle's. Carey squatted down beside the red-haired stranger's chair, yielding to a sudden curiosity.

''You don't think the little man is bluffing?'' he said to the red-haired man.

The latter turned and looked at him searchingly. His gaze fell on Carey's eyes; then his own gleamed with a quick, though partially repressed cordiality, and his lips wreathed into a slow, deprecatory grin. ''Bluffin'?'' he said. ''Shucks! I reckon a man wouldn't be none on the shoot at all if he'd miss that glass the first try. But three times!'' His gaze went to Carey's head, and the grin on his lips widened. ''You're the newspaper fello' across the street,'' he said. ''I've seen your red head through the window an' wondered if you knowed how red it really is. From here, it looked like a fire. Come pretty near to raisin' the hue an' cry when I first seen it.''

''Sure it wasn't your own reflection in the window?'' returned Carey. ''Some folks are mighty nearsighted.''

''Oh, shucks,'' said the stranger with pretended gravity, ''you don't mean to tell me you noticed *my* hair!''

''Couldn't help it if I looked at you at all.''

''So you've been noticin' me.'' He laughed softly. ''Well, I reckon that ain't nothin' unusual. But say! That locoed banty is sure strong on windy palaver, ain't he?'' he said, changing the subject. ''But they tell me there's a right good lot of them wild an' woolly speciments hangin' out in this town. You *sabe* Flash Haddam?''

''Wish I didn't,'' frowned Carey.

The stranger shot a slow, quizzical glance at him. ''Not admirin' him none, eh?''

''He'll tell you I don't.''

The red-haired stranger laughed. ''Carey, your name is, ain't it? Mine's Owen—Red for short. I'm figgerin' on hangin' out here for a while. I figger to get the job the locoed banty is after.''

At this point in their conversation they were interrupted by the reappearance of the little man. He rode around the corner of the building at breakneck pace, and with a shrill yell brought his pony to a halt beside the post upon which the whisky glass reposed. He grinned at the glass, waved a hand grandiloquently at the crowd, and then urged his pony down the street.

The crowd made a concerted movement out of the line of fire, hugging the front of the building, its gaze concentrated on the little man, who was now at the edge of town, though not more than two hundred yards distant.

He yelled as he drew his heavy Colt, kicking his pony in the ribs at the same instant. The animal broke into a dead run and whirled toward the post, enveloped in a cloud of dust. It was over in an instant. As the pony neared the post the little man raised his weapon, and when about thirty feet distant brought it down with a quick, jerky motion. The gun crashed; the glass tinkled to atoms; and the little man rode on a short distance, wheeled his pony and came back, bowing with extravagant politeness in acknowledgment to the applause that greeted him.

He rode up, bowed to Lawler. ''I reckon I'll take your job, stranger,'' he said to Lawler.

''It's like takin' candy from a kid.''

It was Red Owen who spoke. He sat in his chair beside Carey, grinning derisively up into the little man's face. ''Like takin' candy from a kid,'' he repeated, the eyes of the crowd upon him, the little man looking at him with a sneer of defiance. ''I don't like to butt into any man's game, but if I couldn't do no better shootin' than that, I'd take no man's job.''

''You reckon you can do better?'' said Lawler. He seemed to be skeptical.

"Plenty," returned Owen.

"Make your play. If you beat that shootin', you get the job," declared Lawler.

"She goes," said Owen. "I allow I'll break two glasses on the post with two shots."

Owen got up. As he did so, something bright and metallic slid along his leg and dropped noiselessly into the dust at Carey's feet. Carey looked at the object, started, and instantly placed a foot upon the object, grinding it down into the dust. An instant later, while the crowd was devoting its attention to the post and the two glasses that someone placed on its top, Carey stooped, dug the object from the dust and stealthily placed it into a pocket.

There was an amused smile on Carey's face now, a complacent smile, pregnant with knowledge. With a newer and different interest he watched the crowd, the little man, Lawler and Red Owen. The latter had got his pony. Like the little man, he rode to the edge of town. But there was no self-consciousness in his manner, no vainglorious posing. He was very much in earnest.

"Wants that job pretty bad, I reckon," said a man in the crowd.

Red made the feat of breaking the two glasses seem ridiculously easy. With his pony running desperately, he held himself loosely in the saddle, riding smoothly with no more undulations or jerking than one would have experienced in a rowboat on the quiet surface of a river. Came two reports, one closely following the other, and it was done, and cheers greeted the destruction of the two glasses.

Red rode back to the rail, with satisfaction, and perhaps a little triumph, in his eyes. The little man sneered, but received his defeat philosophically.

"Accordin' to returns, you've got the job," he said. "I didn't want it so bad anyway."

Carey's eyes were on the third stranger. Until now, he had sat quietly in his place, apparently not deeply interested. But now, at the little man's words, he got up and walked over to Lawler.

"I'm some glass buster, myself," he said. "I can spill 'em, empty or full. Two, mebbe."

He got on his horse and rode to where the two others had gone. In a flash he was back. Twice his big gun crashed, and one glass was shattered. But the other stood mockingly erect, uninjured, and amid the mingled laughter and jeers the third man rode back to the hitching rail. He was red with embarrassment.

However, Lawler quelled the laughter and jibes with a wave of the arm.

"I reckon it's a heap easier to laugh than to bust a glass with your cayuse on the run," he said. "An' this game ain't got no limit, either to glasses or men. You're all welcome to try it. I want more than three men. I'm hirin' them which has already shot, an' I'll hire any man who can bust one glass. Forty-five a month I'm offerin', an' nobody is barred!"

Another man stepped out of the crowd and mounted a horse, and another glass decorated the top of the post. The fourth man failed ingloriously—likewise a fifth. At the sixth trial, Lawler remarked that there didn't seem to be any danger of the proprietor of the Palace running short of whisky glasses, and there were no more volunteers.

An hour later Lawler, with his three newly hired men clattering beside him, rode out of town over the parsonage trail. The crowd gradually broke up, many seeking the Palace barroom. Carey stood in his place, watching Lawler and the three other men until a bend in the trail hid them from his view. Then he turned to see Castle standing near him.

Carey grinned. "Some shooting, eh?" he said.

"Clever fellows," was Castle's tribute. "Didn't I tell you they were hard cases?"

Carey did not reply until they were inside the *Advocate* office. Then he sank into a chair beside his desk and grinned broadly at Castle.

"Clever?" he said then. "Well, that fits the case exactly. They're clever enough to fool these Red Rock people. They're even clever enough to fool bankers—but not clever enough to fool a newspaperman."

"What in blazes are you getting at?" growled Castle with a puzzled look at his friend. "You don't mean to say there was any shenanigan to that deal, do you?"

"Frame-up, pure and simple," said Carey. "Grandstand play for effect. And it had the very effect Lawler intended it should have. No one will ever suspect him, hiring men that way. But if he had hired three strangers without giving everybody in Red Rock a chance, people would have been suspicious."

Castle's puzzled expression changed to one of incredulity, then to amazement.

"You don't mean——" he began.

"Yes. They are Lawler's men. They came here by prearrangement."

"How do you know?"

Carey held out for Castle's inspection the bright, metallic object dropped by Red Owen. It was a badge, and the fastening had become broken. On the reverse side were stamped the words: Deputy Sheriff.

"For the love of Mike!" gasped Castle. "What if it had been found by someone else!"

"It wasn't—fortunately. And when I hand it back to Mr Owen I shall warn him to be more careful in the future."

"I'll be cussed if I'd give it back to him," declared Castle. "I'd be afraid he'd be sore about it."

"Mr Owen won't be sore," smiled Carey. "We're pretty good friends already. We have something in common which assures mutual admiration and respect." He tapped his head.

"Brains, I suppose," jeered Castle.

"Just hair," grinned Carey.

CHAPTER 11

"I draws 'Shorty,' usual," defiantly confided the little man in satisfying a natural curiosity on the part of some of Red Rock's citizens, "that handle bein' popular with fresh guys which think they're pullin' off somethin' new in alludin' to my ground hooks. So 'Shorty' goes. The rest of my name, which is duly registered an' noted in the Congressional Records—or wherever they keep track of guys which is long on palaver an' short on legs—is Percy Lewelyn Mc Guinness. But," he added, with a cold glare around at the men who stood near him in the Emporium, "I'm warnin' you that I ain't never allowed no one but my mother to apply it to me in one lump. Shorty Mc Guinness will do for you yaps, an' don't you go for to enlargin' on her!"

Owen acknowledged to the sobriquet "Red," with a grin of satisfaction, and in due time it became known that the third man was "Slim" Weaver. Red Rock got the impression that, though all had been hired by Lawler, jealousy existed between them as a result of the shooting match. If, as Carey suspected, the three men were Lawler's deputies and had come to Red Rock to follow out some prearranged plan, they had concealed their real mission with consummate cleverness—the loss of the badge excepted, of course. The finding of the badge by one of Haddam's men, together with the knowledge that it had been lost by Red Owen, would have aroused instant suspicion. Owen was plainly pleased when Carey returned the badge. Carey saw Owen riding into town one day soon after the shooting match, and signaled to him. A little later Owen entered the *Advocate* office. He was a likable fellow, who held his head erect and looked at Carey with steady, quizzical eyes.

"Howdy," he said as he stood in the doorway of the office, glancing about him as if to discover if anyone was listening. "Ketchin' the high sign, I ambles over here as soon as I can do so decent to help you take a load off your mind. I'll take it now, you agreein'."

"Take what?"

Owen grinned. "The badge," he said. "I saw you nail it with your number 'leven. Caught your eye later, an' knowed you wasn't advertisin' no secrets."

"If I had?" said Carey.

Owen smiled. "Much as I'd took a shine to you, I'd have salivated you before I busted the whisky glasses. Accidental of course, it would have been, but you'd have been just as dead, I reckon. I was plumb charmed over your conduct. I've been inquirin' about you some, since. You're on the level. Me losin' that badge was plumb carelessness. I'd looked at the blame' pin that mornin', an' knowed it was loose. She slipped off the under side of my suspender."

"What else is coming off?" questioned Carey, unwisely.

Owen grinned. "Aw, don't make me lose my faith in red hair," he said.

"Of course not," laughed Carey.

After Owen departed and Carey reflected upon their conversation, he realized that he had gained no information whatever. But he was convinced that Hawks's days as sheriff were numbered. He confided to Castle the news of Owen's visit, but the resulting speculation was pointless. And the next issue of the *Advocate* did not even mention the shooting match.

Activity reigned at the parsonage. The bunkhouse, which in an earlier day had been occupied by the cowboys employed by the former owner, was again made habitable, and Red Owen, Slim Weaver, Shorty Mc Guinness and Lawler took up their abode in it. Their presence did not interfere with or disturb the occupants of the ranch house.

There was little for the men to do during their first days at the parsonage, but when one day the new outfit drove some hundreds of cattle—yearlings, cows and the regular quota of other stock—into the parsonage corrals, the place began to take on a busy appearance. There were strenuous scenes during the rebranding process in the corral, during which the three new men showed they could do things other than shoot, and when it was done and the stock turned out into the open range, the little outfit settled down to routine work.

Through various channels the cattlemen of the basin heard of Lawler's activity. Publicly, they criticised him for venturing to attempt to raise cattle in a vicinity so harassed; privately they admired his courage; but when they heard he had adopted a solid triangle for a brand they openly jeered. For it seemed that the adoption of this brand was a tacit invitation to Flash Haddam to help himself to the stock. As a practical problem in pyrography, the merging of the triangle into the star—Haddam's brand—would be ridiculously simple, involving nothing more difficult than the mere branding of the star over the triangle, thus obliterating the latter.

Still, it was not a matter for interference, though Lawler's choice aroused caustic comment in some quarters, much of which bore upon the question of his fitness for cattle raising. Some of this criticism might have reached Lawler's ears, but he gave no sign. No warnings moved him. The nearest he came to showing interest in any opinion delivered within his hearing was when one day he met Carey on the river trail, and Carey asked him if he wasn't daring Haddam by adopting the triangle as a brand.

Lawler grinned at him. "H'm," he said, "you're the fellow Red Owen was tellin' me about. He's plumb taken a shine to you. I'm a heap thankful for you callin' my attention to the mistake."

Lawler's grin broadened as he rode on. If Carey's suspicions had been less strong, he would have felt baffled. However, he was pleased over Lawler's answer and gratified by the subtle expression of confidence betrayed by Lawler. Lawler had shown that he was not the reckless fool that Red Rock thought him— that the triangle brand had been adopted with deliberate purpose.

Reverend Jim was silent concerning the arrangements he had made with Lawler. Blanchard, however, proffered the suggestion, with sarcasm which was not wholly lost upon his hearers, that perhaps Reverend Jim's arrangement with Lawler had been forced by the meager collections following Reverend Jim's sermons at the meetinghouse. "Mebbe you've been dolin' out enough coin to feed a road runner," Blanchard told them, "but Reverend Jim is some husky, an' his grub pile would sure be lookin' pitiful if he depended on you. I reckon Lawler's handin' him somethin' substantial."

Despite Blanchard's speech, Red Rock had no need to feel concern for Reverend Jim. He seemed to be getting enough to eat, judging from his energy in making calls upon his parishioners—and he looked cheerful and contented. He had not referred to his talk with Ben Warren. He wanted to test the strength of the boy's resolutions before mentioning him to Lize. But as the days went, he heard good reports of Ben's activities, and from Dal Thompson, the H-Bar-W foreman, he learned that the young man had joined his father's outfit and was working steadily.

Martha Warren had ridden over to the parsonage—to find the object of her visit absent, he having ridden over to the Arrow. From Ellen, through the medium of subtle badinage, Reverend Jim got the impression that Martha had been disappointed to find him gone. He did not permit Ellen to sense his disappointment, for that would have delivered him into her hands. Martha had left word, however, of the change in Ben's conduct. Words had not been necessary to acquaint Ellen with Martha's joy over the change in her brother.

"It was in her eyes," Ellen told Reverend Jim. "Jim," she added, watching him narrowly, "you have made a staunch friend in Martha."

"I'll be mighty pleased if I've helped to make a man of Ben," he declared. And he told her of his talk with the boy. "He thinks a heap of Lize, in spite of everything."

"I don't think Lize cares much about him," said Ellen.

"How's a man to tell about a woman?" asked Reverend Jim. "They're so whimsical."

"Perhaps a man can't understand a woman," she said. "But one woman can understand another. Men are blind—sometimes."

"You shooting in the dark?" he said, gently.

"No. Meaning that Lize is in love with someone other than Ben Warren."

"Oh, don't," said Reverend Jim disappointedly. "That's too

bad—for Ben. I was hoping they would both quit their foolishness and make a hitch of it.''

"I don't think you will be much of a success as a matchmaker,'' she mocked, "with your man's way of ignoring the things that are always in front of you. Don't you see that Lize doesn't want Ben Warren?''

"She'll have him when she sees he's reformed.''

Ellen made a gesture of resignation. "Yours is a laudable ambition,'' she said with a sober laugh, "though I warn you that you are due for a shock.''

Ellen saw the Reverend Jim Mc Donald later, standing near some alders that fringed the river, talking with Lize. They were fully a hundred yards from her and she could not see their faces, but from Lize's attitude—her bowed head, her rigidity—she anticipated what her answer would be if Reverend Jim importuned her on behalf of Ben.

But Reverend Jim could not see the signs that were plain to his sister. And when Lize still persisted in her refusal to reconsider her decision to reject Ben, he watched her, puzzled and uncertain.

"Why, Ben's reforming for your sake, Lize,'' he told her. "He's straight, now, and deserving, and because of what's gone on before, you ought to feel tickled to get him. He'll make a mighty fine man—give him time.''

"I don't want him.''

"Well,'' said Reverend Jim, stroking his chin, a feeling of helplessness afflicting him. "I expect I'm not such a great success at matchmaking, after all—as I've been told. There's folks that haven't much faith in me.'' He smiled at Lize. "I expect I understand,'' he added, after an interval of silence. "There's someone else, eh?''

Lize's face was scarlet, and Reverend Jim understood *that*.

"Well,'' he said, "it's your life that you've got to live, after all, I expect. And nobody but you can live it. And if a man keeps from meddling, he won't have anything to blame himself for, no matter what turns up. Anyway, Ben can't say that I didn't try, can he?''

He left her and started toward the house.

Watching from the ranch house, Ellen saw Lize turn and look after him. The wistfulness in the girl's attitude brought a frown to Ellen's face. She wondered, as she stood there watching the girl, if those who have sinned do not sometimes ask the world to pay too high a price for their reformation.

But Reverend Jim, unaware of the thoughts in Lize's mind, grinned as he entered the door of the house and caught Ellen standing at the window.

"I expect you hit the nail on the head with your guessing," he said regretfully. "She's soured on Ben. Women are sure too deep for me."

CHAPTER 12

Had Reverend Jim yielded to his inclinations he would have made a visit to the H-Bar-W sooner, for since his first meeting with Martha she had figured prominently in his thoughts. He now intended to stop at the H-Bar-W for a few minutes only, for he had promised to visit the Diamond Dot today. It was thirty-five miles down the river, and he would have to ride steadily to make it and would probably stay overnight, for he had delayed starting, and it was now nearly noon. So when he rode up to the front porch of the H-Bar-W ranch house he did not dismount, but sat in the saddle and hallooed.

There was no answer. He called again, with a like result. Then, patiently, he rode his pony around a rear corner of the house and up to the rear door, expecting to find Martha in the kitchen. The kitchen door was closed, and when there came no response to his calls he dismounted, with the intention of knocking. Then, a piece of paper, affixed to the door with a pin, caught his attention. He read:

"DEAR DAD: *I have gone down to the parsonage.*
"MARTHA"

Reverend Jim was disappointed, and remounting his pony, he sat in the saddle, fixedly contemplating the note. Hexter, of the Diamond Dot, would have considered Reverend Jim's thoughts amusing. An abashed grin reached his face. The Diamond Dot seemed suddenly very far away and the heat too great for the long ride.

"I expect she took the river trail or I'd have met her," ran his thoughts as he urged the pony away from the house, guiding it toward the river. He was in a strange mood, which aroused him to self-criticism. Here he was, headed for the Diamond Dot, deciding not to go there. Instead, stirred unaccountably to dilatoriness, he was going to wander along the river trail, his direction set by the note on the door. This was not like him—not like the Jim Mc Donald he knew. How, when he reached the parsonage, would he explain to Ellen? If Martha had gone there he would not need to do any explaining to Ellen. Ellen would know that he had been drawn back, as metal is drawn to the magnet, resistlessly! So, his face a little flushed because of the knowledge that he was doing something that in the history of the world had been many times repeated by the weak and the strong and by the brave and the cowardly, he rode along, surrendering to the romance in his thoughts.

And then, absorbed, paying no attention to his surroundings, his pony walking through a wood where the shade was deep and the silence disturbed only by the rhythmic beat of the pony's hoofs, he came suddenly upon her. The spot was only a quarter of a mile from the parsonage, and as Reverend Jim suddenly pulled his pony in, he could see someone standing on the porch of the parsonage, watching. He did not speculate upon the identity of the figure, for the blush on Martha's face was more interesting.

She was pleased to see him—he would have been insensible to all knowledge of facial expression had he failed to understand that. But there was something besides pleasure in her eyes—surprise that was sincere and complete, together with a shy reserve and embarrassment.

"Oh," she exclaimed, "Ellen told me you had gone to the Diamond Dot!"

If Reverend Jim's face was red, he was not aware of it. His only conscious emotion was satisfaction over having found her in a place where he could talk to her without anyone overhearing him. He had prepared a reply to this question which he felt Ellen would ask on his return.

"I was intending to. But I got to thinking that I didn't care to hang out at the Diamond Dot overnight. So I postponed the trip until tomorrow."

"Did you stop at the H-Bar-W?"

Reverend Jim was not a clever prevaricator. He had not found it difficult to experiment with white lies to certain people, and in certain circumstances, but lying to a girl he loved was a different matter entirely, and so he did not trust himself to look at Martha when he answered, pretending to be very much interested in the pony's mane. He could not tell her that he had stopped, for then she would know that he had seen her note to her father and would suspect that his excuse for not going to the Diamond Dot was a mere subterfuge. He had seen a quick flash of doubt in her eyes when he had spoken.

"No," he said, "I didn't stop." And then, instantly, keenly alert for advantage, he added gently: "Was you expecting me?"

He looked at her. To his amazement she was blushing. For her note had really been intended for him, should he ride to the H-Bar-W and find her absent. Her father would be away for several days.

"Yes," she said quietly. "I have been expecting you for a long time—ever since Ben has mended his ways. I have wanted to thank you. I thank you now. The last few weeks have been the happiest of my life." She rode forward and held out a hand, which he took, holding it, marveling at the thrill it sent over him. They were very close together, now, and both laughed without any clear idea of the emotions which provoked their laughter. The thrill of contact, of physical nearness, an expression of mutual attraction, dimly comprehended but deeply ecstatic. He longed to hold her hand still longer, but, wisely, he gently dropped it.

"I didn't do much—only told Ben the truth about what he was facing, if he kept on doing what he'd been doing. He couldn't go very far wrong, you know, being your brother."

"He told me you said that." She blushed again. "It was nice of you."

"Just the truth again," he said. He glanced swiftly around, and then back at her, his eyes narrowed.

"Do you know where we are?" he asked.

She looked the place over—calmly, it seemed. Then her gaze

drooped. "Yes," she said. "How odd! It is where we met the other time—the first time."

"So it is," he said. He stroked her pony's mane, wishing the mane was her hair. They were so close together that at times, when their mounts moved, his right knee touched the shoulder of her pony. "It's right where you said I was almost a hypocrite."

"Yes—almost."

"Well," he said, "I was one. I'm confessing. You see, I wasn't wanting to get acquainted with you as a preacher gets acquainted with a member of his flock. I was figuring on knocking the edges off convention."

"And did you succeed?" She shot a demure glance at him.

"Why, I expect there's nothing stiff and formal in our talk right now."

This was true. It was only their second meeting. But she felt— his manner had caused her to feel—that they had been acquainted for years. She did not hesitate when he suggested that they sit for a while in the shade at the edge of the promontory, but dismounted, trailed the reins over the pony's head and seated herself on the grass. He found a place near her.

The view of the river, its valley, and the plain that swept away from it, was magnificent from where they sat. The distant mountains, their peaks aglow in the shimmering white of the midday sun, were fitting guardians of the wide, vast, slumbering country that lay at their feet. In the foreground the river, wild, rugged, picturesque with its rocky buttes, its fringing weeds and brush, its stretches of timber, wound a serpentine way, vanishing as it doubled at a point near the parsonage.

"It is beautiful, isn't it?" she said. "And I have been happy here. And yet, there is a world beyond the mountains that I would like to see. When I look at their peaks it seems to me that they form a barrier which is keeping me here. It is a grotesque fancy, I know, but I believe I am growing to dislike the mountains for that reason. I should like to see those cities of which I have heard. They must be very interesting."

"I expect they are not so awful interesting," he said gravely. "They are like everything else—interesting from a distance. Money mills, cities are. They're hoppers into which human beings put principles and morals and manhood and womanhood and even their souls, at one end, so that dollars will come out at the other. But happiness! Well—maybe there is some, ex-

perienced by people who don't let money master them. The rest
yield to envy and jealousy and an eternal scramble for dollars. If
a man can get happiness out of that he has to deceive himself a
heap. I expect a man could stand it to live in a city for a while,
knowing that someday he would get out of it, back to the open
where he can see the real world. That's what makes some men
patiently endure the things they face. But to stay in the city
regular, with nothing to do but look at dingy buildings, and
smoke and man-made things! I expect not. The open was made
for man, and it's a man's fault if he doesn't live in it. Most city
men have the instinct to get into the open or into the woods. The
man who makes camping trips, or goes fishing or hunting,
is trying to escape. I think no city can show you anything
like that!'' he swept a hand toward the plains and the mountains.

"Yes," she said, "it is beautiful. And there is no danger of
my leaving here just now, for Father is opposed to my going, and
I shall not leave him. He needs me." Her eyes grew more
serious. "I wanted to go—somewhere—to school—years ago.
But Father told me he couldn't afford it. Now he says he can't
afford to leave Red Rock."

"Isn't he prosperous?"

"No one knows. He ought to have money, but it is not visible.
Generosity would have prevented Ben from—doing what he
did. But Father's peculiarities do not include generosity. I have
made him promise, though, to pay Ben wages—good wages. So
you see," she added, laughing, "dollars do answer some good
purpose, after all."

"There have been times when I've found them mighty conve-
nient," he returned. "But I've noticed they are most valuable
when you haven't got them."

She did not smile at this remark, and he noted that her face had
become slowly grave, and now she was looking at him steadily,
her gaze searching, though unmistakably personal. None but the
purely innocent could have asked the question she asked of him
now, without a telltale wavering of the eyes or a betraying color.

"Were you ever as wild as Ben?"

Reverend Jim was astounded. Then, instantly remembering
her lack of worldly knowledge, he was stirred to respect, venera-
tion and gentleness; and his narrowed, probing eyes found in
hers no guile—nothing but frank inquiry.

"Our own faults are never as glaring to us as the faults of

others," he said. "I used to think I was about average, but to other people I must have seemed to be a little wild."

Satisfaction shone out of her eyes, and a smile thanked him. "I have wondered ever since you came," she said. "But if you were wild and got over it there is no reason why Ben should not get over it, too. I should like him to be like you."

"Outwardly or inwardly?" asked Reverend Jim.

She studied him intently, turning her head this way and that, as if to consider the details of his appearance. Then for a moment her gaze grew introspective, as if she were thinking of his character—of what she knew of it. Finally she smiled brightly.

"Well," she said simply, "I would like to have him be like you—in character and appearance. But I suppose, in appearance, I shall have to keep him as he is."

"You are making it hard for me to be myself," he laughed. "From now on it's likely I'll be what you think I am rather than what I am."

"I haven't flattered you *too* much," she said. "If you feel complimented you are welcome to it, but I want to warn you that I made some reservations."

"Of course," he said. "But would you mind being specific. Maybe knowing your reservations would help to take down the swelling in my head. It's got pretty big within the past few minutes."

"One thing is that you do not always mean what you say," she said.

"Does anybody? Do you? Are you sure you would want Ben to be like me?"

"Yes," she declared positively. "Just like you—your slyness and all."

"So now I'm 'sly,' " he laughed. "Go ahead, Martha, and continue the character inquisition—with me as the subject. And after you get through I'll tell you what I think of you—and I shall say exactly what I mean."

"No, that's plenty," she smiled. "But I don't see why people should not say what they think, whether there is a compliment in what they say—or just the opposite. I shouldn't want to get into the habit of saying things that I do not mean."

This conclusion made him smile. She was as refreshing as the prairie breeze that stirred the leaves above their heads.

"But I expect it's pretty wise—sometimes—not to say everything you think," he said. "Don't you think a man might get too good an opinion of himself if a girl kept on telling him things like you've been telling me?''

"If I had thought there was any danger of that I shouldn't have told you," she said calmly.

"I'm trying hard not to give in to it," he laughed.

She laughed with him. But presently she looked at him inquiringly.

"Who is Eliza Ebbets?" she asked.

Now again, suddenly, he was faced with a problem. He had thought of the possibility of Martha's meeting Lize, but had decided that Lize would be careful to avoid such a meeting. But it was evident that such a meeting had taken place. How had Ellen managed it? Obviously, Ben had told Martha nothing about Lize's reputation; it was equally plain that gossip had not wagged its tongues over that particular morsel at the H-Bar-W. He smiled faintly.

"She is Ellen's companion," he said, not caring to discuss the subject of Lize's profession with Martha.

"So Ellen told me," Martha said. "But Ellen also told me she is from Red Rock. I thought I knew everybody in this section, but it seems I was mistaken. Ellen said she did not know where in Red Rock you had got her, and so I wasn't able to place her."

Reverend Jim had two courses before him. He could tell Martha the truth and embarrass her, or he could equivocate and keep the ugly subject out of his romance, so delightfully developing. He chose the latter way. Ellen, he surmised, had wisely evaded. This was as it should be, for Ellen would not know whether or not Ben had told his sister anything about Lize, and certainly, if Martha was to know at all, it was her brother's place to tell her. At any rate, Reverend Jim decided not to accept the responsibility.

He had lied before; he lied now. "Dave Blanchard got her for me," he said. "I didn't ask him where he got her, but I expect she must have been working for him."

"That explains it, doesn't it? She is probably a newcomer. I met her at the kitchen door as I rode over. She came around a corner of the house and almost ran into Ginger—my pony. Bashful, isn't she? I am certain she doesn't like me, though. For Ellen came out and introduced us, and she excused herself as quickly as possible and didn't show herself again."

"Yes, she's bashful, I expect." She wasn't bashful, of course, and she had the hard sophistication of her profession.

Reverend Jim could not defend or accuse her. He merely pitied her. And he was reluctant to say more.

"She is pretty, though, isn't she?"

Reverend Jim did not wish to certify to this, though he knew it was the truth. It seemed like disloyalty to Martha to admit such a truth in her presence. He did not answer.

"Isn't she?" persisted Martha.

"I expect some people would think so."

"And do you think so?"

"Well, now," said Reverend Jim, not yet cornered, "I expect I don't know. You see, a girl or a woman can be pretty to one man, and not so pretty to another. A great deal would depend upon the man's notions of beauty."

"But every man has some notion?"

"Of course."

"And you have none?"

"I wouldn't say that. You see, I have some notions about you, and awhile ago I told you I was intending to tell you about them. And I'm glad you brought this up about Lize, because saying what I've wanted to say about you won't embarrass me."

She laughed, but there was skepticism in her eyes. He had refused to commit himself, and therefore Lize's beauty had impressed him. With Martha looking at him in that manner he could not tell her what he had intended to tell her—that she was the most beautiful girl he had ever met—and so, absently, he picked up a pebble, threw it over the edge of the butte and watched it drop with a splash into the water. When he turned again to Martha he was surprised to see her gazing soberly into the distance, her lips pressed firmly together.

Somehow, Martha was vaguely disappointed. She had had a secret hope that Reverend Jim would not confirm her words about Lize, and that he had refused to affirm or deny—after so much deliberation—convinced her that he had been impressed with Lize's attractions. She told herself that she was not jealous, though she knew that with her first glimpse of Lize had come a disquieting pang over the knowledge that the girl seemed at home at the parsonage. She could not conceal the embarrassment which the revelations of the past few minutes had brought to her, and her face was flaming as she got up.

"I must go," she said quickly. "Dad will be home."

But she did not go just then. Instantly aware of her perturbation, and vaguely conscious of the cause of it, Reverend Jim arose also. His face, too, was red—surprise, knowledge, elation shone in his eyes as he stood before her and looked at her averted face, at the drooping lashes that veiled her eyes. Manlike, with the evidence of her feelings toward him revealed, he could not resist the temptation to speak of them.

"Well," he said gently, "I expect if you think I've taken a shine to Lize you're a heap mistaken."

But it was Reverend Jim who had made the mistake—the second one.

She met his gaze fairly and smiled. She had been hoping for this disavowal, but of course Reverend Jim must never suspect it.

"Mistaken?" she said. "I don't quite understand. I have no right—or desire—to interfere with you and Eliza. And she is pretty—isn't she? And I don't believe I would blame you for taking a 'shine' to her. She really is attractive, and what you do can be no concern of mine."

Reverend Jim's thoughts were troubled as he watched her walk to her pony. She mounted and turned to smile at him.

"I want to thank you again for what you did for Ben," she said. "And," she added, "won't you bring Ellen over to the H-Bar-W sometime?" Then she waved a hand gayly at him and urged her pony down the trail.

Something had been added to Reverend Jim's knowledge of women. Half a minute later he climbed into the saddle, frowning. He did not go far, however, before the frown vanished. Presently an abashed grin reached his face, and he was glowing with pleasure when he rode into the corral yard and dismounted.

Meanwhile, Martha had not ridden far. She had guided her pony into some brush just around a bend in the trail, out of Reverend Jim's sight, and had watched him ride away, regret in her eyes. When he vanished she again brought her pony to the trail. Before her, seated on a rock, watching her gravely, was Lize Ebbets.

It had been Lize whom Reverend Jim had seen on the porch of the parsonage when he had looked in that direction at the time of his meeting with Martha. The Red Rock girl had watched Reverend Jim and Martha until they had dismounted, a jealous light in her eyes. When she saw the ponies unconcernedly grazing, with their owners nowhere in sight, the jealousy in her became bitter. Making her way stealthily through the house, she observed that Ellen was busy with some fancywork. Stealing out again, Lize descended from the porch, ran swiftly past the bunkhouse and the corral and vanished into the heavy undergrowth along the river. Shortly afterward, still pursuing her stealthy tactics, she stole into some thick brush near the promontory at whose edge Reverend Jim and Martha were sitting and had overheard nearly all of their conversation.

Now she smiled easily at Martha's surprised "Eliza Ebbets!" Getting up from the rock, she walked to Ginger and patted the animal's muzzle with grave playfulness, Martha watching her curiously.

Then Lize looked up and said: "Won't you get off and talk?"

Martha instantly complied, for she wanted to know more about Lize. "Why, yes," she said as she dismounted. Facing each other, she said: "When you avoided me at the parsonage this morning I thought you had done so purposely. I am glad I was mistaken."

Lize laughed quietly. "I had a lot of work to do this morning," she explained, "and you came around the corner so suddenly. Besides, we don't have much company at the parsonage."

She led the way to the rock upon which she had been sitting. For several minutes their conversation hinged upon those trivialities which prepare the way for more pithy subjects.

Then, finally, with a covert look at Martha, Lize remarked: "Reverend Jim didn't go to the Diamond Dot, after all, it seems."

"No," said Martha, "he complained of the heat and the distance and postponed going until tomorrow." She gazed down the parsonage trail, and following her example, Lize saw Reverend Jim just dismounting at the corral gate. When Martha turned again it was to see Lize smiling at her with broad, sly significance.

The Red Rock girl had planned her conversation with Martha with much deliberation while she had lain in the underbrush, watching. She knew she must be cool and careful and convincing, and though jealousy was tugging at her, there was no trace of it in her smile.

"You had quite a long talk with him," she said as Martha looked at her. "He is interesting, isn't he?"

Martha flushed slightly. Lize's words had been innocent enough, but there was no mistaking the subtle implication of her manner. Without knowing why, Martha was aware of a stealthy, though bold subtlety in the atmosphere that lingered around her. It gave her a sensation of shuddering repugnance which startled her.

"If you mean that he is an interesting talker, why, yes," she said.

Lize laughed slowly. "Oh, please don't try to evade. Every good-looking man is interesting to every woman, just as every good-looking girl is interesting to every man. Don't you think so?"

Martha sat slowly erect. The sensation of repugnance that Lize had excited was growing stronger.

"I hadn't given that question any thought," she said.

"How innocent you are, dearie! You simply can't help knowing Reverend Jim is attractive. Now, isn't he?"

"Yes—I suppose so."

"Of course he is. You'd be blind not to know that. And of course, being an attractive woman, yourself, you are not blind. You know when a man looks at you a certain way."

"Why——"

"Now, don't pretend, dearie," laughed Lize. "But isn't it strange that attractive men are always flatterers?"

"I hadn't noticed," said Martha.

"You haven't noticed that Reverend Jim is a flatterer?" She laughed once more. "Don't, dearie. You know how men flatter any woman they single out for a conquest. We've got to expect it."

"Conquest?" said Martha.

"You'll learn, dearie," said Lize cynically. "They all have the same line. Only yesterday Reverend Jim said I was very pretty, just what he was about to say to you when you got up and left him."

Indignant, Martha was now rigid. Suspicion filled her eyes. "Were you listening?" she demanded, thinking of their present close proximity to the promontory.

"Listening!" said Lize. "Oh no. I don't have to play the eavesdropper to hear Reverend Jim say that. He tells me personally. I saw you sitting on the grass with him, but I didn't listen. I don't have to. I am pretty sure of Reverend Jim. You see, he wouldn't have brought me over to the parsonage from the Bulldog if he hadn't thought a great deal of me."

"The Bulldog!"

Martha was on her feet now, and her voice was cold with the

dismay and horror that Lize's words had suddenly aroused in her. She stared at Lize, her face pale with lines of pain deepening in it. "He brought you from the Bulldog! Do you mean to say you are one of those women——"

She hesitated at Lize's brazen grin and shrank away from her, leaning against Ginger's shoulder and covering her face with her hands. She had heard her father refer to the Bulldog—always in terms of scathing condemnation; and the girls she knew—her former friends—had whispered to her about the place. Its reputation could not be hidden; it made a loathsome blot upon an otherwise fair community. She uncovered her face and looked at Lize again—noting with a horrified interest her beauty—which once may have been delicate—and it did not seem possible that the girl was telling the truth. She did not want to think that Reverend Jim was that kind of a man.

"You are joking, aren't you?" she said with a quaver of dismal laughter in her voice. "Please say that you are. Why, that would be horrible!"

"Aw, you're actually funny!" derided Lize, staring at her. "Reverend Jim's a deep one, isn't he? He fooled you. But you're not the only one. People here think he took me over to the parsonage to reform me. They don't know; they don't suspect——"

Lize said no more, for she saw that nothing more was necessary. Her face ashen, Martha was climbing into the saddle. Afterward, she turned and looked at Lize and then urged the pony down the trail, holding her head erect, trying her best to conceal the wound that Lize had inflicted, revealing courage that made Lize clench her teeth in reluctant sympathy. But once out of Lize's sight, deep in a wood where the shade was dense and the silence solemn, her fortitude forsook her and she pulled the pony to a halt, bowed her head over the pommel of the saddle and cried bitterly.

CHAPTER 13

For a long time Lize sat on the rock. For half an hour after Martha left her she watched the trail at the point where the girl had vanished, frowning, perplexed, agitated by torturing thoughts. Strangely, she was not elated with her easy victory over Martha. That satisfaction she had expected to feel was not there. In its place was uncertainty which, as the minutes fled, yielded to a gnawing regret and shame. Principle had not died in Lize though environment had stunted it. Some power was fanning it into life again as she sat there on the rock. She gulped hard over the recollection of Martha's glances at the only romantic figure she had ever known; and her face reddened guiltily as she reviewed the words which, spoken to Martha, had wrecked Reverend Jim's character in her eyes.

The afternoon sun waned as she sat there on the rock. Through an interminable time, it seemed, she fought the demon Desire, arraying his pleasures against the newer impulses which had assailed her, while the sun sank into a cleft in the mountains, and purple shadows rose and mingled with the somber twilight. And then, when she knew she had won, and that on the morrow she would go to Martha and confess her sin, she got up from the rock

and stole to the promontory, where she sat, dry eyed, staring into
the darkness.

It was late in the afternoon when Martha reached the H-Bar-
W. She had ridden slowly, and her heart was heavy as she
dismounted, pulled saddle and bridle from Ginger, turned him
into the corral and walked toward the ranch house. She did not
even take the trouble to put the saddle and bridle away, shuddering as she looked at them, for they were associated with the
incident of the afternoon.

The H-Bar-W had never seemed so desolate to her—not even
on the day following that which had seen the failure of her party.
She walked to the kitchen door and removed the note she had
pinned to it that morning, crumpling it and throwing it from her.
It landed in the sand of the yard, and watching it, she saw the
fresh imprints of a horse's hoofs—where the animal had pawed
and stamped impatiently. The imprints came from around a
corner of the house; they went toward the river. They were not
Ginger's, for she had started from the corral gates on her trip to
the parsonage. She knew, now. Reverend Jim had been here. He
had purposely ridden back to the parsonage in the hope of
meeting her. He had lied to her about going to the Diamond Dot,
had lied as he had lied about Lize. What a consummate actor he
was! Resentment took possession of her, and she sat on the lower
step of the little porch, allowing it to riot in her veins.

And then, after her imagination had visited hideous revenge
upon him, she began to doubt. Could it be possible that any man
who was able to look a woman so honestly and so frankly in the
eyes, who had been so apparently earnest in his sympathy, and
who had done so much for Ben—could he be the sort of creature
she had been picturing him—that Lize had pictured him? She
wavered between final condemnation and a hope that there was a
mistake somewhere, until, far out in the basin, she saw a horseman approaching, the moonlight playing upon him; and then she
suddenly remembered that Ben had promised to ride in that
night. She stood erect on the step and watched, and when finally
she knew the horseman was indeed Ben, she was filled with
anxiety and impatience. Ben—she would ask Ben about Lize.
He might know. And if Lize had lied! How she hoped that Lize
had lied!

Ben was terribly slow in coming. She could hardly wait until
he reached the corral gates, but was down off the steps and

running toward him while he was still some distance from the gates; and by the time he reached them she was at his stirrup, her hands grasping at his waist, her eyes luminous in the moonlight as they met his. He pulled his pony to a halt and looked down at her, his eyes wide with astonishment.

"What in blazes has got into you?" he demanded.

"Ben, I'm worried! Do you know that Lize Ebbets is at the parsonage—that she is staying there with Reverend Jim and his sister?"

"Sure," he growled, his face reddening. "Everybody in the basin knows it, an' everybody is talkin' about it. But what of it?" he asked brusquely.

She did not answer this. "Is it true that she lived in—the—the Bulldog?" she went on breathlessly. "Is it true that Reverend Jim got her—took her—from there?"

"Yes!" he almost shouted irritably. "What in blazes is the matter with you?"

"Oh!" she exclaimed as her hands fell from him and were raised to her face, while her voice, broken and hoarse, came through her fingers. "I met Lize today. She said that she—that Reverend Jim had taken her from the Bulldog to the parsonage because—because he—loved her. He told her that she was pretty—that——"

"The four-flushin' devil!" grated Ben. He rose stiffly in the saddle, his face suddenly white, his eyes blazing. She removed her hands from before her face and looked up at him, fascinated by the terrible change that had come over him. When he spoke again—instantly—his voice was thin and icy, penetrating into her consciousness as a steel barb might pierce her heart. For she knew that for some reason her words had aroused the demon in Ben—that death was stalking abroad and that her words were responsible.

"Dad's comin'," said Ben, speaking between great gasps. "He'll be here in five minutes. He ain't feelin' good; he's sick. It's his heart. He had a spell out on the range. You go an' wait for him; get somethin' hot for him. He wanted me to ride on ahead an' tell you. Go on!" he shouted viciously, as she hesitated, watching him fearfully.

"What are you going to do?" she demanded shrilly, aroused to dread apprehension by the awful threat in his manner.

"I'm goin' to kill that damned sky pilot!" he cursed. "Lize is my girl—you hear! An' he can't play me for no sucker!"

He buried the spurs in the pony's flanks, leaning far over the animal's mane, racing desperately toward the river trail. She tried to call to him, to tell him to come back, but the words would not come and she stood, white and shaking, watching him until he vanished into some timber. Then she went toward the house, fear clogging the breath in her throat, whispering over and over: "What have I done? What have I done?"

Coming into the parsonage from a trip that had taken him far out into the plains north of the river, Red Owen was riding beside the promontory where Reverend Jim and Martha had met, when he came upon Lize. Darkness had fallen when Red passed the spot, but there was a silvery moon just peering above the rimming hills on the southern edge of the basin, and in its light as he passed the open space on the trail Red saw a huddled figure at the base of a tree. He reined in his pony, drew his six-shooter and cautiously approached the figure. A man never knew what to expect in this country, and Red was not a man to take chances. So, with his weapon at a poise, he rode closer.

Presently a sharp exclamation came from him; in a flash he was out of the saddle and bending over the figure.

He knew her. He had seen her a few times at the parsonage, and he did not touch her until, having called her name several times without receiving an answer, he gently took her by a shoulder and shook her. She was lying face downward, and there came no response to his action. Peering closer at her, he drew a startled breath, and then his arms went under her, and she was lifted bodily and turned so that she lay flat on her back.

"Holy smoke!" said Red, awed, his voice hoarse with emotion over his discovery.

Five minutes later, with the body of the girl lying across the saddle in front of him, Red came upon Reverend Jim, walking toward him on the trail.

"Lize!" said Reverend Jim when he saw Red's burden. "We've been looking everywhere for her!" He stared at Red, awaiting an explanation. "What has happened, Red?" He stepped to Red's side and looked closely at Lize's face. His own whitened; he spoke sharply to Red. "Hurry, man, get her to the house so that we can do something for her!"

"I reckon that time has passed, Reverend," said Owen gravely. "She was dead when I found her. A fall—or somethin'. The poor little cuss."

That "something," representing the mysterious agency which had brought death to the Red Rock girl, was later rendered definite and intelligible when, with Red and Ellen, Reverend Jim stood over the girl as she lay on a couch in the parlor of the parsonage. Reverend Jim indicated one of Lize's temples, discolored, without a bruise to mar the skin. "Apoplexy, I expect," he said huskily.

CHAPTER 14

Fitfully, like a huge firefly, Reverend Jim's pipe glowed as he sat on the front porch of the parsonage. He was sitting with his back to the side railing, his chair tilted back, his legs crossed. Ellen had retired some time before, depressed over Lize Ebbets' death. Red Owen had sat on the porch, talking with Reverend Jim for a long time, but shortly before he had announced his intention of "turnin' in" at the bunkhouse. Lize's body, covered by a sheet, lay on a couch in the parlor, where it had been placed when brought in by Red Owen.

Reverend Jim had planned to stay awake during the night, or at least until Red Owen returned to relieve him. In the parlor a kerosene lamp was burning, fitfully and dimly disclosing the austere simplicity of the room, and imparting to the sheet-covered form of Lize Ebbets a dismal reminder of the inevitability of the end of life. Reverend Jim had been deeply affected by Lize's death, but as he sat there on the porch, his thoughts persisted in lingering upon his meeting that day with Martha Warren. She had not deceived him, and since he had reflected upon her manner, he had reached a conclusion. "She won't need to be jealous of poor Lize any more," he told himself, "if that's what she meant by acting that way. It's sure a thrilling feeling a

man gets when he finds that a woman he likes is jealous of him."
He wanted to believe that Martha had betrayed jealousy, and he
had wrestled with his vanity for a long time before it finally
convinced him that there could be no other explanation of the
girl's perturbation as she had questioned him about Lize.

He had inquired about Lize from Blanchard. No one knew
from where she had come. She had appeared in Red Rock the
year before, had lived her brief day in her chosen surroundings
and had died in the open with no man's gaze upon her. Men had
been her worst enemies; now she had escaped them.

Her speech had told of past refinement, but to no one had she
uttered a word in confidence. There was no chance, then, that
the friends of her past might be communicated with—if, indeed,
she had such friends; and therefore a quiet spot on the timber
grove must be her final portion. There was peace there, in the
cool, green recesses.

So ran Reverend Jim's thoughts. They gradually became
incoherent and rambling. A rapid drumming of hoofbeats on the
river trail, coming always nearer, he did not hear—or if he did
hear them they lulled him farther into the doze into which he had
been sinking. His pipe spluttered; it turned over in his hand, and
burning embers sparkled on the porch floor. He took no note of
the occurrence.

But he roused presently. A gun crashed within a foot of his
head. A bitter curse followed the report, and he lurched out of the
chair to see in the moonlight which had grown bright and silvery
Ben Warren, a raging, blaspheming figure, struggling in the
grasp of Red Owen.

The boy was powerless in Owen's arms. His gun had been
wrenched from him and lay in the dust at the edge of the porch
while Ben writhed and twisted ineffectively.

Reverend Jim vaulted over the porch railing as Ellen, her face
white as her night robe, opened the front door and stepped out on
the porch, calling excitedly:

"What is it, Jim? Has someone been hurt?"

"Nobody's hurt, ma'am," came Red's voice in calm reassur-
ance. "Me an' Ben Warren was just tryin' a new shot. It wasn't
just what we thought it would be, an' so we ain't usin' it any
more. Them's your sentiments too—ain't they, Ben?"

"I reckon," said Ben. This reply was prompted by Red, who
had released the boy but was standing behind him, the muzzle of
his six-shooter making a deep dent in Ben's back.

"Go in, Ellen," said Reverend Jim gently. "I expect you can trust us not to do anything reckless."

There was a moment's pause, and the gaze of the three men was upon Ellen as she looked doubtfully at them. She went in and closed the door, however, and again there was silence until she had time to reach her room. Then Reverend Jim, his lips straight and hard, turned to Ben.

"You're explaining," he said coolly. "I'd like to know about that new kind of shot which you pull off from the back!"

The boy's face was still convulsed with the fury of the rage that still racked him. "You've been playin' double with me, you sneakin' coyote!" he said in a strained, shaking voice. "You've gone an' made love to Lize——"

"Shut your rank mouth!" said Reverend Jim. "Nobody's been making love to Lize." His hand descended upon the boy's shoulder, the fingers biting so deep that Ben winced under them; and without further words he was led—reluctant and feebly resisting—into the parlor.

His muscles jerked violently when the sheet was removed from Lize's face, but he instantly darted forward and stood looking down at her, his perplexed eyes wide with sudden astonishment and horror.

Reverend Jim turned to replace the sheet, Red watching him. They saw Ben leaping toward the doorway, saw him race across the porch and vault the railing. Stepping outside, they watched him as he ran to a point near the bunkhouse where he had evidently left his pony. They saw him mount and wildly spur the animal toward the Red Rock trail. Then they could hear the racing clatter of the pony's hoofs diminishing.

"Loco," said Red Owen.

Reverend Jim shook his head but was silent.

"Goin' to Red Rock," said Red shortly. "Shucks," he added sympathetically, "I reckon he was sure some disturbed in his mind, tryin' to plug you in the back, thataway. It's a heap lucky for you that I decided to smoke another cigarette before huntin' my budwar." He looked closely at Reverend Jim. "I reckon he was just foolin' himself about you an' Lize?"

"Sure."

"Sure," repeated Red. "He's a damn' fool!"

Just before daylight spread its gray in the east, another horseman appeared on the Red Rock trail. He rode toward the parsonage, and his pony labored hard under heartbreaking speed. The rider was Norman Carey, and in his pale, grim face as he rode, one might have read that he was the bearer of news of dire import. A mile away from the parsonage, with the trail hazardous in spots, he was still riding furiously. The sturdy animal under him brought him to the door of the parsonage in record time. His vigorous knocking brought Reverend Jim out in an instant. A window shrieked, and Ellen's head came out, while from the bunkhouse came Red Owen, barefooted, coatless, his hair tousled, a six-shooter in hand.

"Sheriff Hawks has hung Ben Warren!" Carey called without preface. "They took him in the Palace—a posse—and tried him on a charge of rustling. Hawks and some more of them gave the evidence. They took him to a cottonwood grove near the river. I didn't hear of it until a few minutes ago. It's too late to do anything for Ben. The posse has come back, but if there's such a thing as law in this country——"

"Hawks hung him, you say?" asked Reverend Jim.

"Hawks took him into custody," explained Carey, "charging him with rustling. The posse took him away from Hawks. But everybody knows it was a frame-up—Hawks letting them do it. The members of the posse were masked, too—Haddam's gang, of course. Ben must have got in bad with them."

Reverend Jim and Martha, only, knew of Ben's knowledge of Haddam's guilt in the murder of Snedden; and that, Reverend Jim was certain, was why Ben had been hanged. "Yes," he said thoughtfully, "Ben must have got in 'bad.' "

"Is there anything we can do?" asked Carey.

"Where's Lawler? I happen to know that Lawler——"

"Easy with your gab," said Red Owen at Carey's side. "Whatever you know about Lawler won't bring Ben Warren back. An' Hawks will keep."

When Ellen came outside a few minutes later, Carey supplied new details of the hanging of Ben, and was apprised of Lize's death. But Reverend Jim took no part in their conversation. He was wondering how Martha would receive the news.

CHAPTER 15

Lawler, Slim Weaver and Shorty Mc Guinness rode into the parsonage before sunrise from some mysterious errand. But they could not be considered, since they were comparative strangers to Martha. Red Owen was likewise a strange; Norman Carey knew the girl only slightly, and Ellen begged off—so that it became Reverend Jim's duty, as minister, to acquaint Martha with the news of her brother's death.

Reverend Jim had no ministerial interest in Martha, and so was reluctant to make the visit and rode slowly on his grim errand. He set out shortly after sunrise, and it was two hours later before he reached the H-Bar-W. Lawler and his men left the parsonage about the same time to bring Ben's body back, Shorty Mc Guinness taking the parson's buckboard. Carey had returned to Red Rock before them. Afterward, they consigned Lize's remains to the place in the cottonwood selected by Reverend Jim, and Reverend Jim spoke briefly over her. There was no coroner in Red Rock, and no doctor nearer than Lazette, two hundred miles away.

Reverend Jim's face was grave as he rode up to the kitchen door of the H-Bar-W ranch house and dismounted. It was only yesterday that he had dismounted at this very spot—later to meet

Martha at the promontory, her spirits high, the world beginning to smile for her. Today it was to be different.

She opened the door for him. She was not surprised, for she had seen him coming, but there was the stiffness of formality in her greeting, and her gaze was unsmiling.

"Good morning," she said. She turned quickly from the door before he could reply, and so Reverend Jim knew she was still resentful.

He saw Harvey Warren sitting on a chair in the corner of the kitchen. He looked pallid and worn, but grinned faintly when he saw his visitor.

"Come right in, Reverend!" he said. "Take a chair. You're makin' your rounds early this mornin', eh?"

"Yes," said Reverend Jim, "early." He did not take the chair which had been offered. "I don't intend to stop long," he explained. There ensued a queer silence, for Martha and Harvey Warren were wondering what his visit portended, and Reverend Jim was considering how best to acquaint them with news of the tragedy.

Martha's manner puzzled him. When he had stood in the doorway, she had looked straight at him, and in spite of his dismal mission he had felt delight in meeting her again, in looking at her. He had expected a welcoming smile, even if only a formal one. None came. Instead, he had been met by scorn, hostility. Now she stood near the kitchen table, facing him, her body rigid, quiet and cold.

As he had ridden over to the H-Bar-W Reverend Jim had considered many methods of breaking the news he bore, but now he felt none of them would answer. Equivocate or delay as he might, the blow would be shocking and deadly. Reluctantly, he spoke, knowing they were expecting him to explain the reason for his visit.

He looked straight at Martha and spoke gently: "It's strange," he said. "Yesterday you and I were talking about Lize Ebbets."

"I don't care to discuss her—if that is what you came for," Martha answered.

"No—of course," he said. "It's no use, now. Lize died last night."

He watched Martha. She drew a quick, deep breath.

"Oh!" she exclaimed. It appeared to Reverend Jim that in spite of this shock to her there was a note of relief in her voice.

Martha had seen Reverend Jim coming; she had ample time from the moment she saw him until he knocked at the door to enjoy her relief over the knowledge that Ben had not accomplished what he had meant to do and that Reverend Jim was still alive. But her resentment had not been assuaged by the knowledge that Ben had not killed him. Nor was it lessened now, since she had learned of Lize's death. Reverend Jim's relations with the girl could not be made to appear excusable because Lize was no longer here.

But she had feared for Ben—still feared. Some accident, perhaps, had kept him from meeting Reverend Jim last night. But she was afraid Ben would finally meet him. She meant to warn Reverend Jim of his danger before he left the H-Bar-W. She would have made the trip over to the parsonage the night before if she had not felt it would be futile—Ben would have reached there long before she could hope to; and besides, her father had come before Ben had been gone five minutes, and she had been compelled to minister to him—his heart had bothered him greatly.

She was apprehensive that Reverend Jim had not ridden over this morning merely to tell them about Lize Ebbets' death. And as Reverend Jim was silent for a second time, a cold dread came upon her, and her imagination supplied a picture in which Ben, intent upon his vengeance and with the lust to kill upon him, had been killed by Reverend Jim, or by some of his friends.

She stepped toward Reverend Jim, stared at him, not even thinking of Lize Ebbets. She thought she could see reluctance in his eyes, and regret.

"Something has happened to Ben!" she said, her voice quavering, her hands catching at Reverend Jim's shoulders. "What is it? Tell me—please! Quickly!"

"I suppose I've got to tell you," said Reverend Jim. "But I wasn't expecting it would happen just the way it did happen."

"Ben is dead!" she said, staring wildly at him.

"Yes," he said. "Sheriff Hawks and some of his men arrested him. Then a posse took Ben from the sheriff and hung him."

At her low gasp Reverend Jim stepped toward her. She did not speak, but stood straight and stiff, looking at him with an expression of wild, dumb horror. For an instant only she stood there; and then, without uttering a sound, she sank to the floor.

Reverend Jim was bending over her, to help her to her feet, to offer what little comfort he could, when he heard a sound from

Harvey Warren. The old man had stiffened in his chair; his hands were pressed to his chest; his face was ghastly, his eyes staring straight up at the ceiling. While Reverend Jim watched him, he suddenly became limp, slipped out of the chair and fell, face upward, to the floor.

Reverend Jim went to him, peered closely at him, laid his ear to his chest and then stood erect, shaking his head. The shock had been too much for Harvey Warren.

Reverend Jim turned to go again to Martha. She was on her feet when he faced her. The next instant she was at her father's side, sobbing wildly, calling to him, smoothing his forehead, shaking him. Reverend Jim, helpless, stood near, his face ashen with unutterable sympathy.

He got Martha away after a time, coaxing, pleading with her, and led her outside where she sat on the lower step of the little porch, oblivious to his presence, a slight little figure, crushed by the double affliction.

When he sat down beside her, though, yearning to do something to help her to bear the shock, she pushed him away, got up from the step and re-entered the kitchen, to stand near the doorway with clasped hands, looking at her father. She turned when she heard Reverend Jim enter again and looked at him. "Go away!" she said. "Please go!"

"You can't stay here, you know," he said. "You ought to have someone with you. A woman. I'll take you over to the parsonage. Ellen——"

He backed away when she approached him, and he was amazed to see that she had conquered her hysteria and was now cold and calm. Yet there was no mistaking the scorn in her eyes or the contempt in her voice.

"Please go," she said. "Can't you understand? I *want* to be alone." Her voice was clear and incisive. "I shan't go to the parsonage—or anywhere else with you. And I shall never go there again as long as you are there. You know why, I think. But rather than watch you play hypocrite again, I shall tell you. I met Lize Ebbets on the trail yesterday—near the edge of the cliff where you found me—where you tried to be so clever—tried to impress me with your goodness, your manliness! I met Lize there after you had gone. She told me that you had brought her to the parsonage from the Bulldog—for no good purpose—that you had flattered her and made love to her. She gave me to understand that you are the kind of man—— Oh!" she broke off, her voice suddenly high pitched and quivering with scorn and bitter, lashing contempt. "And I let you touch me! I listened to your hypocritical speeches; I asked you to help Ben! You are not fit to be mentioned in the same breath with Ben—though he *was* wild. His crimes were clean ones, at any rate; he—"

Reverend Jim took a step toward her, his face white.

"Lize told you *that!*" he said. "Why, Martha, I never——"

"Don't lie any more," she said. "Ben knew what you were. He told me last night when he went over there to kill you. I—I almost wish he had; I wish it had been you instead of Ben who had been hanged. I am glad Lize died; you won't be able to reach her any more. I don't want to see you again—ever. Go, now—go back to the parsonage and continue your hypocrisy. But don't come here again. If you do I shall do what Ben failed to do!" She placed both hands against his chest and pushed him through the doorway, then suddenly stepped backward and slammed the door.

Reverend Jim stood on the ground near the porch and stared blankly at the door. Then, mounting, he rode slowly back toward the parsonage.

"Death's breaking records in the basin," he grimly told Ellen, "and leaving lies behind that no one can disprove. Lize told Martha Warren that I am a skunk with women. Martha believes it. Her father's dead, over there—hearing about Ben killed him. You go to her. You're a woman, and maybe you'll understand each other."

"Lize lied, of course," said Ellen, smiling gravely. "She wanted you and was jealous of Martha. It will be hard to explain, of course, because jealousy is unreasonable and prejudiced. And of course she is shocked by the double tragedy and isn't herself. Be patient. Give her time."

But Reverend Jim doubted. Only himself—whom she had termed "hypocrite"—and Lize who would never speak again—could testify concerning his relations with the dead girl.

CHAPTER 16

It seemed to Martha that an age had elapsed since the tragedy which had robbed her of her father and brother, but in reality only a month had passed. To the lonesome girl time now represented nothing more than a dreary space, marked by slow-dragging days during which she ate and performed her household duties from force of habit, and interminable nights that brought tortuous dreams and tearful awakenings. She could not think of the future; she had no plans for it. Someday, she knew, she would leave this place, but she felt vaguely that there was much to be done before that event could come to pass. For the H-Bar-W was now hers—solely—lands, cattle, buildings; and as she had no desire to stay here she must dispose of it all and go someplace where, perhaps, she might forget the horror of what had happened.

Ellen had drawn from her the details of her conversation with Lize Ebbets, and had told her that it had all been a malicious falsehood, but though she made no comment, she was convinced of Reverend Jim's duplicity. She steadfastly refused to visit the parsonage.

She saw Reverend Jim occasionally as he passed the ranch house on his way to visit parishioners in other sections of the basin; twice she had seen Norman Carey when he delivered *Advocates* to her—for her father had been a subscriber. But she did not let either of them see her. She wanted to be alone.

She had forced herself to read the *Advocate*, and in one issue she learned that there was no clue to the identity of the men of the posse that had executed Ben. But the *Advocate* openly charged Sheriff Hawks with incompetency, hinting that he had too readily surrendered to the posse, and concluding with the covert charge that Haddam was at the bottom of it all.

She believed that, for in his talk with her the day he had stood at the porch rail, Haddam had told her that he had been keeping Ben out of the sheriff's clutches. And because, in common with everyone, she knew Hawks was a friend of Haddam's, she was convinced that Hawks would not have acted—or allowed the posse to act—unless so directed by Haddam.

Dal Thompson had come in early this morning. He had reported to her, giving her many details concerning the movements of his men and the cattle, which she only half comprehended, though she gathered that the outfit wagon would not come in for a few weeks yet, there being excellent grass and water in the present location. He had gone away again, telling her to "buck up."

She felt strangely depressed after Thompson's departure and afflicted with a premonition of evil. The sensation was so strong in her that, watching Thompson ride away, she was half inclined to call after him, to tell him to send in a man or two to occupy the bunkhouse permanently, as protection—at least company—for her. But she fought this impulse down, ironically assuring herself that she had suffered all the evil that was likely to come to her. Still, as the day waned, she found herself anxiously watching the parsonage trail and hoping that Ellen would ride over.

Ellen did not come.

At sundown Martha prepared some food for herself and was surprised to find that she was regaining her appetite. Then, after washing the dishes and straightening up the room, she went outside for a breath of air.

A second surprise came to her after she had been outside a little time. She discovered that there was still in her heart a reluctant appreciation of the beauty of the world—that it had not died with her father and brother. The mountains, far and shining through the misty films of the sunset, still held their lure; the

stars, just appearing, she watched, wondering, as a child might
have wondered, at their cold and unchanging glitter. She drank
eagerly the sage-scented breezes that swept over the plains to
her, realizing that it was all good, after all. She felt more
cheerful when she returned toward the house, but it looked so
gloomy and empty that she delayed going in, walking instead to
the stable. She led Ginger out, hobbled him and turned him out
into the pasture to graze. She spent some time, too, in the
garden, and when she finally decided to return to the house
darkness had come.

At the kitchen door she was suddenly overcome with a recur-
rence of the premonition she had felt upon Thompson's departure. Halting, with her hand on the latch, she looked about her.
She could see or hear nothing unusual, and she smiled, reassur-
ing herself, for the great peace of night had descended, and there
was nothing tangible upon which to base her fears. She stepped
into the kitchen, leaving the door open as she went to a shelf near
the kitchen table and took down a kerosene lamp. She placed this
on the table, found a match after fumbling for a moment at the
shelf, and then removed the chimney from the lamp and held the
flaring match to the wick.

To her surprise, as she replaced the chimney, she discovered
that her hand trembled. The strange presentiment of evil again
seized her, and yielding to a sudden, unaccountable terror, she
ran to the kitchen door and peered out.

It was now black outside, and she cast a scared glance at the
door leading into the dining room. It was open, and the room's
interior yawned darkly except where the light from the lamp on
the kitchen table threw a thin, ever-widening streak over the
floor and the farther wall. She found that an inexplicable dread
was upon her, which grew to a conviction that someone was in
the dining room; and she stood motionless, breathing fast, a
chilling fear creeping over her as she watched the door and tried
to peer into the room without going nearer to it, fighting an
impulse to leave the house. She stayed, telling herself she was
foolish. At length she left the door and walked over to the table,
dropping into a chair and resting her elbows on the table top. She
was up again instantly, though, drawing the shade of the window
near the table, for the outside darkness now terrified her. When
she turned from the window she saw Flash Haddam standing in
the dining-room door, grinning at her.

She caught her breath and for an instant rested one hand on the table top to steady herself. Involuntarily the other came up and was pressed tightly to her left side, for it seemed to her that her heart would leap out. Yet, after the first shock of surprise, she found that her fear had left her, and that uppermost in her thoughts at this moment was a sort of humorous satisfaction that her premonition had not been without foundation. Indignation came next. She despised and hated Haddam, but she had never feared him, and she was now conscious of only a fierce resentment. She kept a weapon in the house—a six-shooter that her father had given her—but at this minute it was in one of the drawers of a china closet in the dining room. Had it been in her hand now she might have tried to kill Haddam. But she knew better than to think that the outlaw meditated an attack on her. That was a thing which had never happened in this country among white men, for it would have brought vengeance swift and certain from every man in the vicinity. And so she faced him confidently, concerned with nothing but his unwarranted and unallowable action in entering the house uninvited.

"What are you doing here?" she asked.

"Visitin'," he drawled.

"When did you come in?"

"About dusk."

The secret mirth in his look annoyed her, because she could see no reason for it. But if he had come about dusk, as he had said, her premonition was accounted for. But how had he entered the house?

"Walked in the front door," he explained, as if answering the question in her eyes. "Left my cayuse behind the stable."

"Why didn't you stay outside—where I was—instead of sneaking in here in this manner?"

"Easier talkin' in here. I've got a lot to say to you."

"I've nothing to say to you." She walked to the kitchen door and threw it open. "Get out of here—instantly!" she ordered.

He grinned easily and smoothly but did not move. "Nothin' doin'," he said. "I wouldn't have come in if I didn't intend to stay a while. Set down. There's no use gettin' fussed up. I ain't meanin' any harm to you, an' I'm goin' to go when I get tired of visitin'." He motioned her to a chair—he even pulled one away from the table for her.

Obviously, there was nothing she could do. She could not force him to leave, matching her strength against his. That thought was ridiculous. Nor could she get past him to get the weapon in the drawer, for in spite of his apparent unconcern she knew that he was watchfully alert. He had the reputation of being always ready, as many men had discovered to their discomfiture, when too late. And she knew, too, that no ruse would avail, that he was too suspicious to take chances. Therefore, surrendering, she sank into the chair he had drawn out for her.

"Now I feel like company," he said. He left the dining-room door and took another chair. She watched him in scornful silence.

For a long time a silence, unbroken except by a strange sound that seemed to come from near by—which seemed to her to be caused by voices and the impatient stamping of horses—was maintained by Haddam and Martha. There was nothing that she wanted to say to Haddam. It was useless to charge him with being the cause of Ben's death. He would have denied it— or admitting it, he would have goaded her to impotent fury. Words were futile, now. They would not bring Ben or her father back to her. And yet, sitting there, facing the man, she was tortured by her loathing, her repugnance, her horror, her hatred of him.

Her patience, finally, was at an end. She got up, determination in her eyes.

"It may amuse you to sit here and grin to yourself," she said. "But I have more important things to do. Say what you came to say and get out of here!"

He laughed, but did not move. "Oh, shucks," he said, "don't be in no hurry. We've got all night. Years—mebbe." He laughed, enjoying her perplexity, the startled light in her eyes.

Something secret, furtive, hugely humorous in his manner increased her uneasiness. She associated his manner with the strange sounds she was hearing. Listening more intently, she was now certain she heard voices.

"There are some of your men here!" she said.

"Uh-huh."

"What did you bring them for?"

"Just for company," he laughed. "They ain't botherin' you any—they're gents."

She got up, her breath coming heavily. She felt that somehow he was arranging a trap for her. She was very nearly ready to faint or make a desperate attempt to escape; and she caught the edge of the table uncertainly.

"Set down," he invited again. When she had dropped into the

chair, sitting on its edge, still grasping the table, ready to spring up again, filled with a new terror, her eyes peering through the open kitchen door and the shadeless window in a vain effort to see the faces she dreaded to see, Haddam continued: "Your dad cashed in without puttin' you wise to where he hid the bunch of coin which he's been storin' up for a long time."

"So that is what you came here for—you and your men?" she said scornfully. "Well, you needn't be mysterious about it. I don't know that he ever hid any money, but if he did he said nothing to me about it. I am sorry I can't help you," she added with a pulse of triumph. She thought this would signalize the end of his visit.

He calmly smiled. "Don't mention it," he mocked. "There ain't no hurry. The money will keep." He stretched his legs out comfortably, relaxed, and watched her with an interest that would have been lazy had there not been design in his eyes.

"Lonesome for you here, ain't it?" he said.

"No."

He laughed. She got the impression that he seemed to be listening for something. At first she thought it might be that he was trying to identify the voices she thought she had heard; but now she could not hear them, and so she listened for other sounds—those which, plainly, Haddam expected. And then, after a long interval during which Haddam was silent, his head cocked to one side, and through which she also listened, watching Haddam's face, sound came. She heard it—Haddam heard it—the dull, faint beating of hoofs.

Haddam sat erect and turned to look at her. He laughed, his voice tense with some strange emotion.

"Reckon someone else thinks you're lonesome, too," he said.

Martha heard a horse come to a halt outside. Then, almost instantly came the stamping of other horses. Then silence, followed after an instant by voices. Then silence again.

Haddam swung quickly around, drew his heavy Colt and leveled it at the door. The carelessness that had marked his manner was gone; he was now alert and tense, his shoulders hunched, his eyes narrowed. Martha sensed something of the significance of this—that an enemy of Haddam's was coming— and she was about to shout a warning to the visitor when the sound was stifled at its inception and became a gasp of amazement when she saw Reverend Jim slowly appear from the darkness and become framed in the lighted doorway.

She saw, too, that Reverend Jim had appeared upon the unexpected. He saw Flash Haddam. He saw Martha. His eyes widened with astonishment to instantly narrow and flash with comprehension. His right hand dropped to the holster at his hip. And there it rested. For at the movement Haddam's voice came, cold and snapping:

"Easy there, Reverend Jim!"

Reverend Jim stood, as if he meditated springing backward from the doorway. And then Martha saw another man behind him—saw the man press the muzzle of a six-shooter against Reverend Jim's back, heard the man's voice raised in mockery:

"Don't be bashful, Parson—walk right in."

Reverend Jim entered, with obvious reluctance, but there was a glow of something unfathomable in his eyes as he looked at Martha. He bowed to her, his hat in hand.

"Looks like at least two of us are surprised, ma'am," he said. She thought that his eyes had never seemed so luminous and handsome. She was almost ready to smile at him but remembered Lize.

Reverend Jim heard the door close behind him and was aware of the continued presence at his back. The man who had ushered him in was standing behind him. He looked now at Haddam.

"Well, now," he said, "a man never knows what's going to happen in this country. I'm sitting at home, reading my Bible—my sister gone to bed, Lawler and his outfit away somewhere—when a Diamond Dot man rides up and says Martha Warren wants me at the H-Bar-W. He won't tell me what for, leaving me curious. I'm still curious. Maybe you'd straighten things out for me." He looked at Haddam, then at Martha, then back again at Haddam.

Martha did not meet his eyes, but found herself admiring his quick recovery from his surprise of an instant before. His manner now was that of quiet unconcern for whatever might impend.

Haddam watched Reverend Jim with saturnine curiosity. "It's a celebration," he said. "I'm runnin' it." The six-shooter was still in his hand. It dangled in lazy, careless fashion from his fingers. He went on again, amusedly, but coldly watching Reverend Jim's face. "You recollect me tellin' you once that I was savin' you for the big day? I was meanin' *my* day. The day when I'm boss. It's here. You're helpin' me celebrate it."

"Talking in riddles again, eh?" said Reverend Jim. "You do a lot of it."

Here was a new Reverend Jim—a man she had never seen, and Martha watched him, amazed, fascinated, for she caught a warning of action in his glances. He seemed to have comprehended the significance of what was occurring—of why Haddam had tricked him into coming here, but was pretending not to understand. Martha cynically remembered a day when she had been talking with him on the river trail and she had told him he was more of a thinker than he pretended to be. And he was thinking now, mentally and physically tempering himself for whatever ordeal he was to endure.

"Celebration, eh?" he said. "When is it going to begin?"

"Right now," said Haddam. He looked at the man who had followed Reverend Jim inside. "Get his gun!" he directed.

"Nobody touches my gun, Haddam!" said Reverend Jim. And the wanton light that leaped into his eyes again gave Martha warning of threatening violence. Reverend Jim's right hand was hovering over his gun holster. He had turned swiftly, so that his left side was now toward the man who had entered behind him, while Haddam was at his right. Martha looked at Haddam. He had changed color; a shallow smile reached his face.

"We'll pass that if you're finicky about it," he said. "Set down."

"Standing suits me," said Reverend Jim shortly.

"All right, then. We'll get goin'." He gestured widely toward the outdoors. "There's right smart of the outfit with me tonight," he said. "I reckon right now they're lookin' in the windows, gettin' an eyeful of what's goin' on."

Reverend Jim did not look—he was anticipating a trick. But Martha saw faces at the windows, filling them—all of them blinking against the light, some grinning, other exhibiting slight embarrassment, still others hanging their heads, plainly reluctant to reveal themselves to Reverend Jim's gaze. Among them he would have discovered men who worked on various ranches in the vicinity—some of whom he had seen and talked with at various bunkhouses on his pilgrimages through the basin. Martha recognized them all.

Now Flash relaxed the vigilance which had so far marked his manner, leaning back in his chair and laughing hilariously. Through the open windows came laughter also; and Haddam, hearing it, got up and walked to them and peered out at the faces near them. "We're headin' straight for town, tonight—ain't we, boys?" He walked back to the chair but did not sit in it, for impatience seemed to have seized him.

"Me an' the boys is reformin'," he went on, looking from Martha to Reverend Jim with an insincere smirk. "We're traveling the straight trail from now on—accordin' to what the parson preaches. No one's goin' to be able to say that we're runnin' our irons on anyone's cattle, for we're goin' to be bang-up citizens." And now his grin broadened, and he winked with extravagant slyness at the windows from which came audible snickers of laughter. "We're announcin'," he went on, "that we're hereby takin' possession of the H-Bar-W, that we're firin' the outfit which is now in charge, an' that we're goin' to run things to suit ourselves!"

Martha could not have said that she was completely surprised at this declaration. She had expected some sort of weird action from Haddam, for she had felt that the presence of him and his men indicated such action. And the effect of Haddam's words on her was not entirely visible; she flushed, then paled quickly, but retained her composure.

"And how are you going to get possession of the H-Bar-W?" she asked scornfully. "The law will have something to say about that, I imagine!"

"The law!" Haddam sneered. "You know how much we care for the law! Why," he added with a cunning look at Reverend Jim, his voice filled with a deep significance, "look at the parson, Martha! Ask him if he knows what we brought him over here for!"

The truth suddenly burst upon the girl as she got to her feet and stood staring from one to the other with ashen face and fear stricken eyes. Reverend Jim knew she was looking at him, but he kept watching Haddam, who had correctly read the knowledge in his eyes.

CHAPTER 17

"I reckon you've both tumbled," laughed Haddam. "I'm some surprised that it didn't strike you before. I reckon I'll have somethin' to say about runnin' the H-Bar-W when you're Mrs. Flash Haddam!" He looked at Martha.

Reverend Jim continued to watch Haddam, but now Flash could no longer read his eyes—they were enigmatic.

Martha sank into her chair again, rested her arms on the table top and buried her face in them. No sound came to her. She was too stunned, too horrified to think coherently. She heard a voice presently—Haddam's—and the sound of it partially aroused her. Yet she seemed to have no interest in what he was saying though she listened. He was talking to Reverend Jim, who evidently had been talking to him.

"I ain't makin' no explanations to you, damn you! But there ain't no secret about this: I ain't carin' who knows about it. I've got tired of playin' for what I can grab from the cheap boxheads in the basin—gettin' a steer here an' a calf there, and sneaking around tryin' to sell them—an' then gettin' half what they're worth. The H-Bar-W's about my size. Three thousand head of beeves, good grazin', water, buildin's—an' a woman!" He laughed deep in his throat with triumph, and Martha felt he was

146

looking at her. "I'm goin' to ride a straight trail after this—me an' my outfit. I'm goin' to be law abidin'. Me an' my men stay right here. But we ain't been able to do much business lately—due to the careful watchin' of the folks in the basin; an' we're figgerin' on makin' a cleanup. Some clever, eh? I'm sellin' the H-Bar-W stock at the market price, and I'm keepin' the woman!"

"You're loco, Haddam," said Reverend Jim quietly. "Send your men back to your ranch. You can't get away with it."

"Can't, eh? Who says I can't?"

"Common decency, Haddam. When the people of the basin hear that you forced Martha Warren into a marriage with you they'll rise up and smite you." He met Haddam's sneer with a slight smile in which there was no mirth. "Besides," continued Reverend Jim, "you can't force a woman to marry you. The law won't recognize that kind of marriage."

"Who's goin' to tell the marriage was forced?" jeered Haddam. "How you goin' to prove it? There's honest men here to witness that it wasn't forced. A Pigpen man, four Diamond Dot men, three Lazy J boys an' four Arrows. An' not one of them that ain't a good citizen—accordin' to the basin's knowin'—whose word will go as far as yours. An' myself!" Martha caught the mockery in his voice. "Is anybody in the basin hintin' out loud that Flash Haddam ain't on the level? There's been a heap charged, but nothin' proved. Who's goin' to yawp about a forced marriage? You—you sufferin' sky pilot? If you open your trap about what's goin' on here tonight, I'll herd ride you until you'll look like a prairie dog town after a stampede. You get goin', now, an' hook us up. I've been savin' you for this day, Parson, an' you're deliverin' the goods, pronto!"

Reverend Jim did not speak at once, and when he did speak his voice had more than casual curiosity in it: "Have you found out how your prospective wife feels about it, Haddam?"

Martha turned and looked at Reverend Jim. He had backed away from where he had been standing and was now near the corner beside the great, cast-iron kitchen stove. In the windows were the faces of the men of Haddam's outfit; and there was Haddam, grinning, yet menacing, watching; his glances probing the faces of his victims as if enjoying their consternation. Martha's apprehension was visible, but if Reverend Jim had been startled there was in his manner nothing to betray it. To Martha, it seemed that he was paler than usual, and there was a glitter in his eyes that she had not seen there before. Also, there was a slight twitching at the corners of his lips which was apparently the incipient movement of a derisive smile not yet formed, but threatening, which might come at any instant. And the glitter in his eyes, veiled and guarded, was, she thought, from deep emotions which he was trying—successfully—to conceal from Haddam. And once again she wondered about him—how cleverly he concealed his real purposes, how he could dissemble and equivocate and pretend. That, she believed, was the reason she did not trust him; the reason that, twice, at least, she had almost accused him of being hypocritical. And that he was capable of deceiving had been proved to her satisfaction by the way he had "carried on" with Lize Ebbets while pretending to be interested in herself. Of course she would never forgive him for that, but now, knowing him, she hoped he would find some way of evading Haddam's trap.

But Haddam, alertly watching both of them, grinned again, hugely, as he answered Reverend Jim's question:

"Why, she's goin' to agree peaceable, of course. I'm doin' the orderin'."

"I am not!" she burst out furiously. "I wouldn't marry you under any circumstances. Oh, I hate you!"

Haddam was stirred. He got up and faced Reverend Jim. "She's put it straight up to you, Parson," he said. He walked close to Reverend Jim, tapping his six-shooter significantly. "Get goin'!"

Reverend Jim looked at Martha.

"Not unless the lady is willing, Haddam," he said.

Haddam's muscles tensed; the big gun in his right hand came to a level and was held there steadily, while his eyes, blazing, looked into Reverend Jim's. What he saw there was derision. To his astonishment Reverend Jim smiled at him. Haddam was almost convinced that Reverend Jim would have winked at him in another instant, and that the wink would have expressed mild wonder that Haddam had thought he could be that easily intimidated. The wink's message, interpreted by Haddam, would have meant that Reverend Jim knew there was no danger, that there was another way of settling their differences—a peaceable way. So, though the wink had not come, Reverend Jim's thoughts had been read by Haddam. The blazing light went out of his eyes; his twisting grin apprised Reverend Jim that the outlaw understood him.

"So you've finally figured it out, eh?" said Reverend Jim.

"Figured what out?"

Reverend Jim did not answer at once. He walked to a chair, seated himself, filled and lit his pipe and studied Martha's face. She was watching him in astonishment, puzzled by his manner, and still more puzzled by the way Haddam watched him, plainly bewildered and uncertain. The faces at the windows expressed amazement; the man who had entered the room behind Reverend Jim was scratching his head doubtfully, and the gun in his hand had dropped. They all watched Reverend Jim, who, with his pipe drawing well, answered Haddam.

"That you won't get anywhere by shooting," he said. "You've got the lady and the preacher. Keep the preacher alive and maybe the lady will become Mrs. Flash Haddam. Shoot the minister and the deal is off."

"Hell," scoffed Haddam, "do you reckon I don't know that?"

"Thought you did," said Reverend Jim. He puffed at his pipe and continued to look at Martha.

"Do you think I care a damn about killin' you?" said Haddam, "that I'm goin' to hesitate about killin' you?"

"You don't, of course," said Reverend Jim. "You want to marry Martha Warren. You don't dare take her without marrying her; and if you took her that way you wouldn't be legally entitled to control her property. So let's you and your friends quit bluffing about killing me. After—if I perform the ceremony. Not before."

A great dread seized Martha. Her hands gripped the table edge so hard that the fingers pained her, for as Reverend Jim ceased speaking she saw that a change had come over him. She noted breathlessly that the glitter had gone out of his eyes and that he was thoughtfully considering the situation, considering surrender. She watched him, hoping, praying, trying to catch his gaze so that she might plead with him not to sacrifice her to Haddam.

Haddam was watching Reverend Jim under lowered lids. He scowled, for he had felt something ironlike under Reverend Jim's surface easiness of manner. What Reverend Jim had said was true—though he wanted Martha he did not want her without the H-Bar-W; and if he killed Reverend Jim there would be no marriage. So now, Reverend Jim had "called his bluff." That was what he had been doing, of course, though he had hoped and expected that Reverend Jim would yield.

"There's one thing I'm not bluffin' about," said Haddam. "It's this: That when I'm sure—after all the gas has been used up—that you *won't* marry me an' Martha, I'll blow you to hell rapid! Do you think I've let you go on livin' in this country after you've crossed me like you have unless I figured to use you? You're takin' a minute to think it over: whether to hook us up an' walk out of here on your feet, or whether we'll carry you out." He stood, his face twisted into an evil grin as he watched Reverend Jim.

Reverend Jim was not to be hurried. By drawing meditatively upon his pipe as they all watched him, he created that impression. He calmly looked at Martha again, at Haddam, at the faces of the men at the windows. Then once more at Martha with a slow smile.

"You wanting to see Haddam kill me?" he asked.

"No! No!" she exclaimed, shocked at the thought, shocked more by his calmness.

"But you don't want to marry him, of course," he said. "I don't blame you. But I expect you're in for it, much as you hate him—which ain't as much as you'll hate him after you've lived with him awhile. The cuss ain't got one solitary redeeming trait. He wants two things—he says—you and your property. I'm saying that he don't want you as much as he wants your property. If he wants only the property and will agree to letting you go back to the parsonage with me—to stay with Ellen until he gets rid of the property—I'll perform the ceremony. If he wants both you and the property I'll see him in hell before I'll tie the knot!"

Haddam licked his lips avidly; a flash of triumph glowed in his eyes.

"Why, I reckon I'll agree to that," he said. "There's plenty of time to claim the bride—after I've got the H-Bar-W!" He stepped back, laughing harshly. It was evident that he had harbored a doubt of being able to force Reverend Jim to perform the ceremony. The arrangement proposed by Reverend Jim was obviously welcome to him, as it provided him with a graceful retreat in the presence of his men.

"You're sure the discernin' cuss!" he said to Reverend Jim. "An' I reckon we'll put that deal through right now." He turned to Martha. "Your weddin' is comin' off, ma'am," he told her, bowing mockingly. "The honeymoon ain't comin' off as per schedule, but seein' that the parson has got a constitutional aversion to doin' things in a hurry, we'll have to humor him—

until after the weddin'—bein' that there wouldn't be no weddin' at all if he wasn't so obligin'.''

Martha got to her feet, and now she stood, darting rapid glances about, seeking a way of escape, though she knew escape was impossible. The grinning faces around her told her that this incident must be carried to the conclusion the men looked for— which they would insist upon—which Haddam would insist upon; and to which Reverend Jim had agreed. She couldn't permit them to kill Reverend Jim! She had no right to ask him to make that sacrifice! It happened that at just that instant she looked at Reverend Jim. Haddam was talking to the men at the windows and the glance exchanged by her and Reverend Jim was unnoticed. He smiled and closed one eye at her. It was a gesture which told her as plainly as if he had spoken, that his sudden surrender had been a ruse. In the stress of the moment he had planned something—a way out of the predicament. At least, no matter what his plan, she must trust him. But hers was not a graceful surrender. For when Haddam turned to her and tried to take her hand, approaching her with extravagant politeness and courtesy, she savagely pushed him from her.

Despite the hilarity that now possessed Haddam and his men, there was in the ranch house an undertone of tragedy. It was in Haddam's voice as he laughed; it was in the watchfulness of all of them as they noted covertly Reverend Jim's movements, as, seeming to be occupied with preparations for the ceremony, he rearranged the furniture in the kitchen, shaking his head when Haddam asked him why the big living room should not be utilized.

"I'm running this, Haddam," he said shortly.

He pulled the kitchen table to the left wall of the room, part of which was occupied by the great cast-iron range, and called Martha over, placing her behind it and instructing her to stand there while he retreated almost to the windows through which the men of Haddam's outfit were watching, apparently to consider the effect. His manner was that of an expert in such matters, who, aware of a woeful lack of the necessary equipment, was attempting to do the best he could. Haddam thought so, for he grinned at the men in the windows and told them: "The parson's sure hell for makin' it look regular." Martha thought so, too, as she watched these preparations with heavy heart, shrinking from the ordeal, but thinking of Reverend Jim's wink at her which had seemed to promise hope of ultimate escape. She was still standing behind the table when at last Reverend Jim approached her again. In the wall at her back was a door, opening upon darkness. It led into the water house where, in times of drought, were barrels and other vessels designed to hold the life-giving fluid. Reverend Jim had seen it before from outside; now he was peering into the darkness of its interior, while pretending to be looking at Martha. He was talking in low tones, and to Haddam and the others, now talking and laughing, he might have been consulting her regarding the details of the anticipated ceremony.

"What kind of bars are on the door?" he said. "The door to the water room," he added quickly as she gave him a startled glance accompanied by an upward tilt of her head. "Keep looking down," he said, "as if you are listening to some instructions I am giving you. They're instructions, all right, but not the kind they think you ought to have."

"The bars are heavy," she answered, drooping her head and spreading her hands on the table top. Thus she braced herself to stop the sudden trembling that seized her over the now certain knowledge that Reverend Jim meant to help her to escape Haddam. "They were put there by Father when the water house stood by itself, before the house was built against it. There was a smaller door on the other side. He blocked it with thick adobe—like the rest of the building—when we built the house. There is now only a small window in the rear. The door is heavy, too," she added.

"And the walls are two-feet thick," he smiled. "And the roof. All built of adobe which has hardened almost to the consistency of stone. Well, that seems to be perfect. Now, while I pull this table out a little—getting it into a more proper position for the ceremony—you just sort of wander into the water house. As soon as you get inside, grab hold of the door and get ready to close and bar it—after I come in, pretending to look for you. Easy, now—don't hurry."

While Reverend Jim worked at the table, pulling it this way and that, not seeming to be quite satisfied with its position, Martha backed away until she stood in the water-house doorway. Then, as Reverend Jim moved toward her, she retreated from him until she was lost in the darkness beyand the door. Reverend Jim, unnoticed by Haddam and the others, followed her. Then the heavy door swung against its jambs; the bars were dropped into place, and, their bodies touching, they stood listening. Martha was trembling with excitement, but when Reverend Jim drew her away from the door to the shelter of the heavy adobe wall beside it, she whispered: "Thank you!"

He could not see her but could feel her breath, the touch of one of her shoulders. The scent of her hair told him that her head was close to his chin. Almost, he yielded to an impulse to put his arms around her. Instead, he said: "I thought you were taller!"

She did not answer, for now they heard a commotion in the kitchen, a roar of rage and suspicion from Haddam, and the thudding of his gun butt on the heavy, double-planked door—sounds that were flat and dull in the thick, damp atmosphere of the water house. Faintly, they could hear Haddam's voice:

"Damn your hides! What's comin' off here? Open this door, Parson, or I blow you to hell!"

"Careful you don't shoot the bride, Haddam," mocked Reverend Jim. Faintly, Reverend Jim and Martha could hear laughter rocking the kitchen as the men of the outfit realized what had happened. Then there was a silence which lasted only a few minutes. It was broken by Haddam calling through the door:

"What's the play, Parson?"

"Well, it's changed some, I expect."

"Not much. We'll hang around until you come out. Then we'll bust you wide open!"

"That's what you'd do, anyway, after the ceremony is performed. So I play safe. No ceremony—no busting me. And no dragging Martha Warren away. So it's all as it was before you got me to come here. So far, I'm satisfied, and you've got to be. Try busting the door down and I'll perforate you and your men as fast as you come through. Fuss around the window, and I blast your heads off. The water house won't burn; you can't tear down the walls. It's built on the ground, so you can't get under it. There's water here; and grub enough to last for a week. In less time than that Dave Blanchard and a posse will be out hunting for me, and they'll be tickled to hear what you've been trying to do. Go away, Haddam, and let us alone."

"So that's it—you mangy gospel bleater! I oughtn't to have trusted you!" Faintly, they could hear him stomping through the kitchen, could hear him cursing.

Reverend Jim laughed. To his astonishment, Martha joined him. Relief, he supposed. He spoke to her:

"They'll be talking it over for a while—not having any original ideas. We can't get away for a while yet, I expect, so there's something I want to say to you."

He felt she was retreating from him, and she spoke to him from a distance, confirming his impression.

"About Lize Ebbets, I suppose," she said coldly.

"Yes."

"I don't want to hear anything about her!"

"Well, you can't get away, and we've got plenty of time. So you'll have to listen."

"As soon as you start to talk about Lize Ebbets, I shall cover my ears. I don't want to hear it—I won't hear it! Whatever you were to Lize Ebbets—or she to you—doesn't make any difference to me. Do you understand that?"

"Of course, if you put it that way. Anybody could understand, I expect. But you see——"

"Please!" she protested. "If you insist upon talking that way, I shall open the door and go out to Flash Haddam!"

"So we don't talk about that," said Reverend Jim gently. "And there's other things to talk about. One of them is this: You saw the faces of all the men with Haddam?"

"Yes."

"Know any of them?"

"All of them."

"Me, too. Well, what do you think Haddam wants—you or the cattle or both?"

"I think he wants the cattle. And he'd like to find the money Father seems to have hidden."

"He's a fool for not wanting you," he said, and winced at her scornful laugh.

"You just can't help pretending," she said. "But," she added, "it was clever of you to pretend before Haddam and all of them that you were preparing for the wedding ceremony."

"That wasn't pretending," he said.

"It wasn't?" incredulously.

"The wedding ceremony will take place," he told her, wondering at the expression of her face.

"You can't mean that!" she said.

"It can take place with reservations—now."

"What do you mean?"

"I mean that Haddam can marry your cattle—that after the ceremony he can take them without taking you. You see, he can't get in here to get you, but after he marries you he can go and get the cattle—and sell them. I think that is what he wants."

"But I thought we came in here so that the wedding couldn't take place!" she said.

He laughed. "We came in here to save Jim Mc Donald's life," he said. "Just a selfish move, you see. More pretending. But I'm not pretending I wanted Haddam and his men to make a sieve of me—after the wedding."

"Oh," she said, understanding.

"So we'll have the wedding," he went on. "And Haddam won't get the bride. He won't have a chance to kill Jim Mc Donald. And maybe Jim Mc Donald will live to explain— though I expect he'll never be able to prove—that he wasn't in love with Lize Ebbets."

"And Haddam will take the H-Bar-W cattle—and sell them!" she said, protesting.

"Which is just what I want him to do," he told her, patiently and quietly.

There was a long silence during which they heard cursing from beyond the door. Then Martha said with a suspicious catch in her voice—and somewhat spitefully: "Well, then, if you want me to marry Flash Haddam—why don't you go ahead with the ceremony!"

"Well," he said through the darkness, "that's mighty sensible of you."

"Yes—very," she said hesitatingly. "You understand, perhaps, that if you marry me to Flash Haddam, I can never marry—any—anyone else?"

"I understand that."

"Oh, you do?"

"Yes."

"And you still want me to marry Haddam?"

"I'm waiting for you to say the word. Haddam is waiting."

"Well, then—go ahead. But—but he is marrying the cattle? That is understood? You won't let him come in here and——"

"I'll kill Haddam if he comes in here after you—or if he tries to take you as his wife after he gets the cattle."

"You are not pretending again," she said in a small voice.

"You don't trust me as a preacher," he said. "So I give you my word as a man—as a man who loves you."

He heard her catch her breath with a gasp of surprise. "Oh!" she said, and was silent.

They stood, listening; and presently there was a hammering on the door again, and Haddam's voice saying:

"Parson! Parson!"

"Yes?"

"We're through foolin', an' waitin'. Open up, or we'll blow hell out of the water house."

"Go ahead. What are you waiting for?"

"You damn fool! We don't want to kill Martha Warren!"

"Of course you don't. You want to marry her."

"You're damn tootin'! An' I mean to! An' you'll do the marryin'!"

"That's a deal, Haddam. But there's one condition. As soon as the ceremony is over, you've got to pull your freight out of here, and not bother the bride until she comes to you of her own accord. And you've got to take your men with you, so that Martha and I can go back to Red Rock without being interfered with. Take it or leave it!"

Reverend Jim, Martha understood, was bargaining for his life. She could not blame him for that, but it seemed that everything she had yearned for was slipping away from her. She leaned against one of the adobe walls and cried soundlessly so that Reverend Jim would not hear her and in a reckless moment sacrifice his life for her.

And presently she heard Haddam's voice again.

"We're agreein'," he said. "Soon as the knot is tied we light out for the range. Start things goin'."

A faint cheer reached Reverend Jim and Martha in the water house: the men, demonstrating their satisfaction. Then, Reverend Jim began the marriage service. Haddam's responses were loud, jubilant, triumphant; Martha's were low and reluctant and barely audible.

It seemed like a nightmare to Martha, after it was over and she and Reverend Jim stood in the darkness of the water house—a period of terror which she had endured semiconsciously, for now that it was over it did not seem to her that it could have been real. She stood, listening to the shouts, the oaths and the laughter that penetrated the heavy door—coarse, vile humor that made her shudder. Then, after a while, the sounds diminished and finally the shouts came from outside the house.

Then Reverend Jim expressed an ironic conclusion: "I expect I was right—Haddam married the cattle."

Half an hour after a rushing clatter of hoofs in diminuendo indicated that Haddam and the men had ridden away, Reverend Jim opened the door slightly and peered out into the kitchen. The lamp on the kitchen table was still burning; the door and the windows were open and now unoccupied by faces. Gun in hand, Reverend Jim stole along the walls of the room, knowing he would make an excellent target for any man who had been left behind by Haddam, while Martha stood in the doorway calling upon him to be careful. He vanished into the darkness of the dining room, and, fearing that Haddam *had* left a man or two behind, Martha called to him to return and wait for daylight. When she received no answer to her call she closed the water-house door and leaned against it, waiting, trembling. Fearing a trick when at last she heard a tapping on the door, she waited until Reverend Jim's voice reached her, saying: "They've gone, Martha."

She helped Reverend Jim catch Ginger and saddled him herself, for though she owed Reverend Jim much she could not forget Lize Ebbets. When he offered to help her mount Ginger she shrank from him; she did not wish him to touch her.

"Don't!" she said. "Please don't!"

He stepped back, and when she had mounted he climbed into his own saddle. And without uttering a word to him, for she now had little interest in anything, or where she was going—as long as she went away from the H-Bar-W—they rode down the river trail toward the parsonage.

CHAPTER 18

Martha shared Ellen's bed for the remainder of the night. Ellen spoke comforting words to her after Martha had related the story of the experience with Flash Haddam; but Martha, while listening, had betrayed no sign of interest, turning her back to Ellen and burying her face in her pillow. She did not sleep, though fits of sobbing that came frequently and lasted long betrayed her.

Ellen, her face white with sympathy, watched her silently in the subdued glow of light that came through a window from a midnight moon. Twice Martha fell into a doze to awake with wild sobs that were instantly suppressed.

The third time she awoke in this manner Ellen stole softly out of the bed and went to Reverend Jim's room.

She stood at his side, looking down at him. He had not been asleep, and at Ellen's call he sat up.

"Jim," she said softly, "it's terrible. Have you heard her? The poor little thing!"

"I've heard her. I'm mighty sorry." He kept his voice low; there was a grim note in it.

"She's frantic," said Ellen. "She's had too much trouble for a girl of her age. I'm afraid she will break down. I'm doing all I can, and it isn't enough. Of course you couldn't help doing as you did. You had to perform the ceremony, I suppose, or Haddam would have killed you—to say nothing of what might have happened to her. But if I tell her——"

"It wouldn't do!" said Reverend Jim shortly with finality. "A woman——"

"Please, Jim," she pleaded. "Think of the great load it will lift from her mind."

"I'm sorry," he repeated firmly though regretfully. "I wouldn't have had it happen. But it did happen, and it changes things very much. It puts Haddam—well, I expect you can see that well enough. She'll have to put up with it until—until Haddam shows his hand. If I'm not mistaken he'll do that fast enough. You tell her not to worry—that Haddam is not going to bother her, and that it will come out all right in the end."

Ellen made a gesture of resignation. "I suppose it must be," she said, "but it seems very hard for her."

Ellen left her brother sitting rigid and silent in his bed and returned to her own room, where she found Martha seated in a chair beside a window, staring dully out. She got up as Ellen entered, and began to dress.

"I am going away—somewhere," she said in answer to Ellen's quick question. "I can't stay here."

"You must!" declared Ellen. She took the girl by an arm and led her to another window, where the moonlight shone upon both, and drew the girl around so that she faced her.

"Look at me, Martha," she said then, her eyes shining with sincerity and honesty. "There are some things I cannot tell you, but I want you to believe me when I say that my brother is honorable, that there has been a hideous mistake about Lize Ebbets, and that what he did tonight was for your own good. If you knew him as I know him, you would not doubt him for an instant. I was talking to him just now, Martha, and he told me to tell you not to worry, that everything will come out all right. If you don't trust him," she added as Martha averted her face, "you will trust me—won't you?"

"Yes," said Martha impulsively. "You are the only real friend I ever had."

Meanwhile, Reverend Jim had done very little sleeping. And when just before dawn he heard the beating of hoofs and the sound of subdued voices coming from the direction of the bunkhouse, he got up, dressed and stole out of the front door. A little later, in front of the bunkhouse, he was talking earnestly

with Lawler, Shorty McGuinness, Slim Weaver and Red Owen.
Lawler seemed hugely pleased.

"Why," he said, "if you was to ask me, I'd call that a right
fortunate outcome of the night's work. But I wasn't expectin'
Haddam to go *that* strong. He's goin' to be a hawg!"

CHAPTER 19

Existence during the first few days of her stay at the parsonage would have been intolerable to Martha had not Ellen exerted herself to divert her thoughts from her recent past, and if Reverend Jim had not discreetly absented himself. He had gone, Ellen explained, upon a mission among the cattlemen of the basin. This explanation sufficed for the girl; she was glad he had gone where she could not see him, no matter what his mission.

At Red Rock the story that Haddam had forced Martha to marry him was received with skepticism. Schooled to hear news of Haddam's depredations with at least an outward show of equanimity, the town was shocked into a sullen silence by his latest escapade, and, following Blanchard's example, decided to reserve judgment until the story was verified.

However, in the fertile brain of the *Advocate* editor, the news of the marriage had caused a doubt to be born. This at first concerned the quality of Reverend Jim's manhood, about which, until the marriage, Carey had had much to say in praise. The news of the marriage made him uncertain. He was positive that in Reverend Jim's place he would have refused to do Haddam's bidding. Reverend Jim's acquiescence had a flavor of cowardice, of craven consideration of self which aroused Carey's contempt.

Carey's sense of honor was high. He did not wish to do Reverend Jim an injustice; nor did he want to risk a break in his relations with Ellen—which had grown intimately sweet of late—by acquainting her with his doubts of her brother's honesty and courage. But as the days went, and Reverend Jim made no effort to right the wrong that had been done Martha, Carey resolutely put away his nice scruples and rode to the parsonage.

Carey trailed the reins over the pony's head and stepped to the porch, taking the chair offered by Reverend Jim. His smile was a trifle strained as he answered Reverend Jim's comment on his overlong absence from the parsonage by saying he had been busy. He had a hope that Reverend Jim would mention the marriage, but when, after they had talked upon indifferent subjects for a time, Reverend Jim did not refer to it Carey made the leap.

"According to report, you officiated at a wedding recently," he said. He watched Reverend Jim closely, and saw his face break into an odd smile.

"Yes," he said. "Is Red Rock talking about it?"

"Plenty."

"What's the loud note?"

"Wonder that you'd do it," declared Carey.

"Surprised, eh?" Reverend Jim's words were unaccented; they expressed no emotion. "What are *you* thinking, Norman?"

There was just enough emphasis on his words, slow and drawling, to indicate subtle amusement. It was enough, however, to arouse resentment in Carey; it showed that Reverend Jim was not very deeply impressed with the gravity of the deed, and that he had little or no respect for public opinion.

"My thoughts on the subject are not clear," Carey answered. "Besides, what I have heard has come to me second hand. I don't know the circumstances."

"They were pretty simple." Reverend Jim looked hard at Carey when for an instant the latter turned his head away. Into Reverend Jim's eyes came a glint of knowledge; some emotion tugged at his lips for expression. It was denied. He spoke slowly and evenly: "Pretty simple. I've not been advertising what happened, but I'm telling you because I've got to know you rather well. Flash sent for me—by a man. I went to the H-Bar-W. Flash and his gang was there—and Martha Warren. Flash bent his gun on me and forced me to perform the ceremony. That was all.''

"You objected, of course?"

"I didn't like to do it."

"Why didn't you refuse then?"

Reverend Jim's eyes grew frosty. "Would you have refused, Norman?"

"I would! Flash wouldn't have shot you. He wouldn't dare shoot you. He'd have swung as soon as we could have organized a posse.''

"Comforting for me," said Reverend Jim. "I'd have taken a lot of interest in what was happening to Flash.''

For a moment Carey was silent. Again he looked at Reverend Jim, and somehow he was convinced that he was not a coward. His own attitude was unjust. Reverend Jim must have been convinced that it had been Haddam's intention to shoot him if he refused to do his bidding, and no one could blame Reverend Jim for making the choice he had made. Undoubtedly, in the crisis, he had formed some plan by which to defeat Haddam's aim. But if that were the case his inactivity since the marriage was damning.

"Well," said Carey presently, "there is no use in airing our regrets over what has happened. But do you fully understand Martha's predicament? Under the law in this Territory a woman's property at her marriage becomes her husband's.''

"That's right."

"And do you know that Haddam can sell every steer on the H-Bar-W range without bothering to get Martha's consent?''

"I know that, too."

Carey made a gesture of impatience. The Reverend Jim's unconcern irritated him.

"Then why, in the name of all that's good, don't you do something about it? You don't want that infernal outlaw to profit by the marriage, do you? Go to Las Vegas, to court, and have the marriage annulled! It is not legal! You ought to have gone the very next day! Get ready now, and I will go with you!''

"I'm waiting Haddam out," said Reverend Jim.

"My God!" ejaculated Carey. With dismay he suddenly realized how great had been his faith in Reverend Jim. Deep in him had been trust and admiration. Reverend Jim had destroyed both, and the editor's face slowly paled as a new suspicion seized him—a feeling which was more than a suspicion: a conviction that the marriage had been carefully premeditated, and that Reverend Jim was a spineless creature whom the outlaw was using for his own purposes.

He studied Reverend Jim's face. "What reason can you give for taking that remarkable attitude toward the marriage?" he said coldly.

"I don't seem to have thought of a reason, Norman. Or, if I have reasons I'm thinking them over until I decide what to do." There was a baffling smile on Reverend Jim's lips as he looked at the editor. But it seemed to Carey that there was cold amusement in his eyes—even curiosity.

Carey walked over to the edge of the porch, turning again to Reverend Jim, who was narrowly watching him. Reverend Jim's final words had driven the last spark of trust from Carey.

"Well," he said, "I've got to hand it to you. You've fooled all of us—me more than anybody. I'm saying good-by to you."

Carey stepped down from the porch. Turning again for a last look, he saw Reverend Jim smiling meditatively. He reddened angrily. And then he started and went pale again, for now Ellen was standing in the doorway, looking at him. The girl's face was white, her eyes luminous; she was erect, rigid, and her hands were clenched at her sides.

Carey bowed to her. "You have overheard some of our talk," he said, and as she nodded slightly, he continued: "And you are aware of the remarkable sentiments expressed by your brother." And now he looked at her hopefully, eagerly, anxiously, for upon her answer to his remark he was going to base his expectations for the future. But she said nothing, and so he was forced to ask a question. "Do you subscribe to them?" he said.

"Yes," she answered.

Carey bowed to her ironically. "Good-by, then," he said as he strode to his pony.

CHAPTER 20

The interview with Reverend Jim had aroused the editor's fighting spirit. As he rode toward Red Rock his rage and disappointment yielded to a grim determination to defeat Haddam's plot to rob Martha Warren of her heritage. He decided to have a talk with Lawler, and when he rode into town and saw Lawler talking with some men in front of Hitchens' store Carey motioned to him. Lawler followed him into the *Advocate* office.

"Look here, Lawler," he said, facing the latter near his desk, "there's crooked work going on and it's your place to stop it. I happen to know that you're——"

Carey's face changed color, for Lawler made a quick move, and the muzzle of his big Colt was against Carey's throat, making an icy ring, while Lawler's lean jaws showed ridges of muscle, indicating clenched teeth, and his eyes were glittering pin points.

"Whatever you know, you're keepin' quiet about!" he said in a cold, tense whisper. "There's men with ears, over there! An' they're watchin' me like hawks. I'll blow you to hell an' gone if I hear you let out a single peep about what you know about me or my men—or what you think you know! I reckon I know what's eatin' you. You're some disturbed about Martha Warren's marriage. If that's it you be mighty ca'm—not gassin' about it or puttin' nothin' in type. This thing's gone too far to have it spoiled by somebody with a loose tongue. You promisin' to keep your head shut?''

Carey looked into the cold eyes that were boring into his, and the recollection of another man drawing a pistol on him in the office came to him. But the man who was now facing him was not of Hawks's caliber; he was not bluffing, as Hawks had been, but was unmistakably in earnest.

"You make it plain enough,'' said Carey. "I wouldn't be fool enough to make that mistake, eager as I am to have the law at work here. But I think you ought to get busy.''

"I thought you was goin' to get loud,'' said Lawler, holstering his gun. "You acted plenty excited. If you was me how would you get busy?''

"That was a forced marriage,'' declared Carey. "You can take Haddam in charge for that.''

"You reckon the parson would appear against him?'' insinuated Lawler. "The parson has yawped some about it—to me, but it appears he's goin' to let things slide, not interferin'. An' Martha Warren don't seem to have no regular thoughts about it—settin' around over at the parsonage, lookin' like she was dreamin' an' would never wake up. Besides, I'm runnin' my end of this thing, and what you're wantin' me to do don't jibe with what I figure on doin'. You run your newspaper, an' be careful that Flash don't get you, an' don't get reckless with your gab. There's a heap you don't know, even if you are a newspaper guy.''

He turned and went out of the office, leaving Carey feeling rather subdued, but more suspicious than ever. He sat in a chair beside his desk to think. He had much to think about. Reverend Jim's attitude had made him suspicious of everybody, and he was not in the chair long before he began to dwell upon Lawler's manner toward him—the menace in his eyes, the quick rage he had exhibited at the mention of "crooked work.''

And a conviction grew stronger the longer it abided with Carey: it was that there was some sort of an understanding between Lawler, Haddam and Reverend Jim, and that the three of them were working together to rob Martha Warren of her property. He was baffled, but still determined, when an hour later he went down the street toward Castle's bank.

He found Castle at his desk. Castle stared at him.

"Holy smoke!" he ejaculated. "What's wrong with you? You look desperate!"

Carey did not take the chair Castle offered him, but stood beside the counter.

"Castle," he said, "there's something crooked going on between the Reverend Jim, Lawler and Haddam over that marriage. I'm going to the bottom of it if I have to start a riot in this town!"

"Oh, that's it," said Castle in apparent relief. "I thought something real important had happened. A marriage, now, Carey, a marriage is nothing to get excited about. Most men and women have them at some time or other in their lives, and those that don't have them are wanting to have them. I'd keep my fingers out of that affair if I were you; you're liable to get them pinched. What's developed?"

"I just came from the parsonage," Carey told him. "I thought the Reverend Jim had had time to get the machinery started to have that marriage annulled, and I asked him if he intended to get busy on it. He told me he wasn't going to interfere. Think of it, man! He is going to let Flash Haddam hold the girl and the ranch! He's a crook, and this crime is the limit. It's a damnable outrage! It's the final insult of outlawry gone mad!"

Castle did not share the editor's excitement. "You didn't talk that strongly to the Reverend Jim?"

"I let him know that I am through with him."

Castle bent over his desk. His face was expressionless. "Well," he said, "it's your affair."

"It's yours, too!" charged Carey. "It's the affair of every man with good red blood in him. Those fellows have got to be headed off! It's my opinion that the main object is to sell the H-Bar-W stock. Of course Haddam wants the girl, too, but I suppose he figures she will keep. But we've got to prevent the sale of that stock; that's the main thing right now. They'll keep the girl over at the parsonage; it's likely they'll not bother her until they cash in on the cattle. So she's safe until that time. You've been buying stock from all the cattlemen in the basin, and it's likely Haddam will want you to buy the H-Bar-W. I want you to help me head them off until I can get over to see the judge at Las Vegas!"

"I don't see how I can help you to head them off," said Castle without looking up.

"By refusing to buy any H-Bar-W cattle, of course. You can string Haddam along for a few days. That will give me time to do something. I've had a talk with Lawler about it—that is I tried to talk, but he got on his ear and wouldn't listen. I'm convinced that there's something wrong about Lawler, too; I've got an idea that he's double-crossing the governor. We'll find out, pretty soon. I'm taking the night train to Las Vegas. We'll fix them. While I'm gone, you can pretend to Haddam that you're willing to buy cattle, but haggle with him about the price, and keep putting it off until——"

Castle looked up. "You're late, Carey. I've already made arrangements to take five hundred head of H-Bar-W cattle at a price that suits me well, and I'm dickering with Haddam for the remainder."

Carey gasped and then stood silent, his lips slowly straightening.

"Good lord, Castle!" he said finally. "Knowing the circumstances, you wouldn't deliberately take advantage of that girl's predicament? Just to make a few extra dollars?"

"Business is business," was Castle's trite reply, delivered as his gaze dropped from Carey's. "I'm here to make all the money I can."

For an instant it seemed Carey was in danger of losing his temper. He stood rigid, his hands clenched, the muscles of his face twitching, his lips white. Then his lips curved in contempt.

"You can't mean that, Castle!" he exploded.

Castle looked up again, his face flushing at Carey's tone. "Why can't I mean it?" he demanded. "I'm not the law, am I? It's not my business to take sides in an affair of this kind. So far as I know, the marriage was a legal one and according to law. Haddam has a right to sell the H-Bar-W cattle. If I don't buy them someone else will. I'd be a fool not to take advantage of this situation. It doesn't look so desperate to me as it looks to you. And when you come to consider the matter, you've got to face the fact that Haddam has been pretty thick with the Warrens for a long time—with Ben at least; and perhaps Haddam didn't use as much force at the marriage as you think. The Reverend Jim doesn't seem to be much disturbed about it, anyway, or he'd have acted before this."

"The Reverend Jim is an infernal crook!" declared Carey. "And I'm telling you this, Castle; knowing what you do about this affair, if you buy any of the H-Bar-W cattle from Haddam, you're as big a thief as he!"

He watched Castle, his eyes gleaming with a cold rage. But Castle, except that his face went a little pale, gave no indication of emotion over the charge. He did not meet Carey's eyes, pretending to be busy with some papers.

For the second time that day, Carey was afflicted with nausea. This discovery hurt him worse, he believed, than had the evidence of Reverend Jim's and Ellen's perfidy, for he had sincerely liked Castle; they had known each other a long time.

"I seem to have the misfortune to always make mistakes in selecting my friends," he said when he observed that Castle did not intend to answer him. Then he turned and walked out of the door.

Castle watched him until he could no longer be seen. Then he smiled mysteriously. "Took it hard," he said. "I wonder if he *can* stir up anything?"

Carey tried hard to stir up something. After leaving Castle, he was closeted with Blanchard in the room behind the Emporium for an hour or so. Blanchard listened attentively to him, his face serious.

"It looks a heap suspicious," admitted the saloon-keeper at the close of the conference. "But I don't advise starting anything right now. You do what you say you're goin' to do. Then, if nothin' happens an' Flash gets gay, we'll take a hand." He sighed. "I've seen it comin' for a long time, anyway. An' if it's got to be, we'll make it a hell warmer!"

Carey took the night train as he had threatened to do. At a water tank, ten miles west of Red Rock, the train came to a stop while the engine took water. On a siding Carey saw a string of cattle cars, and he swung down to where the freight conductor stood, talking with a brakeman.

"Where are they consigned to?" he asked of the conductor, indicating the cars.

"Empties for Red Rock," said the conductor.

Carey got back into his car, frowning. He had a hope that Castle would back out at the last moment—that he might have been bluffing, though he couldn't have told why he had hoped that: it was largely a wish. But the presence of the empty cars destroyed his hopes, and when the train went on its way the *Advocate* editor, impatient, fretted at its slow progress, and wakefully listened to the monotonous clicking of the wheels over the rail joints. It had been a bad day for him. But a worse day would come for those who had misled and betrayed him. Justice would be done if he could bring it. He would take it back to where love—sadly crippled—had looked at him that day. For he knew that love had shown in Ellen's last glance at him.

CHAPTER 21

Dal Thompson, grizzled, tanned, his face set in grim lines, was galloping past the promontory when a voice hailed him, and he rode back to find Martha standing at the base of a tree near the edge of the cliff. Delight shone in her eyes at sight of Thompson, for she had been yearning for speech with an old friend.

"I've just heard what happened, girl," he told her, his voice vibrating. "Me an' the boys came in about an hour ago. Flash paid us off an' told us he wouldn't need us any more. It kind of set me back, him presumin' to be boss thataway, an' I asked him what in thunder he meant. I was pretty near flustrated when he told me, grinnin' that smarty grin of his, that him an' you had hooked up double. I could think or talk none lucid, an' soon's I could break away, I busts over here to get it straight. What's happened? If he's done you harm I'll go back an' salivate him if I get turned into a sieve doin' it!"

She told him briefly, and his face reflected his rage.

"An' the parson ain't done nothin' toward breakin' up the marriage?" he asked. "What do you reckon is eatin' him?"

"I don't know," she said, wearily. "I haven't asked him why he hasn't done something. I keep putting it off—I don't know why. I'm afraid, I suppose. I don't know what to do. Ellen keeps telling me that it will come out all right in the end, but the end seems far away. I think she is sincere, and I trust her. I don't know why I trust her, either. I suppose it's because she is a woman."

"You poor little cuss!" Thompson patted her shoulder. "I've been kickin' myself for a fool ever since I heard of it, for not sendin' some of the boys to hang around the house. Then it wouldn't have happened. But now it's done, it's got to be squared. The parson has had plenty of time to get busy. I'm havin' a talk with him. They treatin' you right here? You want to go somewhere else?"

"They are kind and considerate if that is what you mean. Do you think, after what has happened, that I would be welcome anywhere else in the basin?"

"I'm afraid not," said Thompson, his lips straightening. "No, you wouldn't. The fools! But you hang on here a few days yet. I'm takin' a job with Dobble—foreman; he's been holdin' it open for me since Snedden cashed in. I didn't want to take it— but I'm takin' it now. I'm havin' a straight talk with Dobble about you. When I get home with him he'll be tickled to make a place for you. But first, I'm gassin' to the parson."

"You won't be rough, Dal?" she said, putting a hand on his arm; for now, since someone had come to champion her, she suddenly felt a thrill of the old confidence in Reverend Jim.

"Rough!" laughed Thompson. "Oh no! Just a quiet, confidential confab. But after it's over we'll know somethin' definite. You wait here."

He jumped on his pony and rode toward the parsonage. He arrived at the front porch as Carey was vanishing down the Red Rock trail, in time to see Reverend Jim and Ellen, standing very close together, talking earnestly.

He was off his pony and standing at the edge of the porch before the exclamation of surprise which sprang from Ellen's lips could die away; and with three or four long steps he was standing before Reverend Jim.

"I reckon you don't know me; but I've seen you, Parson. My name's Dal Thompson. I'm the former H-Bar-W foreman, let out recent by the new boss, Flash Haddam. I don't know what's bein' pulled off here, an' I ain't wastin' any time guessin'. But somethin' is wrong—my real boss ain't gettin' a square deal. I ain't never had no truck with parsons—don't know how to swap palaver with them; an' mebbe I'm seemin' a little blunt in my remarks. Howsomever, here they are: It takes a day to get to Las Vegas, where there's a court, an' a day to get back. That's two days, accordin' to the figurin' I learned at school. That's settled then. Well, I'm addin' a day for accidents or delay. That's the limit. In three days I'm visitin' you again. You'll show me the papers from the Las Vegas court, knockin' this marriage out, or hell will be poppin' so loud you'll think you're goin' through hell in a hemlock coffin! I reckon that's all!''

He turned his back and walked to his pony, mounting and spurring the animal toward the promontory. Reverend Jim had not spoken; he did not speak until he saw Thompson bring his pony to a halt at the promotory. Then he turned to Ellen, who was regarding him with a fixed smile.

"I reckon I could depend upon that man," he said, then.

"I found the parson right agreeable," said Thompson to Martha as he reined in near her. "He'll hustle right over to Las Vegas an' get the marriage busted up. I reckon he means well enough, but he's been waitin' for someone to offer him a suggestion. I'm goin' to light out for Dobble's place now; some of the boys is waitin' for me, not havin' decided definite on what they're goin' to do. I'm takin' some of them over to Dobble's with me. I reckon some more will find jobs other places made vacant by Haddam's men leavin' them. Lord! If we had a real sheriff! Haddam's whole gang is at the H-Bar-W. They're raisin' old Ned with the house—rippin' an' tearin' it apart—pullin' up the floors an' bustin' the chimney in.''

"Looking for Dad's hidden money!" said Martha breathlessly. "I hope they find it! Then perhaps they will go away!"

"Haddam's a hawg," said Thompson. "I ain't got no such hope. Let them hang around here, for the limit has been passed a right smart while ago. I'm findin' out if there's any *men* in this basin. If there is I'll be back with them in three days. If there ain't I'm comin' back alone. So long, honey!"

He was gone, with a grin and a wave of the hand, and Martha stood for a time, thankfully watching him. Then, when he had vanished, she walked to a grassy spot near the base of a tree on the cliff edge and sank down upon it.

She had lost her repugnance for this place, for she could not forget that here had begun what had promised to be a romance for her; and, even though Lize Ebbets had brought it all to an end, there still remained thoughts that lingered and allured her. And so, although she kept her face averted, she was secretly pleased when she heard a step turn from the beaten trail, rustle in the grass and halt within a few feet of her. She knew it was Reverend Jim.

"Dal Thompson told me he had quit the H-Bar-W. You were talking with him. Did he quit?"

Martha turned and faced him. "Haddam discharged him—the others, too. Thompson heard only a little while ago what had happened—to me. He came right over. Haddam and his men are tearing the ranch house to pieces—searching for Dad's money." She looked up in time to see his lips come together in straight lines 'You might do something about it—don't you think?"

"I expect not—just now. Haddam will not bother you. He thinks he's got a right to do what he's doing."

She got up and stood stiffly before him. "He has no right!" she declared. "You know he hasn't. He forced me to marry him! Ellen tells me that everything will come out all right, but you— you do nothing. You might have prevented Haddam discharging Thompson and the others—if you had acted. Thompson told me a few minutes ago that you had agreed to have the marriage annulled within three days. If that has been your intention right along why haven't you done it before this?"

"So Thompson told you I had agreed. Well, Thompson was traveling a little fast. I'd like to be able to tell you what is in my mind. But I can't. You trusted me on the night the wedding ceremony was performed, and you must keep on trusting me. There's other ways of breaking up the marriage. But it will take a few days."

"Other ways?" She looked at him with quick doubt, then scorn, while a sudden fear that he did not mean to do *anything* possessed her. "There *is* no other way," she said.

"You'll have to trust me, Martha," he repeated.

"I don't trust you!" she said vehemently. And then, suddenly, she broke under the strain of the misfortune and trouble that had come to her, and charged him with being responsible for all her misfortunes, while he stood with bowed head and flushed face, listening to her, speaking no word in reply. She told him, in an excess of scorn, of how he had pretended to her all along; that she now believed the marriage had been prearranged; that he had known what Haddam intended to do—and she cited his quick compliance to the outlaw's demand that night to prove it—his significant wink at her, seeming to promise protection and assurance of ultimate escape for her. She finished by referring to Lize Ebbets.

Reverend Jim's face had grown slowly pale. He took a step toward her.

"I expect I've got to——" he began, then paused, shaking his head. "You wouldn't believe me, anyway, no matter what I told you," he said. "Feeling like you do, you'd think I was pretending again. I expect I do look pretty bad to you right now, but—if you give me time—— Shucks! I wasn't ever in a mix-up like this before." He took another step toward her, speaking again, his voice vibrating with earnestness. "It certainly must seem like a riddle to you—everybody doing things so mysteriously. But there'll be an end pretty sudden now. And then you'll find out that——"

"Go away!" she said shuddering. "I don't want to listen to any more of your lies! I want to be alone!"

"Well, I expect that's best, after all."

She heard him as he turned and walked away. A little later she saw him at the parsonage.

Dusk had fallen when she left the promontory and made her way down the trail. She felt that it would be impossible for her to stay at the parsonage longer; her denunciation of Reverend Jim had made the thought intolerable. She would not go until morning, though. She did not know where she would go; she could make no plans, for her thoughts were confused. She had very little money—no friends, except Dal Thompson. But she would go somewhere; she had decided on that. Upstairs in her room she flung herself down on the bed without undressing.

CHAPTER 22

At ten o'clock in the morning of the second day following Norman Carey's departure from Red Rock on the train, the leaders of a trail herd passed the *Advocate* office. Other cattle—five hundred odd in all—followed, strung out in the straggling formation peculiar to the peripatetic habits of their kind.

Castle's cars had arrived the day before. They were on a siding that paralleled the corrals, and for several hours after the coming of the herd there was much bustle and activity. It was after noon when the last car was loaded, and the sweating, wearied cowboys sought the saloons.

During the work, Castle had sat on a flat-topped post of the corral fence, tallying and watching Haddam direct the activities of his men. After it was over and the cowboys had gone Castle climbed down, and accompanied by the outlaw, went into the bank building. Castle walked to his desk, laid a paper in front of Haddam, and said shortly:

"Sign it."

Haddam read:

Received of Justus Castle ten thousand dollars as payment in full for five hundred H-Bar-W steers.

*

Haddam grinned and signed his name with a flourish.

"You got them cheap enough, but not as cheap as I got them."

Castle took the receipt, placed it in an iron safe in a corner of the office and returned, passing over to Haddam a bulky leather bag. "Here's your coin," he said. "Count it."

"I'm takin' your word," grinned Haddam. "I'm obliged to you—you saved me a long drive. Fellow who used to buy my stock in San Pablo got foul of the law which seems to have come lately in these parts. I'd have had to drive to Willets—three hundred miles. Drinkin'? Well"—at Castle's negative—"I'm loadin' in a few. The boys is takin' whisky over to the H-Bar-W—my new home. Goin' to clean up, after. I'm takin' the bride home, an' the parson is hittin' the breeze to hell! So long."

He strode out, and Castle watched him go down the street and enter the Emporium. Also, Castle saw Red Owen lounging in the doorway of the Palace. And farther down he saw Shorty Mc Guinness leaning idly against a building, and Slim Weaver sitting on the top rail of a hitching rack, swinging his legs, and Lawler sitting on the steps of the empty *Advocate* office. Castle looked thoughtful.

When Norman Carey got off the two o'clock train at Red Rock Flash Haddam and his men had departed. Hilarious over their potations in the Emporium, their slickers packed with bottles out of which they were to drain inspiration for that celebration about which Flash had spoken to Castle, they had ridden out of town in high spirits. Red Rock had watched them in sullen silence.

Carey was travel stained, pale and grim when he alighted from the train. He did not stop at the *Advocate* office, but went directly to the Emporium. Standing in the rear room, facing Blanchard a few minutes after his arrival, he told the saloon-keeper the result of his journey.

"The judge at Las Vegas wouldn't interfere. He said Reverend Jim would have to appear before him personally, and would have to unreel endless miles of red tape in order to set the machinery of justice in motion. Wanted to know, if a crime had been committed, why I didn't bring charges against Haddam before the sheriff. Smiled at me when I told him Hawks couldn't be depended upon. Said that it was evidently a matter for the governor to decide. I jumped a train and went over to Santa Fe.

The governor was polite and attentive, but also referred me to Hawks. When I mentioned my suspicions about Lawler, Reverend Jim and Haddam being in the plot against Martha Warren, he settled back in his chair, looked at me as though he doubted my sanity, and then said: 'Hum! That seems to be quite a muddled affair. I'll look into it.' That was all I could get out of him. It's mighty indefinite. The girl will be robbed and Haddam and his bunch out of the country before the law will take any action. Castle's cars didn't come, eh? I didn't see any signs of them on the siding. That conductor missed his reckoning."

"They came, right enough," said Blanchard. "They pulled out of here an hour ago, carryin' five hundred head of steers."

Carey's face whitened through the dust upon it. "That settles it, Blanchard. We've got to take the law into our own hands!"

"Looks like it," agreed Blanchard. "I was hopin' it wouldn't come to this. But we'd be fine speciments if we was to set here, idle, an' see them make a monkey of Martha Warren. It's come to a showdown, an' we'll deliver the goods. I've already talked to some of the boys about it, an' they're ready. There's about twenty who are a heap eager to bust things up. I'll get a dozen more. Mostly they're cattle owners who have got a grudge against Haddam. If a thing is to be done it's always wise to get it done quick an' have it over with. There's no time like the present. We'll clean up right, an' get a new start! The first thing is to hawgtie Hawks, so's he can't interfere!"

There followed an earnest conference in the rear room, in which a dozen men participated. One result of the conference was immediate and startling.

Sheriff Hawks was sitting in his office—a little frame shanty down near the station—dozing, his feet on his desk, when a dozen men with handkerchiefs covering the greater part of their faces burst in upon him. He started up, but sat abruptly down again when the cold muzzle of a six-shooter made a dent in his back. Before he could ask a question his weapons were taken from him, a gag was forced into his mouth; a forty-foot rope was wound around his legs and arms, and he was carried out of the back door of his office and into the door of the rear room of the Emporium, where he was placed on the floor and a guard provided for him.

While this incident was taking place, several other men suddenly appeared before the telegrapher at the station. This man was known to be a friend of law and order, but the quickly formed vigilance committee was taking no chances, and despite the telegrapher's protestations, his instrument was disconnected and whisked away. One man climbed a telegraph pole near the station and cut the wires; another man did likewise on another pole. But as it turned out, this precaution was unnecessary, for the operator signified his intention of joining the committee forthwith.

Red Rock had suffered long; it had patiently waited for the law to come; and when the law did not come it had waited, still patiently, for the appearance of a man with courage and initiative. He had come—rather two had come—Carey and Blanchard. And that spirit of fair play which is deeply rooted in the hearts of the citizens of the republic, had leaped, responsive, to their call. In an hour, as word passed concerning the contemplated action, thirty men of the basin were assembled in the Emporium.

There was no demonstration. Method ruled. Several men were detailed to guard the trails from town, lest a Haddam sympathizer be among them who would try to get away to warn the outlaw. Preparations went on swiftly, with few words; and within two hours from the time Carey had stepped from the train, the thirty riders were ready. Led by Carey and Blanchard, they rode down the river trail into the basin.

They rode, as the afternoon shadows began to descend over the far mountains, into the clearing near the parsonage. Blanchard—for Carey had evaded this duty—dismounted and walked to the front door of the parsonage, where Ellen was standing with Martha at her side, watching them.

"Reverend Jim anywheres around?" asked Blanchard.

"He hasn't been here since morning," Ellen told him. She stood with clenched hands, looking at Blanchard and the other members of the posse, at the rifles they bore, at their stern faces. Her eyes were worried, frightened. "He left at five o'clock. We saw some H-Bar-W cattle away over there on the trail, and my brother left before they passed. He said he was going to the Arrow. Is anything wrong? What do you want with him?"

"Where's Lawler? An' Slim Weaver, an' Shorty Mc Guinness an' Red Owen?" demanded Blanchard, ignoring Ellen's question.

"They aren't here, either. They went away together—shortly after Flash Haddam and his men passed here—some time ago—going toward the H-Bar-W. What do you want?"

Blanchard ignored this question as he had ignored the others. He motioned to the posse, and several of the men dismounted and ran toward him. Gruffly he ordered the men to surround the house, but stepped inside himself. He was gone some time, and when he emerged he looked grimly at the girls—patting Martha's shoulder.

"Buck up!" he said in answer to her dreading, wondering glance at him. "It'll soon be over now."

Without another word to the girls, the riders mounted and rode away, the girls watching them until they faded into distance.

As the posse went, the horses loping steadily, the twilight deepening, Carey, riding beside Blanchard, turned to him with a question:

"Did anyone see Castle?"

"Sloped, I reckon," grunted Blanchard. "Ed Martin said he saw him hittin' the breeze out of town just before you come in. He was heeled."

Twilight had turned into threatening darkness when the posse reached the edge of the clearing near the H-Bar-W ranch house, but there was still light enough to distinguish objects clearly. The posse halted for a conference before taking action. Carey advised a rush on the house, for without doubt Haddam and his men were inside, celebrating, as they had boasted they intended doing. Their horses were in the corral, their saddles scattered about, evidently where they had thrown them in their haste to be about the business of celebrating. But no light shone through the windows of the house, and the distance from the house to where the posse waited was too great to hear any sounds that might have come from there.

Carey did not like the silence, and he spoke to Blanchard about it as they prepared to go forward, suggesting that perhaps Castle had not gone far from Red Rock—that he might have lingered near the town, and then, having seen the forboding preparations of the posse, he might have ridden on to warn Haddam. In that case, the outlaw and his men might be lying in wait inside the house. But the posse decided that in any event a rush would be no more dangerous than a slow advance. So, deploying the men, Carey taking the left end, which would bring him to the rear of the house, they rode forward.

Carey bowed his head low over the pony's mane in expectation of a fusillade of bullets from the house. But no bullets came. Indeed, no sounds at all, except the rapid clatter of hoofs behind him, telling him that a dozen or so of the members of the posse were following him closely, greeted the editor's ears. There was no sign of life in the house, or from it. Carey pulled his pony up at the kitchen door, yielding to a quick disappointment, for the door was open, and the interior yawned emptily—he could see through it to the front door, which was also open.

But as he peered closer into the kitchen he saw a figure huddled grotesquely on the floor near the door—the body of a man. A bullet wound disfigured his face—Carey could see blood dripping from it. He uttered an exclamation and was about to dismount, when he heard an answering exclamation from one of the men who had ridden past him, only to jerk his horse to a halt at the corner of the house nearest Carey. The other members of the posse were riding forward to the first man's side, and Carey joined them.

Another exclamation leaped to Carey's lips, but was smothered, turning into a gurgling gasp of amazement. For within the radius of a big "L" formed by two great wings of the ranch house—which had prevented the editor and the posse from seeing until now—were many men and horses.

Carey recognized most of the men. They represented every ranch in the basin, and there must have been at least fifty of them. A long, grim line they made—a line which bristled with pistols and rifles. Carey's amazement grew. For in the line were Reverend Jim, Lawler, Shorty Mc Guinness, Slim Weaver and Red Owen. Lawler and his three men each had a weapon in hand; Reverend Jim did not. But he stood a little in advance of the line, his coat off, his heavy Colt in its holster, and he was talking.

Carey urged his pony forward a little, in breathless curiosity and wonder. And then he saw, ranged along the wall of the ranch house, a number of other men. They, too, were armed. There were about twenty of them, and they stood with their hands above their heads. Carey recognized many of this group, too— they were friends of Flash Haddam—his men.

The outlaw himself stood well out from them. His hands were also elevated, but there was an expression of malignant hatred on his face, mingling with rage that was terrible in its ferocity.

It was evident to the editor that there was a mistake some-where, and an abashed feeling was stealing over him. Unmistakably, Reverend Jim and Lawler and his men were members of a second posse. And when Carey's eyes, roving rapidly, rested on the face of Justus Castle, who was armed with a rifle and was standing with the posse, and Carey saw a wide, derisive grin on his lips, the editor began to believe he had come very near to making a fool of himself. Conviction came with growing illumination of the situation.

For now Carey heard Reverend Jim's voice. He was talking slowly and clearly, while two men of the posse were relieving Haddam's men of their weapons. Obviously, Carey and his posse had arrived too late to witness the surprise which had resulted in the capture of the outlaws.

Reverend Jim made an heroic figure in the dusk. His hat was shoved back from his forehead; he loomed big and muscular with his coat off, his slim waist girdled with a cartridge belt, the holster with its huge weapon bulging at his hip. It was the first time Carey had ever seen Reverend Jim's gun and gun belt clearly, and he was amazed to discover that it was a replica of those worn by professional gun fighters he had seen, and that it created in his mind the same impression of deadly utility and accuracy. And Reverend Jim's eyes, gleaming with a wanton light, were narrowed and coldly alert as they rested upon Haddam. No longer did he seem to be a preacher; instead, he was the personification of a ruthless and deadly destroying force. His voice, too, had changed. It was cold and bleak and his words came with metallic sharpness. He talked directly at Haddam, and Carey listened, amazement and incredulity fighting within him for the mastery. It seemed to Carey that Haddam, too, was amazed at something he saw in Reverend Jim, for he was incredulously staring, as if trying ineffectually to associate this fighting man with the "parson" he had known. He kept looking from Reverend Jim's eyes to the cartridge belt and gun, so professional in appearance, with evidence, moreover, that they had been in service for some time, as their softness and pliability and the various scuffs on them told him. So would a man look at an apparition. So would he look at a man whom he had once seen, but whom he had forgotten, and was only just now beginning to strive to remember.

Fascinated by this scene, and with the implications it portended, certain that Haddam was slowly becoming aware that tragedy was at hand, Carey, his eyes straining to see what was behind it all, and his ears attuned so that he would not miss a word, watched both men.

"We've got the goods on you, Flash," said Reverend Jim,

"though it didn't come in just the way we expected it to come when we came here to get you. Your marrying Martha Warren hurried it up a little, too, for we were figuring to get you with Lawler's triangle brand. We would have got you, too—give us time. But you made it simple for us by marrying Martha. Castle's got your receipt, showing you sold him five hundred head of H-Bar-W steers—which you had no right to sell. He's got the signatures of all your men, saying that they were working for you—that they had a hand in the stealing. You've got to hand it to Lawler and Castle for working you that clever. You've given us the evidence, yourself. Maybe you don't understand," he said as Haddam scowled at him. "Lawler and his men, and Castle and myself, were working together to get you to sell the H-Bar-W stock."

"You make me sick," snarled Haddam, hoarsely, for from far back in his memory was coming a name which he was now trying hard to remember—which, when it came, would tell him for certain the identity of this man who was talking to him, who was watching him so closely that not a muscle could move except that he interpreted its purpose. A name which would identify this man with a name that he fearsomely admired—had admired for many years. "I'm married to Martha Warren, ain't I?" he said, while he struggled with his recreant memory. "I had a right to sell them H-Bar-W steers!"

Reverend Jim's voice grew a tone softer—though it was still hard and metallic and icy.

"Listen, Flash," he said. "I'm not a preacher. I'm never going to be a preacher. The bishop knows that. He was against letting me pull this off, but when the governor sent for him and told him he had to have me, why, he caved right in and I came right over, bringing my sister with me to make it strong. I expect there'll be people that will blame me, but if you'll look deep enough, you'll find that law and religion are twin sisters, and that God has no special use for thieves and murderers.

"Besides," Reverend Jim went on, his shoulders beginning to hunch a little as he saw a certain light begin to dawn in Haddam's eyes, "the bishop was feeling kind of sore because you chased another preacher out of Red Rock, and because he thought you had bullied and killed people long enough. Right human of him—wasn't it? It helped him a lot toward giving his consent. There were times, Flash, when I did feel like a preacher, and so I didn't have to pretend much. But pretending made it easy for me to get acquainted with the good people in the basin, and when I started out to get them this morning, I found them all ready and waiting for me. They didn't know I wasn't a preacher, and I expect they're as much surprised as you are. And I expect none of them are offended, for I've done nothing contrary to God's rules, and I've tried mighty hard not to lose my temper—though I've come pretty close to it, watching the way you've carried on.''

Haddam's body had slowly fallen into a crouch, for now had come that revelation of identity for which he had been striving. He had edged away from the men who were relieving his confederates of their weapons, and his right hand hovered close to his gun holster.

''Arizona Jim Mc Donald!'' he said in a hoarse, throaty whisper. ''Tombstone gun fighter! A parson—hell!''

His eyes gleaming with a terrible hatred, he continued to back away. His fingers, curved like the talons of a bird of prey about to seize a victim, descended to the butt of his gun. He had merited the sobriquet ''Flash'' bestowed on him as a tribute to his rapidity in drawing a weapon, but Reverend Jim's lightning motion made his movement seem fatally slow in comparison. For Haddam's fingers had just touched the butt of his weapon when there was a glint at Reverend Jim's hip, a spiteful crash, and Haddam's wrist, broken by Reverend Jim's bullet, dangled oddly.

Haddam shrieked—cursed—his eyes ablaze with malevolence, and reached with his left hand into his shirt front. There came another crash, simultaneous with the movement, and smoke curled from the muzzle of a gun held in the hand of Shorty Mc Guinness. Haddam's head snapped back, a black mark showing in his forehead for just the instant that intervened between the crash of Shorty's gun and the outlaw's huddled fall. He lay face down in the sand. Carey shuddered and gasped. Reverend Jim looked at Mc Guinness.

''I wasn't figuring to kill him, Shorty,'' he said gently. ''I told the governor I'd bring him back, so's he could make an example of him.''

Shorty grinned coldly. ''I reckon that'll be a hard job now, Reverend,'' he said.

CHAPTER 23

Norman Carey led the Red Rock posse back toward town. A full mile ahead he rode, for he was in no humor to listen to the badinage which would have been dinned into his ears by the other members. Besides, humbled, crushed, he intended to stop at the parsonage to make his peace with Ellen. He was reasonably certain of her forgiveness, for he remembered a regretful light in her eyes on the occasion of his last meeting with her on the porch, before his trip to Las Vegas. He was glad it was dark when he arrived at the edge of the porch—while he was yet some distance from the house he had seen Ellen there—and Martha—and he rode directly to them. They met him at the steps, and both girls were eager and anxious.

He was not required to make the apology he had wanted to make—that he expected would have to be made; for at his approach Ellen ran toward him from the steps, and as he dismounted her hands were gripping his shoulders, and her face was very close to his as she asked quickly:

"Is it over, Norman? Is Jim—are any of the men—hurt?"

"All safe," he said. "Nobody hurt but Haddam. He's dead—Shorty shot him. One or two more, perhaps—the outlaws. But it's all over, and I've been wondering if you can forgive me for being such a mystified, credulous, unbelieving fool!''

"Forgive you?" Her hands patted his shoulders. "I didn't blame you much. Anybody would have suspected there was something wrong, I suppose. Even Martha wouldn't believe me when I told her—after your posse had gone—that Jim isn't a preacher, and that of course she had not been married to Haddam. But you know, now, that Jim isn't a preacher, don't you?''

Carey smiled admiringly. "I'd swear to that," he said. And he heard Martha murmur lowly as she went to one of the slender columns of the porch, leaned her head against it and stood looking into the dim shadows that spread over the H-Bar-W trail.

Part of the posse rode to Red Rock in company with the captured outlaws. Accompanied by Sheriff Hawks, they were hustled aboard the midnight train and whisked away to Las Vegas—Reverend Jim, Lawler, Shorty Mc Guinness, Slim Weaver and Red Owen doing the honors. Passing the parsonage, Reverend Jim had stopped only for a moment to speak a word to Ellen. Though he did not stop long he found time to refer to the editor.

"Carey seeing things different?''

"Much.''

He patted her cheeks. "Hook onto him," he said. "He's man's size." He nodded toward the house. "She know?"

"How could I keep from telling her?"

"I expect she still thinks I'm a mean man—that Lize and I——''

"I suppose she will always feel that way," answered Ellen reluctantly.

"I expect she will. Well, I'll be getting along. I'll be back the day after tomorrow. They won't get a trial for a month, maybe. Shucks," he added as he started away, only to return. "I forgot to tell you. Here's some good news for Martha. Castle says her dad banked all his money with him. It's hers when she says the word. He's got the ten thousand he paid Haddam, too.''

Red Owen found Reverend Jim to be a gloomy traveling companion on the way back to Red Rock three days later. Lawler and the other two had elected to stay in Las Vegas until after the trial. Owen endured Reverend Jim's gloominess until the train was near Red Rock, and then he spoke of it.

"What's eatin' you, Jim? You win, an' then you act as if you was goin' to requisition the mourners for your own funeral!"

"I'm not going to win what I'd like to win," said Reverend Jim, staring glumly out of the window.

Red's eyes were illumined with sudden knowledge. He spoke gently. "I reckon Martha's on your mind a heap right now. She won't forgive you none because she thinks you was thick with Lize Ebbets? Now, I'd call that bein' in mean luck. But I reckon that when once a woman gets an idea like that in her head, it's a heap of a chore to get it out. I'd wait her out if I was you. Someday, when she gets to knowin' you pretty well—as well as a lot of other folks know you—that suspicion she's got will seem like nonsense to her."

When Reverend Jim and Red Owen returned to the parsonage it was to discover that Martha had gone to the H-Bar-W. Thompson and the other men had resumed their old positions.

Satisfaction reigned over Red Rock because of the outcome of Reverend Jim's brief incumbency as director of things religious, but there was no satisfaction for Reverend Jim. Blanchard, seeing him several times, remarked that it was his opinion that Reverend Jim's job had suddenly palled on him—that he needed excitement, and that the outlook for excitement in Red Rock was no longer good.

But Blanchard was wrong. Only Ellen and Red Owen knew the real reason for his long silence, his lack of cheerfulness after his successful campaign against the outlaws, and they kept their knowledge to themselves.

Reverend Jim had no hope that the wrong Lize Ebbets had done him would ever be righted. He had no faith in Owen's suggestion that he "wait her out," for he had sounded the depths of Martha's character, and he knew that he must be, and would continue to be, a man whom she could not trust.

He was sitting on the porch of the parsonage on the morning of a day about a week following his return from Las Vegas, smoking his pipe and meditating over Lize's action, when, glancing down the river trail, he saw Martha and Ellen riding toward the parsonage. To his surprise, they alighted at the promontory, which had been the scene of his short romance. Ellen had ridden over to the H-Bar-W earlier in the morning, but she had said nothing about bringing Martha back with her. Reverend Jim forgot to pull at his pipe, and it spluttered out.

Martha and Ellen were at the promontory a long while—so long that Reverend Jim grew impatient and relighted his pipe, puffing at it vigorously. And then, a little later, he saw Red Owen riding toward them—watched while Owen dismounted and vanished.

He started out of his chair when he saw Red reappear, for Red's movements were rapid, as though excitement stirred him. He mounted with his pony at a gallop and came tearing up the trail at a speed that threatened his neck. He rode directly toward the porch, and Reverend Jim ran to meet him.

"Whoop-eee, you old horse thief!" he yelled. "It's all off, for certain! Ellen's found a message from Lize Ebbets, writ on a stone, squarin' things for you! An' Martha wants to see you, immediate!"

Reverend Jim was convinced of the soundness of Red's news by seeing Ellen riding away from the promontory—alone; and a new light leaped into his eyes as he turned and squeezed Red's hand. Well on the way to the promontory he passed Ellen, who gave him a significant, encouraging smile.

And then, in a few minutes, Reverend Jim turned from the trail to face the promontory. Martha was standing at the edge of the cliff where they had met before. She smiled when she saw him, then dropped her gaze from his, a touch of crimson in each cheek. In her hands was a flat rock, several inches in diameter, which, as Reverend Jim came near, she held out to him without a word. He took it from her hand. Scratched on the rock, in crude, wavery characters, were the words:

MARTHA: *I lied to you about Reverend Jim.*

LIZE

"Ellen found it a few minutes ago," said the girl, her gaze still downward, the flush in her cheeks growing deeper. "I'm sorry I misjudged you. But Lize—"

"I'm sorry, too," said Reverend Jim, "sorry that I can't thank Lize." He took her arm and led her to the grassplot where they had sat before, and stood looking at her, his face grave and earnest, reflecting so completely that honesty which she had doubted, that her remorse deepened. He took the stone in one hand, raised it and held it out over the edge of the cliff. Then he released it and it struck the water with a resounding splash.

"That will make a million ripples," he said, "raising as big a fuss in the water as it raised between you and me. But in a minute or two they will all disappear, and the water will be smooth again." He placed his hands on her shoulders, and this time, unlike another time, she did not shrink back but stood, meeting his eyes, her own glowing with promise. "I hope no ripples of trouble will ever come between us again," he added, as he drew her closer to him—she yielding, trembling a little, and looking up at him until, awed by the happiness that had come to her—and which was in his eyes, she closed her own.

The moon, rising over the far mountains, found them still on the promontory.

"Those cities you said you wanted to go to," he said selfishly. "You won't be going to them soon, I hope. Or would you want to go to them on our honeymoon trip? For of course, you'll——"

Half gayly, half longingly, she waved a hand at the distant mountains, while the other tightened on his arm.

"This is my world," she said. "I love it, and I shall never leave it."

"Well," he said, smiling, "I'll not coax you to."

On the porch of the parsonage Ellen looked at Red Owen, who was interestedly examining a finger.

"They're staying long," said Ellen. "I had a hard time getting her to come here with me, but I finally managed it. You should have seen her eyes when I picked up that stone and read its message to her. For a moment I felt guilty. If I hadn't known, for certain that Jim and Lize were as far apart as the poles, I wouldn't——"

She paused and leaned toward Red.

"What on earth is wrong with your finger?"

"Shucks," grinned Red. "I cut the durned thing with that piece of slate that I was writin' on that piece of stone with. I reckon Lize couldn't have done it better herself, though," he finished with some pride.